Play Dirty

ALSO BY LORA LEIGH

Rugged Texas Cowboy

MOVING VIOLATIONS SERIES
One Tough Cowboy
Strong, Silent Cowboy
Her Renegade Cowboy

THE BRUTE FORCE SERIES
Collision Point
Dagger's Edge
Lethal Nights

THE MEN OF SUMMER
Dirty Little Lies
Wicked Lies

THE CALLAHANS
Midnight Sins
Deadly Sins
Secret Sins
Ultimate Sins

THE ELITE OPS
Live Wire
Renegade
Black Jack
Heat Seeker
Maverick
Wild Card

THE NAVY SEALS
Killer Secrets
Hidden Agendas
Dangerous Games

THE BOUND HEARTS
Intense Pleasure
Secret Pleasure
Dangerous Pleasure
Guilty Pleasure
Only Pleasure
Wicked Pleasure
Forbidden Pleasure

ANTHOLOGIES
Real Men Last All Night
Real Men Do It Better
Honk If You Love Real Men
Legally Hot
Men of Danger
Hot Alphas

PLAY DIRTY

Copyright © 2024 by Lora Leigh

All rights reserved.

Designed by Jen Edwards

A Bramble Book
Published by Tom Doherty Associates / Tor Publishing Group
120 Broadway, New York, NY 10271

www.brambleromance.com

Bramble™ is a trademark of Macmillan Publishing Group, LLC.

The Library of Congress Cataloging-in-Publication Data is available upon request.

ISBN 978-1-250-90481-2 (trade paperback)
ISBN 978-1-250-85545-9 (ebook)

Our books may be purchased in bulk for promotional, educational, or business use. Please contact your local bookseller or the Macmillan Corporate and Premium Sales Department at 1-800-221-7945, extension 5442, or by email at MacmillanSpecialMarkets@macmillan.com.

First Edition: 2024

Printed in the United States of America

0 9 8 7 6 5 4 3 2 1

Play Dirty

LORA LEIGH

BRAMBLE

Tor Publishing Group

New York

A broken heart whispers
A saddened heart sighs
But broken dreams . . .
Those scream into the night.
The pain too great to contain.
The wound too deep to heal . . .
For lost dreams
Broken hearts
Shattered hopes . . .

Play Dirty

PROLOGUE

"Does it hurt, Jack?" The whispered question had fourteen-year-old Jack looking up from the arm he was cradling as he tried to breathe with shallow breaths to keep his ribs from hurting so bad.

He looked straight into the pretty summer green eyes of seven-year-old Poppy Porter as she stood outside her parents' back gate watching him with concern.

Dressed in a warm coat and winter boots that he envied, her red hair covered by a green wool cap, she looked like a cheerful winter elf that he'd seen in a book when he'd gone to school.

She stepped closer, placed the small bag of trash she carried next to the dumpster he was hiding behind, and tilted her head to the side. No doubt to see the bruises and cut lip on the other side of his face.

"Get out of here, kid," he muttered, feeling as though he were freezing from the inside out as he huddled amid the snow and cold against the dented dumpster, out of sight of the narrow road on the other side. "And don't be so fu—" He cut off the explicit word as her eyes widened. "Stop being nosy."

She bit her lip, her gaze going from his thin short-sleeved shirt and ragged jeans to the sneakers he wore without socks.

"You can have my gloves." She extended her small hands. "I don't think my coat would fit you, though."

He was a big boy, and not just for his age. Easily three times larger than little Poppy. He wanted to roll his eyes at her offer.

He started to speak, but he heard a familiar truck motor as it turned up the alley, the sound rough, sputtering a bit, and closed his eyes in resignation as it stopped on the other side of the dumpster.

No way would a seven-year-old know how to lie to Toby Bridger, Jack's father.

"Hey, kid, you seen that brat of mine? Jack?" Toby's coarse tone had Jack's teeth gritting in hatred.

She blinked back at the adult's harsh tone.

"A little while ago," Poppy answered guilelessly, a bit hesitant. "He was over by the market walking down the street."

Jack stared at her in shock. Hell, he almost believed her himself.

"What the hell was he doing there?" Toby snarled as though she should know.

Poppy shrugged, but retreated a step toward the still opened gate to her backyard, her expression uncertain.

"He was walking. He looked like he'd been fighting again," she said, as childlike and innocent as possible. "I can get my daddy . . ."

"Fuck it!" Toby snapped at her before gunning the truck's motor and quickly driving away.

No more than a second or two later, Jack heard the motor grinding and accelerating away from the alley and into the next one.

"Get in here!" Poppy demanded, glaring at him as she stepped to the gate and held it open. "My daddy says I can't lie worth nothin', so he might be right back here." She frowned as he hesitated, stepped to him, and tugged at the front of his shirt. "Right now, Jack Bridger, or I'll go get my momma and she'll scold you for staying out in the cold like a ninny."

Why he followed her, he didn't have a clue. But he did. Like a dumbass dog desperate for kindness, he limped along in her wake. Across the yard, up the steps to the porch, and into a kitchen so warm and fragrant he was certain he'd died and gone to heaven.

The first person he saw was Poppy's father. A tall, soft-spoken man who stared at Jack with an implacable expression for only a moment before he turned his gaze to his daughter.

His expression softened then, gentled.

Before he could speak, Poppy's mother stepped into the kitchen. A redhead like Poppy, freckles scattered across the tops of her cheeks, wearing jeans, a T-shirt, and socks, Melissa Porter instantly moved to Jack.

"Cole, get the first aid kit," she ordered Poppy's father, her voice soft, soothing. "Let's see how bad this young man has been hurt." She smiled at him. "Have a seat, Jack; we'll check you out before you join us for lunch. I have a pot of soup nearly ready."

He sat still beneath Mrs. Porter's gentle hands as she checked his arm, his bruised ribs, while Poppy watched, intent. Why a seven-year-old cared, he wasn't certain.

Once Mrs. Porter satisfied herself that there were no broken bones, she cleaned up the cuts, letting Poppy watch, as though she were teaching the girl early how to care for others. Who did that? he wondered. Then antibiotic salve was placed on the cuts, with several Band-Aids applied to the worst. Around his lower arm she placed an elastic wrap to ease what she thought might be a bad sprain.

He didn't tell her he knew the arm had been fractured. Been there, done that. The elastic helped with the pain. He wasn't about to leave the warm house before he absolutely had to.

And Jack could smell that soup. A scent that had his empty stomach aching to be filled. It surprised him, though, that she knew who he was, even more that she seemed to give a damn.

"Awful cold to be out today without a coat, Jack," Cole commented as his wife finished patching him up. "You forget yours?"

"Yes, sir," Jack mumbled. Truth was, he didn't have a coat or gloves, or even socks to wear beneath his threadbare sneakers.

"Poppy, would you find one of your sisters? I need her to hunt down some clothes and boots that the boys have outgrown. I just bet Jack could wear them . . ."

An hour later, he was dressed in clean jeans, T-shirt, and long-sleeved overshirt, with a heavy winter coat and gloves lying over a chair waiting for him. On his feet were thick socks and a pair of warm winter boots with a little extra room in them to ensure he could wear them all winter.

In front of him was a bowl of soup—thick chunks of beef and vegetables and a fragrant broth he knew he'd remember the taste of forever—and bread that Mrs. Porter had heavily smeared butter on.

It was a moment's respite. A fragile few hours, no more than two, before Poppy's father leveled a questioning look across the table.

"It's going to be dark soon, son. I'll give you a ride wherever you're heading," he told him.

The message was clear. For all the man's kindness, he was reminding Jack this wasn't a place he could stay.

"He could just stay tonight, Daddy," Poppy piped up from where she sat next to her father. "Mac-Cole's not home. He could sleep in his room."

A warm home, blankets, more soup. Jack would've sold his soul in that moment if he'd thought those things were possible. But even before he lifted his head from the soup and saw Poppy's father's face, he knew better.

Such things weren't meant for the likes of him.

"No. I can't stay," Jack spoke up, despite the concerned look the little girl shot him. "I'm supposed to be at my uncle's soon," he lied. "I'll be staying there for a while."

He lowered his eyes to his nearly empty bowl, regret slicing at him. He had an uncle, but he wouldn't be staying the night there. He had no idea where he was going to hide, but he knew he'd have to find a place.

"I'll give you ride." Mr. Porter's voice was firm. "Finish your meal and we'll head out."

It wasn't much longer before Poppy's father drove him away, believing Jack's uncle in neighboring Kenova would shelter him.

Jack could have told him there was no shelter. In his life, the only true peace he'd ever known was his time in the Porters' kitchen as a seven-year-old imp had all but ordered her parents to care for him.

That hour or two, and no more.

Poppy stared at the images on the evening news that night, barely aware that she was crying. That her heart was breaking for the boy she'd tried so hard to help that afternoon.

It was dark, police lights flashing red and blue in front of a shack outside of town while two police officers escorted a handcuffed Jack to a cruiser.

"The son, Jackson Lee Bridger, has confessed to killing the father, but hasn't commented in regards to his mother. Officials say the inside of the shack they were living in was a bloodbath . . ."

Poppy turned to her daddy, her gaze meeting his, and in his eyes she saw his regret but his resolve as well. His expression was stoic, unapologetic. He'd done what he felt was best for his family, she'd heard him tell her momma, and now she knew why he'd said it.

"I'm sorry, baby girl," her daddy whispered, shaking his head as her older brothers and sisters turned to them in confusion.

Poppy rose from where she'd been sitting on the carpeted floor and tried to speak. She tried to, but tears clogged her throat, choking her as she fought them back. Turning to the hall, she ran from the room and to her bedroom, knowing she couldn't blame her daddy, because she knew he was a really good daddy. And she knew in that moment that her heart was breaking, because she doubted anyone but her cared about what would happen to the wild, often dirty teenager with too many bruises and a temper that got him in too many fights.

CHAPTER ONE

ELEVEN YEARS LATER

Poppy stared into the full-length mirror with a critical eye, determined to look her best.

She couldn't do anything about the curls her red hair held on to so stubbornly. The deep curls fell to her shoulders in abandon, one insisting on laying over her forehead, but tonight, they looked softer, less frizzy than normal. Her makeup was minimal, a light application of mascara, a soft gray shadow over her eyelids, making her emerald-green eyes seem brighter. Some gloss along her lips.

The flirty skirt she wore ended just above her knees, the blouse, a lighter shade of blue, barely covered the low band of the skirt. It was just low enough to hide the hilt of the little dagger, secured in its leather sheath and tucked inside the band of her skirt.

Her fingers glanced over the wooden hilt, her heart giving a hard beat of remembered excitement at its presence. The little knife was for her protection, since she couldn't seem to keep her butt at home instead of sneaking out and attending parties she had no business going to, she'd been told.

Jack had looked so stern and disapproving that night he'd given her the dagger at one of those parties. He'd spent that evening in the relative solitude amid the vehicles parked at the edge of the clearing, instructing her on how best to use it to protect herself.

He wasn't the boy she'd ordered into her parents' home all those years ago. This Jack Bridger was harder, stronger, and even more handsome than he'd been as a boy. His black hair was cut military short and all she wanted to do was bury her fingers in it and test the feel of it. The gray-blue color of his eyes was mostly somber, but the color would darken whenever he saw her.

And when she saw him, her heart would trip. Race. She was in danger of stuttering and all she could think about was having him hold her against him, his lips moving on hers, kissing her with the same need for her that she felt for him.

She touched her lips with her fingers, her stomach tightening, heart racing. Tonight, she promised herself. He would kiss her tonight. She'd felt it coming the past few weekends. He was always at the parties this summer, hanging around until she arrived, watching her the entire time she was there.

He'd dance with her a few times, then if she didn't walk back with her friends along the heavily traveled path that ended across from her home, she suspected he was the one who called her brother, or one of her friends' brother's.

Tonight, he could take her home himself, she decided. She belonged to him. She'd known that for years. She'd waited for him, dreamed of him. Tonight, he'd see that.

Jack was late arriving at the party. Every summer he, as well as Poppy's brothers, Mac-Cole, John David, and Evan, along with Caine Crossfield and River Dawson, if they were home on leave, did their best to make certain five young women remained safe while allowing them to try their wings and test their freedom.

This summer, Jack's attention had been fractured between keeping his hands off Poppy and tracking the bastard who had more than once made the claim that he was going to have Poppy that summer. Whether she wanted him or not.

That weekend, Jack was going to make certain Wayne Trencher understood how dangerous focusing on Poppy was to his health. Trencher was a known sexual predator, a monster. Jack had no problems making monsters disappear. The US government had actually trained him in doing just that.

Wayne Trencher had managed to slip away from him, though, and the next thing he knew, the little bastard had shown up at the party Poppy and her friends were attending. As he drove to the clearing where the party was held, he flipped open his mobile phone and called Mac-Cole.

"Leave a message," Mac-Cole's recorded voice requested.

"Get your ass to that party," Jack snapped. "Trencher evaded me and I just received a call that he's there and so is Poppy."

He disconnected the call and pressed his foot heavier on the gas as he drove as fast as possible to the turnoff that led to the dirt road winding its way to the clearing.

Arriving at the party half an hour later, much later than he normally arrived, he parked the truck as close as possible and hurried to the music- and laughter-filled area where everyone met and socialized. Music throbbed through the clearing that had been lit up by a combination of work lights and vehicle lights.

Catching sight of Poppy's friends, he noticed Poppy wasn't with them and felt tension beginning to gather tighter inside him.

"Sasha, where's Poppy?" He stepped to the young woman generally accepted as the leader of the small group.

He could feel a warning chill crawling up his back.

"She got tired of waiting for you," Sasha informed him, flicking him a disgruntled look. "She texted a bit ago that she was walking home. Geeze, Jack, she only comes here to see you."

She'd walked home.

He swung away from the group of young women and hurried across the clearing to the path that led to the street directly behind her parent's home. As he hurried through the crowd, he didn't see Wayne Trencher either.

The warning chill at his back became ice racing through his veins and he had a feeling the only person that meant anything to him was being hunted by a monster. A monster that may already have her in his grip.

Moving along the path he knew she often used when returning from one of the parties close to her home, Jack made it about half-way through the woods when he heard the scream, the sound coming from a shack hidden about ten feet from the path amid the overgrown brush.

Jack hadn't felt fear since he was fourteen, let alone the terror that exploded in his gut and ripped through his mind. Within seconds he threw his body into the door of the shack, instinct and primal fury obliterating any thought at the sight of Poppy being held beneath Trencher's much larger body.

"Please . . . ! No! Oh God . . ." she screamed out again as Jack moved toward them.

Grabbing thick, greasy hair, he tore Trencher away, then with one arm around Wayne's neck dragged him from Poppy, even as he realized Trencher's body was a heavy, slack weight. Dropping him to the floor, Jack saw the small dagger sticking out of his chest. The same dagger Jack had given her in case she needed protection when she'd begun sneaking out to the parties.

Crouching down, Jack checked for a pulse, and finding none stared back at Poppy as she knelt on an old, stained mattress Trencher had thrown her onto.

"I killed him." Shock rounded her eyes and whitened her face. "I killed him, Jack."

Blood stained her pretty blue skirt, saturating the blouse as well as her small, delicate hands.

"He was a rabid animal, Poppy. That's what you're supposed to do," he told her, keeping his voice calm, unaffected.

But inside he was damned near breaking apart.

He'd been too late to protect the only person in his life who mattered.

Gripping the dead man beneath the shoulders, Jack dragged him from the shack and hid the body in the heavy foliage that grew close to the building. Once he finished, he rushed back to Poppy.

There, in the middle of that dirty floor, she'd managed to straighten her knee-length blue summer skirt. Her panties lay to the side, shredded, and Poppy was shuddering with anger. Not fear, but pure feminine anger.

Though it wouldn't take the fear long to arrive.

"Poppy." Sliding to his knees beside her, he touched her face, stared into her brilliant green eyes. "Honey . . ."

God, what could he say? There were no tears, but fury and horror filled her emerald eyes and her body was shaking like a leaf in a storm.

"Jack." Pulling back, she stared down at her hands as though they weren't her own before lifting her gaze to him once again. "I felt him . . . I felt him . . . He was going inside me, Jack. I had to . . ."

"It's okay, baby." He pulled her to him, rocking her, feeling an unfamiliar dampness in his eyes. "You stopped him before he could do more than just try. I swear, you stopped him . . . All he did was try. That was all you felt . . ."

He rocked her. Sitting on the floor, he drew her across his lap, held her, stroked her hair, kissed her forehead, and did something he'd never done in his life. He soothed another person.

His Poppy.

"He was going to make me do it," she ground out, that anger still reflecting in her voice as her head rested on his shoulder. "I told him I'd kill him, Jack."

She looked up at him, her ashen face drawn into determined lines even as she shuddered in his embrace.

There was no remorse in her. She'd just killed the man who had assaulted her, but she wasn't crying or hysterical. Shock had stolen the color from her face, and there was a noticeable tremor racing through her, but she was sitting in his hold, fists clenched now as she fought the continued anger.

"It's okay, baby," he whispered, touching her cheek with the tips of two fingers. "You did what you had to do."

"Do you hate me, Jack?" she whispered then, her voice trembling, the question shocking him. "Do I disgust you now?"

Poppy stared into the hardened features of Jack's face, the chill in his eyes, fearing that any tender emotions he may have felt for her were gone forever.

She'd just killed a man. Blood stained her hands and her clothing, proof of her carelessness in protecting herself. Jack was a strong man—nothing but a strong woman would complement him. Strong women didn't let things like this happen. Did they?

"Disgust me?" His brows furrowed as his thumb whispered over her lips before his hand dropped to her shoulder. "Never, Poppy. You could never disgust me."

But this event would change her life forever, and she was smart enough to know that. That one impulsive decision to walk home rather than listen to one of her brothers bitch at her because she'd gone to the party could destroy her life.

And possibly Jack's as well.

What had she done?

For a moment, the implications of what had happened overwhelmed her and threatened the fragile hold she had on the chaos churning in her mind.

"Take it away for a minute, Jack." Her breathing hitched as she fought the fear threatening to tear through her. "Just for minute. Make it go away . . ."

Before he could question her, or answer her, she lifted up to him and laid her lips on his as they parted to answer her.

He froze.

Poppy felt Jack's body tighten, his muscles bunching as though to push her away from him. She knew it could be her last chance for the kiss she'd dreamed of—she wanted at least one kiss. Just a single taste of what she'd been longing for.

She could never have expected his response.

As she prepared to move back, to break the fragile contact, his lips slanted over hers, his tongue moving to lick, to taste hers. Pleasure swamped her. His kiss was hot, experienced, and sent the most incredible sensations rushing through her.

She'd been kissed before, but never like this. Like she was a banquet, and he was a man starved for the taste of her alone.

Arching to him, her hands gripped the short length of his black hair as she fought to get closer to him. To feel the warmth of the hard, hot body seeming to surround hers.

Heat built inside her—the need for more, to feel more of him, taste more of him.

Her head fell back along his arm as his lips moved from hers, traveled to her neck, caressing the tender line of flesh. Every cell in her body was tuned to him, reaching out to him, desperate for his touch.

"Jack," she whispered as she lifted closer to him, needing so much more of him.

"Remember this, Poppy," he whispered, his voice hoarse as his head lifted, the blue in his eyes darkening the gray until they were the color of storm clouds. "The pleasure, the hunger. This is how it should be, baby. When the nightmares come, remember, this is how it should be."

He pressed her head to his chest, and Poppy could feel the calm, steady acceptance emanating from him. The purpose.

Jack was there with her; she'd never convince him to leave if she called the police. And no doubt, his DNA was there in the shack now anyway.

Then, a horrible realization locked inside her and the implication of what she had done tightened around her heart like a vise. If she called the police, they'd never accept the fact that she'd killed Trencher.

Jack had given her the small dagger she'd used to kill her rapist. It had been a gift the year before. It could be traced back to him. And he would take the charge to protect her. She knew he would.

"Jack, what are we going to do?" she whispered, easing up and pushing her fingers through her hair as she stared around the single room.

"It will be okay, Poppy . . ."

It was there in his voice. A deadened sound that assured her he was preparing himself for whatever the results of her actions brought down on him.

Poppy stared at him as a furious denial resounded in her head.

"You think I'll allow you to take the blame for this?" she asked him, moving from his lap to kneel in front of him. "You didn't do this."

He shrugged as though it didn't matter. "Who would believe you killed a man?" he asked her gently. "Even I would never accept that, honey."

She inhaled, fighting to find another answer.

"You're a SEAL," she said then. "Aren't there ways to hide the body? To make certain he's not found? Or if he is found, to ensure he can't be traced back to us? There has to be a way, Jack."

The man had tried to rape her, and when she'd warned him she'd never let him get away with it, he told her dead little girls didn't carry tales. He would have killed her. He'd intended to kill her.

Jack was silent for long minutes, and she could feel him either considering those options or considering her ability to be strong enough to keep the secret.

"He would have killed me, Jack. He had no intention of letting me leave this shack," she informed him. "I don't feel bad about killing him. And I won't have you take the blame for it. I know that's what you're planning to do."

She saw the quirk of his lips, the acknowledgment that she was right.

"I won't let you." She reached out for him, her hands gripping his arm as he sat on the floor, strong, imposing despite his position. "I won't allow a stupid decision to walk home destroy both our lives. Do you hear me?"

Jack stared at her, knowing in that moment that every part of who and what he was belonged to this woman. She was stronger than he had ever imagined. She was only eighteen—so young, so fragile—but what he saw in her eyes went far beyond her age.

"I can protect you, Poppy . . ."

"You think taking the blame will protect me?" she argued desperately. "It won't, because I'll never stay silent about what happened. I'll tell the world you're lying."

Jack doubted anyone would believe her. But he had no doubt there was enough DNA on the floor to prove she was there, to prove something had happened.

He grimaced at the thought. He couldn't let her accept the blame when she had nothing to feel guilty for. This was on him. He was supposed to protect her, and he'd failed.

"And no one will believe you," he sighed, rising to his feet and extending his hand to her. "Come on, baby . . ."

The door to the shack burst open, and Jack rounded on the man forcing his way inside. He pushed Poppy behind him, intent on defending the only person in his life who had defended him.

Armed, dangerous, green eyes filled with fury, the intruder took in the scene before lifting his weapon and aiming at Jack.

"No! Oh God, no . . ." Before he could do more than reach for her, Poppy was around him, moving to stand between Jack and the furious visage of her older brother. "Please, no, Mac . . . It's my fault. It's all my fault . . ."

CHAPTER TWO

EIGHT YEARS LATER

Jackson Lee Bridger settled into the chair in front of the desk where Homeland agent Ian Richards and his wife, Kira, waited silently. A tall, sandy-haired retired SEAL, Ian was a direct contrast to his delicate wife. His skin was darkly tanned from hot Texas summers, his brown gaze hard and assessing. Kira, her long black hair now showing the slightest silver through the strands, a peaches-and-cream complexion, and pretty, direct gray eyes, seemed softer somehow, though Jack doubted that was actually the case.

In front of him lay several pale cream files stamped "TOP SE-CRET," the red print like a stain across pale flesh.

He stared at the closed files in front of him, knowing that at least some of the information contained within had the power to break more than twenty years of careful self-control and deliberate disregard. In all those years, Jack could count on the fingers of one hand the times actual emotion had filled him since he'd been fourteen. And each time, it had been for the same person.

The office he'd been shown to was windowless, the single lamp on the corner of the desk the only illumination. The perfect setting, he supposed, to begin the task of betraying the only person he had ever allowed himself to really care for.

"Sure you want to do this, Jack?" Ian asked, his piercing brown eyes intent.

Jack's brow arched mockingly. "Oh, I don't know, Richards . . . might be more interesting than that court-martial I been waiting on." All shit aside, it was about the truth, but that wasn't why he'd agreed to take the mission.

He had taken it not for his own freedom, but for Poppy.

He owed her this. She'd saved him once, but he'd been too late to save her from a nightmare later. He wouldn't let himself fail her again.

"Just to be clear, we don't believe Miss Porter is involved in anything criminal," Kira told him, her gray eyes somber. "I've met her. She seems quite genuine and friendly, if a little reserved at times. But I could find no proof she was involved in what's going on there. She's our best way into position, though, to get the trust needed to ensure you're offered a specific job."

Yeah, Jack thought, she could be reserved, but only where people she didn't know were concerned.

He stared at the name on the top file and couldn't help but quirk his lips in faint remembrance.

Her parents, self-proclaimed bohemians, had given her one of those cutesy summer names that most kids grew up hating and only kept because to do otherwise would have hurt parents they loved.

Poppy Octavia Porter.

And everyone called her "Poppy." There was no nickname, nothing to soften the fact that her parents were smoking some bad-ass homegrown when they'd come up with that name. And they fully admitted to that fact. The first thing they'd done after Poppy was born, at home with the help of a midwife, had been to light up and come up with a name. Her mother, Melissa Ann, had abstained from the smoke during her pregnancy, but since she had no intention of breastfeeding, she'd seen no harm in it.

The family thought it was hilarious that Poppy had refused to take the infant formula they had on hand for her, though, and Melissa had been forced to breastfeed the furious child while under the influence.

He'd heard the story a thousand times, and he had to admit, he thought of it often.

With her red hair and green eyes, Poppy was charming as hell, mischievous, and filled with laughter. She lived up to her name rather than resenting it, and though there was no gossip or evidence that she partook of her parents' favorite pastime, it was well known that despite the red hair, she was rarely temperamental.

She loved her parents and siblings, always arrived to help fix dinner for the entire family at her parents' home on Sundays, and always joined at her parents' for holiday gatherings.

Her favorite drink was the moonshine her cousins deeper in the mountain made, or straight Kentucky bourbon.

She dated often, but never seriously, met with a small group of friends most nights for dinner, and loved dogs, though she didn't own one of her own.

She was always smiling, laughing, but Jack knew for a fact that the shadow in her green eyes came from a trauma few could understand. One he knew wouldn't be listed in the file, because he'd made certain that that one event couldn't return to haunt her.

Poppy was the only good memory he had of home, and she was one of his greatest regrets.

What he was about to do to her didn't sit well with him. Hell, it downright left a bad taste in his mouth. He would have preferred to involve any other woman in it, because he knew he was only going to end up hurting her in the end.

He was going to betray a woman who prided herself on her

loyalty to her friends and her family, as well as on her business integrity. Yet somehow, she was smack-dab in the middle of a den of vipers, with no clue of the danger that could strike at any time.

She was the only way into a very tight circle of Barboursville, West Virginia, residents that included the two men she worked for and involved their business dealings.

Poppy Octavia Porter was the manager of the commercial and residential properties two friends, Caine Crossfield and River Dawson, owned in the tristate area of Kentucky, Ohio, and West Virginia. They were friends of her older brothers; she and their sisters had been close since grade school, and she'd stepped into the job straight out of college when she was just twenty-two.

Now, at twenty-six, she was a trusted and valued friend and employee, and treated more like family. And she could get into every property they owned without suspicion or notice.

"You're certain Crossfield and Dawson are involved in this?" he asked them, just to be certain.

"We know that one, if not both, are involved. We're certain Crossfield is. Dawson . . . we still need proof," Kira answered him.

"Poppy's not involved," she reassured him. There was no way possible that she'd do more than break the speed limit.

He'd kept up with her through friends. Stories about Poppy abounded with equal parts amusement and fondness.

"Are you sure you can do this with a clear mind, Jack?" Ian asked, his voice much harder than his wife's. "Going in emotionally involved won't help anyone. Especially her. This is a military operation, and it has to stay that way. You cannot reveal your true purpose for being there."

Emotionally involved? He would have laughed if he could have dredged up any humor in the situation.

"I'm certain." He nodded, lying out his ass. "It has nothing to do with emotion. I keep up with home on a regular basis, and everyone knows her. If she was capable of being dirty, there'd be a hint of it elsewhere. As for Caine Crossfield or River Dawson, either would be capable of it."

"At the very least, she's in danger," Kira pointed out. "They buried one of her friends last month. A young officer with the city that we know stumbled onto something or someone involved in this. He was killed before we could get to him. She works with them. If she stumbles onto anything, she could end up just as dead."

No doubt Poppy was fixing to get into trouble. Someone was becoming overconfident, careless. And Poppy was as curious as a damned puppy. Always had been.

"Her position with the two suspects almost ensures the same could happen to her. Both Crossfield and Dawson feel betrayed by their country due to their time in the Special Forces. Their discharges for 'medical with extenuating circumstances' left them bitter and angry." Ian breathed out roughly. "They were blamed for their commanders' fuckups, hence the extenuating circumstances."

Yeah, it happened. Crossfield and Dawson had been able, natural leaders. Their commanders had been head cases. The two men hadn't taken it well.

They'd returned home and built the Crossfield-Dawson properties, and according to the evidence gathered thus far, one or likely both men were using those properties as staging points for other parties to smuggle drugs, arms, and a variety of other highly illegal items across the nation.

"One of our men got into her house when we first began the investigation. There was nothing to be found in the house that could lead back to Crossfield or Dawson or indicate her guilt in their suspected crimes," Ian stated. "You'll need to check it again, make certain nothing's changed."

Jack rifled through the files, his gaze narrowed. There were files of each person in Poppy's circle of friends. When he found nothing, his gaze lifted to Ian's.

There was more; he sensed it. Something dangerous enough to pull Jack from a life behind bars and sign the orders necessary to ensure he stayed out.

He was charged with the murder of three contract black ops agents, and he didn't deny killing them. He had. They'd all participated in the rapes of four young girls as their families were forced to watch. Supposedly an exercise in extracting an admission of guilt from the older male members of the family in regard to terrorist acts against the US.

Those families hadn't been involved in shit other than trying to survive and managing to piss off the commander of that little group.

Yeah, Jack had killed each of them without remorse. And what he'd do to anyone that dared to hurt Poppy would be worse. But to protect her, he had to get to her. To get to her, he had to finish this little meeting.

"You've left something out here," he told the other man.

Ian stared back at him, his gaze chips of ice as he held Jack's.

Jack knew what Ian was doing. It was something he was damned good at himself. They couldn't read minds, but Jack, like Ian, could read men.

Experience, hunter's instincts and knowledge, an elevated inborn, preternatural survival instinct, whatever the hell psychologists were calling it these days. It was the ability to evaluate and read a man's strengths and weaknesses and determine their risk almost instantly.

Turning to a file cabinet behind him, Ian pulled another file free, one much thicker than the files Jack had before him, and handed it over.

Taking it, Jack placed it before himself, opened it, and for the first time in years found himself genuinely surprised and completely aware of the danger in this assignment, not just to Poppy, but to the country.

Artificial intelligence.

It was a word, a subject, that even those working on it tended to shy away from discussing. They'd heard rumors of advances in the area, and they had seen the mechanical canines the Army was trying to introduce. They'd laughed at them, of course, but in the back of every man's mind was a hint of trepidation when they saw them.

This wasn't a mechanical canine.

This would be undetectable, such a true replica of a human that it could destroy all sense of security in the nation if it were known to exist.

"Sentient?" he asked, feeling the ice, the granite hardness of the killer he was settling into.

"We're not certain." Ian and Kira pulled two chairs to the table and sat down. "Our scientists say no, but the man that built it was radical. His ideas were so outside the box that no boundaries existed as far as he was concerned."

Heinrich Gustav had been a man born out of time, Jack realized as he scanned through the pages.

He'd terrified some of his fellow scientists, acknowledged geniuses in Gustav's fields of research, to the point that he'd been cut out of every research project he'd worked on. Then, he, his wife, and their young daughter and son-in-law had disappeared and never been seen or heard from again.

"Any idea where to find Gustav?" Jack lifted his head to stare back at Ian.

"None." Ian shook his head and sat back in his chair as he ran his fingers through his still thick hair. "He, his wife, Lorna, their daughter, Charlene, or 'Charlie' as she was often called, and their son-in-law, Duncan Renaud, disappeared years ago. How four minds so highly intelligent were allowed to just slip away, I can't fathom."

Jack returned his attention to the file, trying to process why those minds, once so dedicated to aiding society, would have conceived of building a weapon such as the one described in the file.

"Rumor is it's being shipped into the states a few pieces at a time, with the end destination being the tristate area of Kentucky, West Virginia, and Ohio, most likely into a Crossfield-Dawson holding or warehouse," Kira told him. "Once all the components are in place, it'll be assembled and the programming uploaded. We're still getting intel, though in bits and pieces, from our asset. We're hoping that by the time you're in place, and your teams assembled, we'll have more information for you."

"We suspect Heinrich and his wife are deceased," Ian interjected. "There are rumors that the entire family was killed and the AI will be controlled by whoever provided the funds for the research. No word yet on who that generous benefactor was," he sneered. "It's one of the pieces of information Homeland considers high-priority. That and disabling whatever form the AI assembles into."

"Not many groups could afford this or get their hands on the needed components," Jack murmured. "Iran maybe, China definitely. Russia isn't even in the running but could be aiding and abetting."

"Or all of the above," Ian growled.

"Stationary or android design?" Jack murmured. "Gustav researched biomechanical flesh; it could be android."

"The quantum programming would take far more room than any droid could house, according to our experts," Ian objected. "But whichever, we have to find it, dismantle it, and destroy it if we can. Even our government can't be allowed to possess a weapon like this."

On that, Jack agreed.

"What's the ultimate assignment where the AI is concerned?" Jack questioned. "What or who's the target?"

"World chaos?" Ian snorted. "Who the fuck knows at this point.

It's one of those pieces of intel we're waiting for. All we have so far is that the target is here, in the US, and of prime value. If our information is correct, it's able to use satellite and land connections without detection to achieve its goal. It's the end of the world as we know it. While you're getting in position to hopefully locate it, we'll work on the intel and get it to you ASAP as it comes in."

"In position for what, Ian?" Jack lifted his gaze, nothing more, and stared back at the other man. "Why do you need four Navy SEALs in place under Crossfield's and Dawson's noses so bad that you're willing to bring me out of a court-martial to see to it?"

A possible stint in Leavenworth was the least of what he was looking at. The cell he'd been sitting in for weeks could become a permanent home. If the general pushing for it had his way, Jack would never see daylight again.

Ian leaned forward once again. "Because the one solid piece of intel that we have out of the area is that Crossfield and or Dawson is looking to acquire a small spec ops team for some reason. Word is, several teams are already en route and or being considered for the contract, whether for backup or security, we don't know. Military required, preferably Special Forces–trained but with no government loyalties. They're planning something big, and we need to know what . . . fast. At best, we figure six to eight weeks before the components are in place and assembly can be completed."

Jack sat back in his chair and regarded the SEAL and his wife, knowing that neither of them could see anything more than he allowed: a cold, hard sociopath who just might not give a damn but for the single weakness they hoped he had.

He let a grin edge at his lips. "I'll take a bad-conduct discharge, effective immediately, but with all military pay and benefits. Because knowing the powers that be as I do, they'll come calling again once this op is completed. I have complete kill-authority within the mission parameters, as well as all authority in protecting my team as well as Poppy. I get my full military pay, because holding down a job will be for shit while this is going on, plus operating funds, and no one looks over my shoulder or questions missing weapons, cash, or other items in possession of any enemy combatants I'm forced to take out. And I'll take that in writing."

Ian glared back at him.

Yeah, he was asking for a lot, Jack knew, but so was Ian. If the AI was even close to being everything they suspected, then life expectancy on this op could be limited.

"We could just put you back in that cell."

Jack grinned without amusement at that. "You could. But you pulled me out for a reason." He scratched at his stubbled cheek before laying his hands on the table once again. "I know Caine Crossfield and River Dawson personally. To say they'll believe I'm rogue is an understatement. But, I'm also the only man you'll get close to Poppy, and I'd say you've figured that one out already. So." He straightened in his seat. "Throw me back in my cell or get my terms typed up and signed and back to me while I go over this information you have."

Ian's expression only got colder, but Kira's lips twitched as she reached into the bag she'd carried in and pulled out another file.

"Your agreement, including the pay package, which is slightly better than you mentioned. You'll find it quite satisfactory. Similar agreements are waiting to be signed with the men you'll be commanding. All we need is your signature." She laid the agreement in front of him.

"Jack, just because the men you killed stepped over the line, that didn't make it right," Ian said quietly as Jack read over the papers. "They were still agents of the US government."

Jack paused, remembering what three agents of the US government had done to four young women as they forced the girls' families to watch.

"I couldn't kill their government," he drawled, his smile cold. "So, I killed their attack dogs. How's that?"

The couple was silent for long moments before Kira spoke.

"There were better ways to handle the situation," she said.

He lifted his head after signing the agreement, remembering—and remembering never failed to ice over any sense of loyalty that might have had him regretting his actions.

"No, there wasn't. I handled it the only way that ensured they never raped another child." He spoke with a tight, hard line to his lips and a flat, killing look in his eyes that Kira couldn't hold. "Now, I need some time with the files to acquaint myself with the operation. A few hours, if you don't mind."

They were thick files.

"Kira and I have a house in Barboursville for the summer," Ian told him, the fact that Jack's answer didn't sit well with him apparent. "We're your and your team's backup. You'll meet your team once you reach Barboursville. Lucas Royce from Huntington, Hayes Granger from Ashland, and Hank Brady from Kenova. You're team lead. They'll contact you once their agreements are signed and they're released and reach their home locations. Once you've gained enough notice, I'll set up a meeting. My known affiliation with the Fuentes Cartel and as the head of that cartel, Diego Fuentes's son, will only give credence to your cover and the story that you're not above breaking the law. Whoever's involved in this won't accept anyone with an appearance of loyalty to their country. They want killers, so let's give them what they think they want. Or at least the appearance of it."

His cover.

Unfortunately, it wasn't so much a cover as that it simply aligned with the facts of his life. He was a troublemaker even before he'd killed that team of agents with his bare hands after he'd walked in on the scene of their crimes. He questioned authority, didn't heel worth shit, and had "accidentally" killed more than a few detainees known for crimes so heinous they should have never been left breathing.

The killing didn't bother him. Monsters breathing did. He'd made it this long because he was damned good at his job and got along great with his team. He'd just been kept on assignment and away from other teams whenever possible. That last operation was just the stick that broke the camel's back.

"I know Poppy's a friend . . ." Ian began.

"Sir, I've been considered a functioning sociopath without the ability to form friendships or emotional attachments since the age of fourteen when I sliced open my father's throat," he reminded the other man with chilly politeness, knowing it was best if the world believed every word of the unofficial diagnosis. "According to Navy psychologists, my patriotism, sense of boundaries, and respect for my country are the only reasons I wasn't in prison before now. Or dead. Friendships denote emotional attachments, of which I have none. What I do have is a knowledge of honor and decency. Right and wrong. And that's my law. Plain and simple."

He wasn't a sociopath—he was realistic, and liked to think he knew right from wrong. His own self-interest wasn't all that drove him. He felt compassion, though he wasn't big on empathy. He could be manipulative if he had to be, though he wasn't narcissistic. He was confident, certain of his abilities, and determined.

He had his own code he lived by, and Poppy was the only person in the world he'd willingly sacrifice himself for.

He'd die for Poppy. He'd sacrifice for her. Because when it had mattered, she'd been the only person who gave a damn about him. She'd been the reason he'd been fostered with a good family after he'd killed his father—because Poppy had cried when she'd seen his arrest on the news. Because she'd asked her father to allow the bruised, bloodied boy she'd found hiding in the garbage to be allowed to spend the night in an empty bedroom. And her father had refused. To ease his daughter's tears, her father had ensured that Jack was given a chance at a good life.

Because of Poppy.

He was aware of the other two watching him carefully, intently, for any signs of weakness or "attachment" where Poppy was concerned.

"You're extremely well qualified and trained, and the perfect personality type for this job." Ian sighed. "But this is home, people you grew up with. That changes things sometimes. And I've been advised to tell you to watch the body count. We don't need a bunch of dead criminals. A few live ones for trial would be nice."

It was a waste of taxpayer money, if anyone wanted his opinion. He was fine with killing the monsters of the world. Killing those monsters kept the world a safer place for Poppy.

"Yeah, it can change things for other people." Jack nodded, ignoring the warning and focusing on the first part of Ian's statement. "But think of it this way. My way, no one gets off on a technicality. Your way, it happens, often. Why don't I just promise to hide most of the bodies if needed, and we'll call it even."

"Thing about hiding bodies, they eventually turn up," Ian warned him.

"Not the ones I hide," he snorted. "I promise you: They'll never be found anywhere except hell. And the devil's a jealous old bastard."

Even the dust from those bodies would never be found—he'd make certain of it. He could play the gentleman when needed. Death wasn't always the best punishment, just more effective in some situations. Destruction could come in any number of ways.

CHAPTER THREE

BARBOURSVILLE, WEST VIRGINIA
ONE WEEK LATER

Jack's home . . .

Bridger was seen in town . . .

Damn Jack Bridger's back . . .

There goes the neighborhood, Bridger's back . . .

OMG Jack Bridger is looking fine, girlfriend . . .

Poppy stared at the countless messages on her smartphone as she tried to make her sleep-deprived brain work.

Jack was back.

It was too early on a Sunday morning to force any semblance of rationality to actually work. She hadn't even had that first cup of coffee yet. She needed a lot of coffee to make sense of the myriad of messages still popping across her phone.

Poppy! Stay away from Bridger until we talk! her brother's text popped up as she swung her legs out of the bed. He's trouble now.

She stared at it in bemusement, frowning.

What the hell was his problem?

John David and Jack Bridger had been friends at one time, she thought. Well, sort of friends.

She pushed her fingers through her hair, grimacing at the bed-tangles that had knotted through the curls and wishing she had her mother's and sisters' temper. Then she could just throw her phone across the room and be done with it for the day.

Her mother and sisters had no problem whatsoever doing things like that.

Instead, hearing yet more messages popping up, she turned off the sound and forced herself to stand up. To leave the heated-blanket warmth for the AC cool until she could get to the controls and turn the damned air off.

The phone vibrated with each message, though, and the feel of it was beginning to irritate her.

Turning the AC off, she slipped through the house to the kitchen window, opened a slat, and looked out, refusing to admit to the fact that her adrenaline was pumping without the infusion of caffeine that it normally took for it to do that.

She looked out just in time to watch the wicked black pickup pull into the back of what was usually a deserted house across the street. Said truck pulled a trailer carrying a tarp-covered motorcycle behind it. The truck came to a stop at the closed garage doors and as Poppy watched, the driver's-side door pushed open and he stepped out.

Jack Lee Bridger.

He turned in her direction, all six feet, five inches of what looked like pure, hard muscle dressed in boots, jeans, and a T-shirt that stretched across broad shoulders, a wide chest, and a set of abs that appeared so hard they should have been illegal.

A darkly tanned, unsmiling face, eyes that were neither gray nor blue but a mix of both, and thick straight black hair that was long enough to give his face a hard, savage appearance.

As he stared at her window, he tilted his head to the side, then lifted his hand, two fingers almost appearing to offer a casual salute as they reached his shoulders, before he turned and let her admire a fine, fine male ass . . .

Oh my God. He knew she was at the window.

She hurriedly stepped backward, allowing the slat to fall back into place as she realized she'd been holding her breath.

He couldn't know she lived there, she assured herself. She'd just bought the house a year ago from old man Ralph Milton and his wife when they'd gone to Florida to live with their daughter.

Only she knew that she'd bought this particular house because it was directly across the alley from the house Jack had bought several years previous.

She hadn't seen him in years. Eight years. She refused to list the number of days, and coming up with the number of hours wouldn't have been hard, but her brain wasn't quite with it when she first woke.

Inhaling roughly, she tugged at the sleep top that barely met the band of her gaily striped pajama pants and told herself he was just being a smart-ass because he could tell someone was watching him.

He was a Navy SEAL. Had been for years. They knew stuff like that, right? The hunter-and-hunted kind of thing? They could tell when someone was watching them. At least, that's what she'd read and seen in television movies.

Her phone vibrated again.

Turning it over in her hand, she frowned down at the new message.

Call me when you wake! It was John David again. The damned busybody. We need to talk about this! Stay the hell away from Bridger, Poppy!

She narrowed her eyes on the message, her lips pursing as she considered telling him to mind his own damned business. It was, after all, her life, not his.

Thank God he was out of town at some lawyer thing in California. Otherwise, he'd probably be on her doorstep with his demands and tight-assed judgments.

For a moment, she leaned her head against the wall next to the window, forcing herself not to fling open the door and run across the alley to throw herself into his arms as she had the last time she'd been in town when he returned home. But she wasn't a girl now, she was woman, she reminded herself. And Jack had made it a point to avoid her when he was in town ever since that same summer. She forced herself not to remember the last time she'd done more than catch a glimpse of him. A time or two he'd acknowledged her with a nod or a somber look, but he hadn't approached her and he'd always disappeared before she could approach him.

The past was a cruel bitch, she thought painfully. A single bad decision to walk home alone through the woods had destroyed a friendship she'd valued and that chance for more that she'd dreamed of having with him.

"He'll just be home for a minute," she whispered as her phone vibrated again. "Then he'll be gone again."

Just for a minute.

She could survive not speaking to him, not basking in the warmth she'd always felt around him at least that long, couldn't she?

No, she couldn't.

Because she'd missed him that much. Because each year it got harder to keep from searching him out, from forcing him to acknowledge her presence.

Shaking her head at the thought, she moved to the coffeepot and popped a pod into the device. Placing her cup beneath it, she waited for the liquid caffeine to begin filling the ceramic mug. The two-times-the-caffeine brand of coffee would hopefully fire her brain cells with a hint of logic and give her the boost she needed to get to the next cup before she was forced to shower and get dressed.

Sunday afternoons were dinner at home, and unlike most weekends, she knew exactly what to expect today. The topic of conversation would no doubt be Jack Bridger: why he was home, how long he was staying, why he hadn't sold the house, why he had even bothered coming back.

She knew, because it happened at least once a year.

The first four years she was in college in Louisville and came home only on weekends. He'd arrive weekdays, always in the winter when the roads were predicted to be hazardous due to the weather. He'd stay a week or two, then leave.

The past four years, after she'd graduated, she'd glimpse him, but other than a few times she hadn't been close enough to speak. And each time she drove by his house it had been empty. But this time he hadn't just ridden in on the motorcycle or driven a truck. He'd brought both.

Did he intend to stay for a while this time? Maybe return home?

Armed with her coffee, she slipped to the window again and opened the slat just barely enough to peek through the side.

The back of his truck was loaded with stuff. A recliner, a new, still-in-the-box television. He had a huge duffel bag, and he was pulling a still boxed microwave from the backseat.

She should at least wave to him maybe. He kept glancing over at the house. Her mother used to say she hadn't raised dummies. And evidently neither had Jack's mother. Somehow, Jack knew who was in the house, and he obviously expected something from her.

An acknowledgment perhaps?

Just a smile and a wave.

A woman simply didn't ignore a man who had been willing to take the blame for a death she'd caused. No matter how deserving that death.

Biting her lip, cup of coffee in hand, she unlocked the door, opened it, and then pushed open the storm door and leaned against the frame as she stared across the alley.

And she couldn't help but smile. Because Jack Bridger never smiled, and since she was a girl she'd tried to make him smile every time she saw him. Just a little bit.

He sat the box on the ground and straightened, staring back at her with that damned somber, God-only-knew-what-he-was-thinking expression as his gaze went over her slowly.

She was dressed decently, even with pajamas on, but still, she was bra-less, panty-less. Unprotected. Not that the thought worried her, as it would have at any other time. She could be naked and be safe with Jack.

At least, years ago she could have been.

As she stared at him, she saw the difference in his face, in his expression. Nine years had matured him in definitive ways. His face was harder, not cruel-looking, but merciless perhaps, where it hadn't been before.

He was broader, stronger, and God knew he'd been strong before, even as a teenager. And his stare reminded her that he knew her. In ways no one else did, he knew things about her that no one else, she hoped, would ever know.

Tilting her lips again in goodbye, she stepped back and closed the doors on the chilly mountain morning, and the man. The sun wasn't even fully up—she should still be asleep, she thought; maybe this was all a dream.

If she didn't look out the window again, she could pretend it was exactly that. A dream. She wasn't up at the butt crack of dawn, and Jack Bridger wasn't really back.

And she really didn't care either way.

Maybe her mother was right—unlike her siblings, she did like lying to herself.

Holy Mother of God.

Jack breathed out hard, blinked, then stooped, picked up the new microwave, and carried it into the house and to the kitchen. Where he grabbed a beer from the fridge, popped the cap, and tilted the bottle to his lips. He didn't stop until it was empty. Then went for a second.

Poppy had grown up for real.

The vibrancy and sheer charisma that woman possessed, even at eighteen, had been off the charts. She was the only person in existence who made him want to smile, made him want to be better than what he'd been born into.

And he admitted—always privately, and only in moments of weakness—that he judged everything he did by whether or not he believed Poppy would understand. For all her sweet temper and easy smiles, she could be a bloodthirsty little thing when it came to the idea of justice.

She'd killed the man sexually assaulting her and would have reported it if she hadn't been terrified he'd be blamed for it instead. Deception never sat well with her, and he knew she'd struggled that year to accept what had happened.

Thankfully, her brother Mac had been there for her. Once he'd walked in on the bloody scene and learned what had happened, he'd agreed with Jack: No one would believe she'd killed a man. Hell, there were times Jack knew that Mac had struggled to believe it.

Wiping his forehead with his wrist, he gave another silent sigh at how damned pretty she'd turned out.

Those fiery curls hung around her face and shoulders, and her face was sleep-tousled as she leaned lazily against the doorframe in rainbow-striped pajama pants and a dark blue sleeveless top that barely met the waistband. No bra. He'd noticed that first off.

But she'd greeted him, lifted her cup and given him a little smile before retreating back into the house.

He could pretend that little coffee wave was an invitation, he told himself as he glanced at the beer. He'd been up all night driving and had a lot to unload from the truck. He could use a cup of coffee.

He grimaced at the thought.

Damn, none of this was going to be easy, and none of it would be right or fair, but he was committed now. The fact that she was innocent wouldn't change anything. Her association with the suspected guilty parties and her known fondness for Jack were going to be her downfall.

Moving to the still open door, beer in hand, he gazed at the little single-story house she'd bought the year before. With its wide back porch, white picket fence, and attached garage, he admitted it suited Poppy.

It was, as some of his former team members' wives and girlfriends would call it, "cute." There were flowers along the side of the house, a weeping cherry off to the side of the wide porch with a black iron bench beneath it.

He watched the kitchen blind shift again as he took a sip of the second beer. He knew he should be getting the house ready so he could get some rest. The bed still had to be made, the television set up.

Ian had made certain he had internet access and cable turned on. Thankfully. The bastard hadn't offered to help unload the truck, though.

Damn. A cup of that coffee would be good, he thought again. Damn good.

What he was going to do was for her own good. He was protecting her, he told himself. And he definitely didn't deserve her, but by God, he was going to claim her. She'd owned him since he was fourteen years old, and now he was back for good. She was grown.

It was time.

The firm knock at her front door thirty minutes after she'd stepped back into the house didn't surprise her. There was a resigned sense of fatalism instead. She'd known, perhaps not consciously, but still, she'd known that this time, Jack would be there.

Just as she knew who was knocking at her door now.

An old country song her mother still listened to drifted through her head. Something about the devil knocking.

Wiping her palms down the hips of her hastily donned jeans, she straightened her sleeveless summer blouse, then ran her fingers through her damp hair as she walked to the door.

She congratulated herself for not running.

Unlocking the dead bolt and doorknob, she opened the door and stepped back.

"Lord, it's the devil," she murmured, unable to stop the smile that curled her lips. "Would you look at him!"

The familiar quirk of his lips. Not a smile, but an acknowledgment.

"Terri Gibbs," he named the singer as he stepped into the house and those dark gray-and-blue eyes seemed to soften. "Hello, Poppy. It's been a while."

"Yes, it has been." She nodded, moving to the coffeepot for the cup she'd placed under the one-cup coffee maker. "I'm surprised you're not avoiding me this year as you usually do."

"I didn't avoid you before," he told her quietly, as unsmiling and somber as ever. "I gave you distance. There's a difference."

She ignored the excuse. "You want coffee? It's two times the caffeine."

She turned just in time to catch the arch of his black brow, as though he was surprised.

"Caffeine used to make you jittery," he reminded her.

"Now it just wakes me up." She grinned, brushing back a curl that seemed to insist on slipping over her eye. "I don't have regular caffeine if that's what you're after."

She slipped the pod into its chamber and started the brewing anyway.

"The more pick-me-up the better," he assured her, his deep, dark voice still calm, almost lazy.

She didn't bother asking if he wanted cream and sugar. Jack was a pretty no-nonsense kind of guy, always had been. And cream and sugar were nonsense when it came to coffee.

Brushing back that wayward curl again, she handed the cup to him as he stepped to the counter.

"You're lookin' good, Bridger." She grinned—she couldn't help it. "If you're going to stay more than a day or two, you'll have the women lining up for your attention."

He grimaced. "God save me. I'd like to get the house fixed up, and the yard. Enjoy the summer a little maybe."

She hoped her cup hid her surprise as she sipped at her coffee.

"Staying awhile, are you?" She glanced down at her bare toes.

The sassy toe ring, the chip in her polish. She should have slipped her sneakers on.

"Maybe." He shrugged. "See how I like retirement."

There was no hiding her surprise now. "Retirement? What are you, all of thirty-two? Who retires at thirty-two?"

"Me," he stated without explanation. "It was time."

She imagined that more than a decade as a Navy SEAL could disillusion a man. She'd always had the feeling Jack had been born disillusioned, though.

"So, you're home for good?" she asked, ignoring the vibration of her phone in her back pocket.

Her brother was insistent.

"Maybe." He glanced around the kitchen, then back at her. "How are you doing, Poppy? Good?"

Was she doing good? She had a good job, good friends. A nice house.

She nodded. "I'm doing good, Jack. You?"

"Normal." His expression didn't change, but his eyes seemed to soften.

They'd always done that. They were the color of gunmetal and ice normally, but the color would soften, become a little darker whenever she met his gaze.

She'd liked that. It made her feel as though the hard, normally reserved young man he had been thought of her as a friend. As someone special.

"And what's normal for a retired Jack Bridger?" She smiled back at him, despite the painful thought.

He shrugged, and by the twist of his lips she sensed a bit of discomfort. "Ain't been retired long enough to find out, I guess."

He sipped at his coffee, just watching her as though he had nothing better to do, and nowhere to be. For a moment, she was seventeen again, slipping out of her bedroom window to join her friends in late-night teenage fun. And no matter where they went, it seemed Jack was sure to show up. He'd find a beer and a place to sit, and for the most part, just watch.

Until he began fighting.

Before the night was out, he'd end up in a fight, and everyone knew that when that happened the local police or sheriff would be there soon. Her friends would get her out of there, she'd slip back to her room, and the next day she'd go looking for him. Just to be certain he was okay.

Finishing her coffee, she continued to hold the cup, not wanting him to rush away.

"I'll take another cup of that coffee to go, if you can spare it," he finally said. "I still have a long day ahead of me before I can crash."

"Do you have everything you need? Sheets, blankets?" she asked, taking his cup. "Pillows?"

Her brothers were always forgetting the oddest things when they traveled.

"I'll get what I need later, if I forgot anything." That shrug again, as though it didn't matter. "Coffeepot. Coffee." He accepted the second cup, glanced into it, then back at her quizzically. "Where do you get your coffee?"

"Walmart," she drawled. "Coffee aisle. Two times the caffeine right on the box."

He nodded, then stepped closer.

Poppy felt her heart pick up in speed, felt adrenaline and heat begin spreading beneath her skin.

His hand reached up, pushed back that damned curl that kept falling forward, then he brushed his knuckles over her cheek as his head bent.

And did she move?

Did she step back?

"I haven't forgotten that kiss you gave me when you were eighteen, Poppy," he whispered, his nose nearly touching hers, the heat of his body surrounding her. "I think about it. Often."

Poppy blinked, stepped back, and shook her head.

She remembered the kiss, remembered how she'd begged for it. How desperate she'd been to wipe away the memory of having Wayne Trencher's lips on hers.

"If I were you, that kiss would be the least of what I remembered, Jack," she sighed heavily. "What you did for me . . ."

"Do you still have nightmares?" he asked her softly then.

Poppy inhaled deeply, pushing back the need to crawl into his arms as she had done that night.

"Mac mentioned they got pretty bad for a while," he said.

Yeah, he and Mac talked whenever Jack came in. He avoided her, but not her brother.

"Not often," she told him.

The night she'd been attacked still had its moments that haunted her, though. The feel of her legs being forcibly parted, the feel of her flesh itself being parted even as she rammed the blade of that little dagger straight into his chest in a blow filled with rage and fury.

She jerked away from the memory.

"Is that why you stayed away when you were in town all these years?" she asked, fearing, despite his insistence that she not report what had happened, that she'd somehow disappointed him.

"God, no." He frowned back at her. "I wanted you to have time to put distance between you and the memory, I guess. Time to heal, and to grow up."

"I healed." She gave him a short nod. "Mac found a doctor I could talk to, so I had a year of therapy while in college. I grew up."

"You did indeed grow up," he agreed, the dark rasp of his voice stroking over her senses and heating them.

"Still." She attempted a smile by the twist of his lips. "You didn't have to avoid me. I've missed you."

And she wouldn't go further. She wouldn't beg for his attention.

"As I said, I didn't avoid you." His gray eyes seemed to darken before he gave another short nod of his head. "Thanks for the coffee," he murmured, stepping back, his gaze flashing for a moment, steel ice, before it softened again. "I'm sure I'll see you soon."

He turned and left the house, his movements quiet for a man his size and oddly graceful.

But, she knew how easily he could move.

How deadly he could be.

As the door closed behind him, she covered her mouth with

her hand to hold back the need to call him back, to have him hold her. And she would have, if it hadn't been obvious that he felt the need to escape.

It had been eight years.

But she hadn't forgotten. She didn't think she ever would.

CHAPTER FOUR

Her parents' home was chaos when Poppy arrived. Four nephews tore through the house like mini-hurricanes as her sisters, the oldest of the six Porter siblings, and their husbands sat at the large kitchen table and chatted with their parents and two brothers, John David and Evan. The oldest of the three boys, just a year younger than the twin sisters, hadn't returned yet from a trip he'd taken with his infant daughter to see her maternal grandparents in Virginia.

Mackenzie Cole Porter, or Mac-Cole as he was often called, had been her lifeline in the year after Jack left town following Wayne Trencher's death. There were days Poppy knew that if he hadn't been there, she would have become lost in the fear and shattering knowledge of what had happened, what could have happened.

John David rose from the table as she entered, his blue-gray gaze intent, his handsome face pulled into almost wary determination as he faced her.

Dressed in gray slacks and a white short-sleeved shirt, he looked every inch the district attorney he was. He was elected into the position at a young age the year before. At thirty-two, he was known for his tenacity and the fact that he ran his office honestly, and without prejudice.

"Can we talk a minute?" he asked as the rest of the family watched them both, almost warily.

"Thought you were out of town," she grumped, heading for the hall outside the kitchen. "Make this little discussion fast. I'm not in the mood for a long, drawn-out argument."

She was aware of him moving behind her, and as she entered her bedroom, she turned to him as she placed her bags on the bed.

"You see Bridger yet?" he asked, standing in front of her with his "prosecutor's face," as she called it. All serious and intent, his gaze eagle-sharp.

"He walked over this morning for coffee," she told him, crossing her arms beneath her breasts and frowning back at him. "Why?"

A grimace pulled at his lips as he raked his hands through his thick, short hair.

"I have friends in the military, Poppy," he told her heavily. "I got a call from one last week, informing me to watch for Jack's return. He was discharged from the SEALs on a bad-conduct charge, but word is, he killed three men, private military agents for the US overseas, when he learned they were interrogating a small terrorist cell. One they suspect he was working with.

"Two days before he arrived a known suspected criminal figure, Ian Richards, moved into a house with his wife for an indefinite time. Two informants in town reported that Richards is waiting for him to hit town so they can connect. Richards ran the Fuentes drug cartel for a year in Colombia before Diego Fuentes disappeared, and he's rumored to head it now. Drugs, Poppy," John David emphasized quietly, knowing how she hated the impact illegal drugs had had on classmates from both high school and college.

"Jack wouldn't do drugs," she said, shaking her head in denial, certain that somehow, someone had to have their information wrong. "Not after what his father did while high on them. He hates drugs."

"Nine years ago he did," John David agreed, his expression determined, though his gaze softened as he watched her. "I know you always liked Jack. You felt sorry for him as a kid, you crushed on him when he became older. But for eight years I know he's avoided you. It's been apparent."

Poppy felt the humiliating flush that raced over her face at his charge. How many other people had noticed how he took pains to be certain he wasn't in her presence?

"That doesn't make him a junkie," she retorted.

Rubbing her hands over her arms, she turned toward the bed, then reached for the neatly pressed black skirt and tailored blouse she'd brought for work the next day.

"I didn't say he was a junkie. But others, men I trust, say he's a murderer. He was behind bars awaiting a court-martial when the evidence against him suddenly disappeared and his JAG attorney filed a wrongful arrest. The information just disappeared, Poppy," he stressed. "Now, he's back in town and a man that could have easily facilitated that disappearance because of his former SEAL status is waiting for him. That's no coincidence."

Unfortunately, Poppy agreed with her brother's assessment—coincidence could only stretch so far. But she'd often heard both Evan and Mac-Cole talk about how far the truth was stretched in military gossip as well.

"It doesn't matter anyway," she said, shrugging after she'd hung the clothes in her closet. "As you said, he avoids me. Even to the point that others have noticed over the years. I had the feeling he just stopped by this morning to reinforce the point that he wasn't interested. I don't think you need to worry about him deciding I'm suddenly his heart's desire."

"The man isn't capable of having a heart's desire. According to his medical files, there's a suspicion he's a high-functioning sociopath. Men like that aren't capable of emotion, Poppy. You know that."

Her lips thinned. Jack did not have antisocial personality disorder, no matter what anyone wanted to believe. Not before and not now.

He felt things; he just refused to show it. He'd always been like that. He regretted, he felt remorse, and he'd always been fond of her.

At least, he used to be.

Moving to her laptop case, she retrieved it from the bed and placed it on the table next to the headboard.

This morning, his eyes had softened as he watched her, and for a moment, just a moment, she'd seen a flash of heat in his eyes when he'd told her he remembered the kiss they'd shared when she was eighteen.

John David's voice softened. "I know you've always felt something for him. Half the time I think you've just been waiting for him to come home and realize you're here. He hasn't realized it yet, and he's not going to start now."

She barely controlled her flinch at the unintentional cruelty she felt at his words.

"How silly," she snorted, flashing him a derisive look.

John David shook his head as he stared at her almost pityingly.

He didn't mean to be so damned arrogant and judgmental, she knew. He only became like this when he tried to protect her or convince her to use more caution. She could be impulsive, he often reminded her. And too trusting.

"You rarely date, and when you have, every man you've dated has stated that the relationship didn't work because of your lack of sexual interest," he pointed out.

She clenched her teeth, then breathed in deeply to contain the anger she could feel brewing inside her.

"So, since I don't sleep around, because I want to wait until it feels right, I'm somehow in the wrong?" she questioned him, only barely managing to hold on to her temper. "Maybe out of that group of would-be lovers, someone should inform one to brush his teeth, and another to wear deodorant. And then there was the one that wanted to shove his tongue down my ear canal, and another that informed me in no uncertain terms that any wife of his wouldn't work, but would stay home and breed for him while taking care of the house and making his life comfortable." She gave a roll of her eyes as she spread her arms out before dropping them to her side. "Yeah, those were some wonderful candidates as lovers, I'll agree with you."

His lips twitched. "God, Poppy, I swear I know who you're talking about, and I can't believe you went out with him."

She sniffed, not at all happy with his sudden amusement, mostly because he was actually right. Until the past year, she'd been waiting on Jack.

"If I decided to sleep with anyone, then my three brothers"— she held up three fingers—"older brothers, mind you, will know about it before whoever it is leaves my house the next morning. You would have something bad or insulting to say about him, and Daddy will be uncomfortable if I bring him to dinner, because you know how old-fashioned he turned out after his and Momma's wild hippie-wannabe days. And every one of you would start pressuring me to get married and have babies." She all but sneered when in fact she wanted to cry, because there was a time she'd dreamed of doing just that.

He glanced away, regret crossing his face, but she knew that his attitude wasn't going to change.

"You're probably right," he finally admitted on a sigh. "Just promise me you'll give me a chance to find out what Bridger's into before you—"

"He ignores me and avoids me," she reminded him, her voice tight as she forced herself not to curl her fingers into fists. "Doesn't matter if I felt something for him, John David. He doesn't want me, so that pretty much makes this conversation the height of idiocy. Now will you please leave me just an ounce of pride here and drop the damned subject? Or I can go home and tell Momma and Daddy why I won't be here for dinner."

And she would do it. It wouldn't be the first time she and John David had butted heads and she'd left the house. Usually because he had some dumbass opinion on a decision she had made.

His eyes narrowed at the threat.

"And don't give me that look," she snapped irritably. "It's never bothered me in the past, and it won't now."

She didn't give him a chance to reply or argue, but pushed past him and left the bedroom as she fought to hold her hurt inside.

She simply couldn't believe what he'd told her about Jack. Drugs were Jack's sore point. He hated them, and she'd seen his anger when he learned someone around him was using. He hated it. He would refuse to associate with those who did drugs.

At least, he had in the past.

She couldn't even say for sure what he would do now, but she knew if that had changed, Mac-Cole would know it, and her brother had never mentioned it to her.

Of all her siblings, only Mac knew how she felt about Jack for sure. It was Mac she'd question after Jack left town each year, Mac who'd listened quietly the few times she'd given words to her regret that what she'd done that summer seemed to have destroyed her friendship with Jack. And it was Mac who had assured her that she was wrong.

He wouldn't lie to her, but if he'd felt Jack was a sociopath, or somehow dangerous to her, he would have surely told her.

Unless he was certain Jack wasn't interested in her anyway and he had nothing to worry about. Unlike John David, Mac didn't like hurting her, and if he thought there was no chance of Jack showing interest, then he might not warn her against him.

Stepping back into the kitchen with the rest of the family, she moved to her parents for their customary hugs, kissed them on their cheeks, and sat at the table before the rush to fix dinner began.

One of the twins brought her coffee when she returned to the table with her own. Her brothers-in-law teased her because she still wasn't bringing home a man to meet her parents and crazy family. Her nephews rushed in for hugs and a willing ear to hear about their boyish adventures.

She listened, laughed, related a few amusing stories from her job, and let herself fall into the routine. All the while, she was aware of her brother's often probing looks and the suspicion in his eyes. She was confident there was nothing for him to see, though. She'd learned how to bury fear, nightmares, and pain. A single summer night when she'd forced a friend and her brother to cover up her crime had made her learn how to hide parts of herself.

Parts of herself she knew only one man could heal. A man who had no intention of trying, and no desire to.

Someone in Ian's group had been watching Poppy for a while, Jack knew. The file they had on her was extensive, right down to her habits, favorite foods, where she liked to shop, and the fact that she normally stayed the night with her parents every third Sunday of the month.

She'd left with a leather overnight bag and garment bag just before ten that morning—because she had meetings scheduled Monday morning—and she'd kept her eyes on his house until she pulled from the parking lot in the three-year-old SUV she'd just bought that spring.

She'd pinned the front of her hair back, likely to keep that unruly curl in place, he thought. He had a fondness for that curl, because it seemed that no matter how long or how short her hair was, she'd had trouble with it staying in place.

He remembered brushing it back so he could kiss away her tears as he held her on the floor of a dirty shack.

Closing his eyes, he remembered the salty tears, her determination to replace the horror with at least a few moments of pleasure. He remembered her anger, her strength, and her refusal to give in to the hysteria he could feel racing through her body.

And he'd kissed her as a man.

At twenty-four he'd been experienced, hardened even then, already a SEAL, a killer. But that night, for one moment out of time, he'd been a man who wanted to love a woman. Who regretted the fact that if he could love, he'd have already given his heart to the young woman he held that night.

Because that kiss, as much as he hadn't held back with her, was still like a dream. The one and only moment of tenderness he'd probably ever felt for anyone else in his life. And he was about to betray that woman in the worst possible way.

He was going to use her to take down those she believed were friends. Two men she cared for, thought of as family. How could she forgive him for that?

As he waited through the day for nightfall, he worked at cleaning out the backyard, cut the grass, did some light maintenance.

As night fell, he drove through the alley behind the Porter home to ensure her vehicle wasn't there before returning to his own house. Then he showered and prepared to slip into Poppy's home.

It was one in the morning before he got up from his chair as he watched her house, tucked his service weapon at the small of his back, and slipped silently through his back door.

Her house was directly across the alley. Neighboring vehicles included several work vans and trucks, giving him reasonable concealment as he made his way to the back door.

Any security cameras were currently being jammed. Just as Poppy's home security system had been deactivated. Once he returned to his house, he'd reactivate them as though nothing had happened.

It took no time to unlock the back door, though he cursed her foresight in having nothing growing around her back porch. Thankfully, the roof provided enough shadows that he felt reasonably safe.

Stepping into the neat kitchen, he gazed around, his lips quirking at the night-light on the counter. Not enough illumination to shadow him against the blinds, but enough that he could easily see.

She had one in every room.

As he went through the house methodically searching for any paperwork or files, he learned quite a few things about her. Most he already knew, though. She had the same group of friends that she'd had at seventeen. She was impeccably neat, if you discounted the several junk drawers he found, drawers that held everything from safety pins to ink pens, screwdrivers, and rubber bands.

He went through her office, the guest bedroom, laundry closet, linen closet, and washroom before he stepped into her bedroom.

He could smell her there. On the mirrored dresser, he found a bottle of the perfume that gave her a spicy, ethereal scent, and made note of the name. She had makeup in one drawer, hair products in another. Frilly underclothes and pajamas in several others. The normal female stuff, with nothing hidden or pushed out of sight.

At the top of her closet, he found a large shoebox. In it were pictures, mementos, letters. Among them were several pictures he'd forgotten existed that had been taken of him with a younger Poppy. And several taken of him in the past nine years that she'd somehow gotten a copy of.

He stared at the last one taken of them together, the summer she turned seventeen. Damn, she was even prettier now than she had been then. Putting that picture in his back pocket, he replaced the box, then turned to her nightstand.

Buried beneath several books was a device he knew he should have expected but hadn't.

God help him. He was going to go to hell for sure for the images that suddenly filled his mind.

The vibrator with a clitoral stimulator attached and the sweetest fucking scent surrounding it.

Son of a bitch.

He replaced it hurriedly, but couldn't help but imagine Poppy, thighs spread, her head thrown back in pleasure as that fucking feminine toy did its job while she held it in place.

His cock swelled to full erection at the thought, his balls tightening. What did she think about, he wondered, while she let that damned toy have her?

Who did she think about?

He palmed his hardness through his dark pants, knowing that this discovery was going to fucking haunt him. Every time he looked over at her house when she was home, he'd wonder if she was lying there, wet and wild, moaning, whispering his name as that goddamned device fucked her.

He closed the drawer quickly and rose to his feet.

Not a file or a scrap of paper that couldn't be explained. There wasn't a laptop or a tablet, either, though he quickly realized she'd have taken that with her.

Tablet or laptop, either would be easy enough to get into once she connected it to her internet again. The small device he had attached to the back of her router ensured that.

All too soon he slipped from the house, and taking his time, making certain he wasn't seen, he made his way to his back door and into the house.

Locking the door behind him, he slid the added security of a metal bar across it and made a mental note to bring up the subject of security with Poppy at some point. Getting into her home had been far too easy, and he knew by the locks she used, and the fact that she had a lock on her bedroom door, that she took her security seriously.

Because she was afraid.

Because she didn't feel safe, even eight years after her attack. She'd been grabbed by Trencher in the dark and dragged into that dirty shack where he'd assaulted her. Now, the darkness was something she no longer trusted.

She did get horny, though . . .

Damn, he was not going to let himself become distracted by that thought again.

Pulling the secured mobile phone he carried from a side pocket of his black cargo pants, he quickly activated Ian's number.

He made his report noting Ian's obvious disappointment that there was nothing to be found. How anyone could imagine Poppy was involved in whatever was going on astounded him.

After finishing the call, he sighed and headed to the bedroom.

He'd been looking forward to a good night's sleep, but he doubted the hard-on torturing him would allow for much of that.

Nor would the thoughts of Poppy and that damned vibrator.

He wanted to watch her use it, he thought. Wanted to watch her work it inside herself, see what it did to her, and show her just how much better he could make it.

Fuck!

He'd never get any sleep . . .

CHAPTER FIVE

Three days later, and Poppy still couldn't make sense of the information her brother had given her or make it fit with the man she'd always believed Jack to be. It tormented her, filled her thoughts and left her chest tight deep into the night.

For some reason, all these years she'd thought she knew Jack inside and out. It had taken her brother to make her realize that there was really no way that was possible.

Until he was fourteen, she'd known who he was, but hadn't had any interaction with him. Mac and John David knew him, often mentioned that he'd come to school in dirty clothes, his face bruised. He was always angry, they said, and always confrontational. Mac had always spoken of Jack as though he felt sorry for him. John David had been critical sometimes.

When Poppy had found him hiding in their garbage, shivering, white but for the bruises that marred his exposed skin, her heart had instantly melted for the young boy. He'd been so determined to make her leave, but obviously desperate to hide from the father everyone knew to be a bully and drug user.

Once she'd gotten him into the house and her mother had given him clothes her brothers no longer wore, shoes, and a hot meal, Poppy had seen a gleam of fragile hope and thankfulness in him.

After her father had left the house with him to take him to his uncle's, she hadn't seen him for another four years. When he was eighteen, he showed up on their doorstep with flowers for her mother and a gift card to a building supply store for her father to thank them. Her mother for the food and clothes, her father for finding a cousin of her mother's willing to take him in.

The cousin—a retired Navy SEAL—and his wife were childless, and had no knowledge of Jack before Cole Porter contacted them, but they'd immediately taken custody of the nearly broken Jack.

After that, for the next eight years, he came back to Barboursville for a few weeks every summer, sometimes a few months. He'd stay in the old house his parents had died in, working on it, keeping it repaired, and he always made a point to send her mother flowers and to find a chance to say hello to Poppy.

Just a few weeks out of the year. They didn't talk much until she'd turned fifteen and began sneaking out with her friends to the summer parties. And he was always there. He'd talk to her awhile, let her flirt with him a little, and make certain no one bothered her or her friends. And she suspected he was the one who called her brother Mac each time to let him know she needed a ride home. Because it was always Mac who showed up to collect her and her friends.

For a few weeks out of the year, those years between fifteen and eighteen, Poppy found herself watching for him, waiting for him. Certain she loved him.

Then Wayne Trencher had struck and thrown her entire life off-kilter After that horrifying night, see'd rarely seen him. Other than a wave here and there, once or twice a hello, they hadn't spoken.

Her mother still received flowers with a thank-you card, her father and Mac talked to him whenever he was in, but he'd avoided Poppy.

And still, she would have sworn she knew him to the depths of his soul if John David hadn't made her realize that just wasn't possible. The painful realization was like a dagger to a heart that just refused to accept that it could be true.

Standing in the wide window of her third-story office, Poppy watched the traffic below. The building sat close to the middle of town, the third floor dedicated to Crossfield-Dawson, though the two men owned the whole building and leased the two floors below to various other businesses.

She watched the pedestrians going to and fro, small groups gathering across the street in a tree-shaded, grassy area with half a dozen picnic tables. Across from the postage-stamp-sized picnic area were several restaurants and some of the smaller shopping establishments that led into the Barboursville mall. Trees lined the street, and the scene was peaceful. Tranquil.

It was a busy area, drawing shoppers and business professionals from Kentucky, West Virginia, and Ohio.

Crossfield-Dawson owned quite a few of the outlying commercial real estate properties, and made a healthy profit from them. She knew they did, because she handled the leases herself and negotiated the contracts on many of those larger properties.

She knew she should be going over several of those leases that were coming up to re-sign, notating those whose monthly rent needed to be adjusted, and poring over the dozens of financial spreadsheets she had on each one. There was a box under her desk, filled with files and papers she needed to go over, that she kept pushing out of her way. The new receptionist had insisted they belonged with her.

She knew she should be working on them.

Instead, she was staring down at the street, her gaze moving over the area as though there were answers to be found there.

She brushed back the curl she could never keep in place, glaring at her image in the window for a second.

Her red-gold hair was more or less confined to the neat French braid she'd pulled the curls into that morning. All but that one corkscrew curl in the front that refused to be confined.

There was a delicate arch to her brows over her deep green eyes. She considered herself passably pretty. Lightly freckled along her cheeks and the bridge of her nose, with high cheekbones and what her father called "Cupid's bow lips" that smiled more often than not.

The white blouse and cherry red slim skirt she wore with black heels made her legs look longer. The tailoring of the blouse complemented her breasts. She wasn't a beauty, but she wasn't a hag, she thought. Still, other than that one time she'd begged Jack to kiss her and take away the memory of Trencher's kiss, he'd never shown interest in her.

She was going to have to stop this, she told herself. She had to accept the fact that she simply couldn't love someone who had never taken the time to allow her to get to know him. Jack had saved her by giving her the means to save herself, her brother Mac had once told her, and she was going to have to accept that their relationship went no further than that. Because the man she thought she knew and the one John David had received information on were two different men.

As she resumed her seat at her desk, a sharp knock on the door announced one of her bosses, Caine Crossfield, as he pushed open the door and stepped inside.

He was nearing forty years old, and his handsome features and charming smile, combined with his dark blue eyes, made him one of the most sought-after bachelors in the state. He was a former

Army Ranger, his career cut short ten years before when the Humvee he was in activated an IED. The explosion had hurled the vehicle into the air and tossed it like a child's plaything, breaking multiple bones in his body.

"Poppy, we have a problem with one of the storage facilities on the other side of town." He carried a file in his hand that he tapped against his leg impatiently. "The lessee, Gordon Tessalon, is bitching about security and driving me crazy."

Gordon Tessalon had been an ongoing problem for most of the year.

"Did you email the file?" she asked, knowing he hadn't.

He stopped short of her desk, glanced at the file he carried in his hand, and let a sheepish smile curl his lips.

"I brought it with me?" he offered without apology.

She shook her head at him, not for the first time, and extended her hand demandingly. "Hand it over, dinosaur."

He grimaced at the accusation. It was well known he didn't care for electronic files but preferred the feel of the paper files and the sense of control they gave him. No electronic gremlins to suddenly go haywire and delete something, he often said.

"We're not required to supply security, Caine," she reminded him. "The security he's demanding is on the sister facility a couple of miles away, and three times what he pays on his lease." She flipped through the file, checking the company's contractual promises. "Additional security is the lessee's responsibility at the site Tessalon is on. He's just still pissed because he wanted in to the secured facility after we'd already assigned all the units. But I'll call him if you want."

Tessalon used the storage facility as a shipping point. From Columbus to Barboursville, then trucks distributed various farm equipment and parts to the tristate area.

"Tell him I said to 'bite me,'" he suggested. "Take care of this today, if you don't mind."

The sharp order had her brows lifting in surprise.

"I have a meeting with him after lunch, actually." She frowned back at him. "Is everything okay, Caine?"

"Peachy," he grunted with a mirthless twist of his lips. "Sorry, Poppy. I know I sound like a little bitch. Shoulder's giving me hell today and River's out of the office this week. I'm not in the best of moods, I guess."

He never was when River failed to come in for whatever reason.

"I'll handle Tessalon this afternoon," she promised. "I won't be coming back to the office, though. I have a meeting with a potential client at five this evening to discuss the Storing House in Hurricane for possible lease. I'll need to get ready and reacquaint myself with the lease on it before we meet."

"Excellent." He nodded. "I wondered if you'd ever manage to get any interest in the house. It's about time."

She stared at his back balefully as he turned and left the office, the irritable reply causing her to clench her teeth to hold back a retort.

She was the property manager, not the agent in charge of acquiring clients for it, and he damned well knew it.

Two hours later Poppy stepped into the lobby outside her office to make her way to the elevator and a meeting she really wasn't looking forward to.

Why a distributor for farm equipment and parts needed so much security she couldn't quite figure out. One thing was for sure: She was going to have to make him understand it was his cost, not Crossfield-Dawson's. Even if they would acquire the system once Tessalon left the lease. Tessalon had agreed to the terms; he could live with them.

Jack had just thrown his leg over the Harley when Poppy stepped from her back door that evening. Juggling a slim leather briefcase, her purse, and her keys, she locked the door, then turned and quickly made her way down the steps to the cement walk leading to the alley parking area.

It was all Jack could do to keep his jaw from dropping and to force himself to breathe.

How the hell she managed to tame all those fiery curls into a sleek, shining, straight ribbon of hair that fell below her shoulders, he had no clue. But she'd done just that. She'd also dressed in a killer soft green, figure-hugging dress that left her shoulders bare, showed a hint of cleavage, and ended just above her knees, while matching heels encased her delicate feet.

She looked like a million bucks, distracted as she talked into the Bluetooth connection at her ear, and apologizing ever so sweetly for being late but adding that she was on her way.

Son of a bitch. Poppy had a date?

Crossing his arms over his chest, he glared at her as she made her way toward her vehicle, certain his head was about to explode at the thought. He'd been trying to catch her home for three fucking days to invite her to a barbecue party outside of town, and couldn't seem to do it.

She'd reached the end of the walk before disconnecting the call and looking up, only to come to a hard stop when she caught sight of him.

What the hell was that expression that flashed across her face? Regret. Anger. Now that just didn't make sense.

"Got a date?" he asked, ensuring his tone didn't hold the pure animalistic growl that wanted to escape. He even managed a fucking smile. Kinda.

Guilt flickered in her gaze. "I'm late," she muttered, just loud enough for him to hear the words. "Goodbye, Jack."

Now, didn't that sound final enough?

She hurried to the SUV, climbed in, and started the motor.

Within seconds she was pulling away and heading to the main street. And she didn't even look back.

"Oh, sugar girl," he sighed, shaking his head as he watched the SUV disappear around the corner. "That shit just ain't gonna work with me."

Pulling up the GPS device attached to her SUV on his smartphone, he waited, watching closely for a good ten minutes before she pulled into one of the nicer restaurants in Huntington. Upscale, pricey. Oh yeah, his Poppy thought she had a date.

Starting the Harley, he revved the engine, then pulled out and followed her.

He had no idea what she thought she was doing, but it was a mistake on her part. He'd seen the look on her face—whatever was going through her mind, she obviously believed he had no hold on her.

He'd had a claim on her since he was fourteen years old, and he guessed it was high time he made that clear to her. For damned sure, it was time to make certain there were no more dates with other men for the foreseeable future. Or forever.

Jack knew he wasn't exactly a good person. His personal code wasn't always agreeable with society's image of who and what a man should be. No doubt it wasn't Poppy's idea of who he was. But he'd thought they could make it work without any undue difficulties.

When his woman thought she could go out with another man, though, there were undue difficulties, ones that needed addressing quickly.

A relationship with her wasn't just imperative to the mission he was on, but to him. He hadn't taken the mission because of the threat to national security or any other pie-in-the-sky fucking reason. He'd taken it because of her. Because she would have expected him to, and because she was no doubt in danger herself. That he couldn't allow, any more than he was going to allow this date.

His men were due to report in at midnight. Before that meeting occurred, this had to be taken care of. He was either going to let Ian know she was no longer the key into Crossfield and Dawson's little group, or he was going to report the mission was good to go as planned.

Until then, he had to break this little date up, get Poppy back to her house, figure out what the hell had happened, and ensure it didn't happen again. All before midnight and despite the pure male outrage burning inside him.

Damn that woman.

"As you can see in the floor plans, the house has all the amenities you were looking for plus quite a few extras." Poppy sat back in the upholstered chair after dinner and stared across the table from the potential new client, Steven Armstrong. "It's located in Hurricane, a halfway point between Barboursville and Charleston. It has its own private airfield, indoor-outdoor heated pool, a large ballroom, and balconies on each of the six upstairs bedrooms. I think you'll find that it's more than suited to fit your needs."

The Storing House was extravagance at its finest, hidden in the mountains in a lush valley filled with prime hunting and fishing.

"It looks incredible," Armstrong murmured as he went through the pictures she'd brought.

"The Realtor can meet you whenever you're ready to go through it, and should you decide it's what you're looking for, we can meet again to go over the lease." She gave him her best business smile, then gave the waiter a shake of her head as he paused at the table with a wine bottle to refill their glasses.

Dinner had been exceptional, the wine smooth and the dessert rich and luscious, but she was ready to go home now.

Steven Armstrong was nodding slowly as he went over one of the four reports she'd brought on the house.

"It looks perfect for my needs, I admit," he finally decided as he laid the papers on top of the open file and looked up. "I'll have my assistant contact Ms. Westbrook in the morning to arrange a time to meet. If everything works out, we could discuss the lease within the next few days."

It was all Poppy could do to keep the satisfaction from her expression. Cool and professional, she inclined her head in agreement.

Armstrong closed the file, his handsome features now shifting from business to charm. Just what she was hoping wouldn't happen.

She glanced discreetly at the small watch she wore on her arm, a silent indication that it was time for her to leave, then caught the waiter's eye with a nod for the bill.

"Dinner's on me," he told her as she glanced back at him.

"Crossfield-Dawson is more than happy to pay for the meal." She smiled. "My bosses would have my head otherwise, Mr. Armstrong."

"Well, we couldn't have that," he told her, frankly admiring. "Tell me, Ms. Porter—"

"Steven? I didn't realize you were in the area." Smooth, cultured, and amused, a feminine voice spoke behind Poppy in a familiar, welcoming tone.

Poppy knew who it was before the woman and her husband paused at the table to greet Armstrong.

"Kira. Ian." He rose to his feet with a pleased smile and kissed Kira on the cheek before shaking Ian's hand.

Kira Richards was beautiful. She had to be in her fifties but appeared much younger. As did her husband, the son of a cartel kingpin whose date-rape drug had destroyed dozens of lives across the nation more than a decade before.

"Allow me to introduce Ms. Poppy Porter of Crossfield-Dawson," he said, nodding to Poppy.

"Good evening." She nodded at the couple.

"Join us for drinks," Ian Richards all but ordered, his grown eyes a rich, almost honey brown as he looked back and forth at them. "I'd like to discuss a security concern, if you don't mind."

Steven didn't appear ingratiating or overly pleased, which she gave him kudos for, but he nodded all the same.

"Shall we?" He turned to her as though it were assumed that she'd agree.

"I have to decline. Work tomorrow." Poppy excused herself as she made to push her chair back.

Ian Richards was there instantly, easing it back and allowing her to rise to her feet as he smiled down at her pleasantly.

She murmured her thanks before turning to the waiter and signing the check that would put the bill on the Crossfield-Dawson account, along with a nice tip.

"You should join us," Ian said. "I hear we have a friend in common. Jack Bridger."

There was a gleam of calculating interest in Ian Richards's gaze that she found distinctly uncomfortable.

"We're acquainted," she informed him. "I wouldn't say 'friends' exactly, but he is a neighbor." She gave the couple another cool smile. "If you'll excuse me, it's late, and I need to get home." She turned back to her client. "It was a pleasure to meet you, Steven," she said sincerely. "I look forward to seeing you again soon."

She didn't run from the restaurant, but she didn't hesitate or waste time leaving, either.

The Richardses' appearance wasn't welcome, as far as she was concerned. She'd met Kira several times at the small boutique in town that Poppy's friend Lilith owned. She'd liked the woman, and hated that she hadn't known who she was at the time.

Leaving the restaurant, she was aware of the Harley parked not far from her SUV and the man sitting on it as the motor idled with a dangerous throb.

Her eyes narrowed, lips thinning as she wondered just what the hell he was doing there. Probably waiting to meet with Richards, she thought caustically.

How could he have changed so much in eight years? she asked herself as she got into her vehicle and started the motor. Making herself accept that he could have changed that much was the most difficult challenge she'd faced in years. Jack had always been a hero in her eyes. A Navy SEAL, one of the good guys. A man who'd risked his own freedom to save her.

The drive home was short, uneventful, but afterward she wished she'd paid more attention to the traffic behind her. If she had, she would have known that the Harley was following her before she turned into the back street that bisected their homes.

Parking, she turned the motor off and left the vehicle as he parked the bike in the area across from hers and hurried to the back walk to the house.

She couldn't deal with talking to him. What he'd want she had no idea. He hadn't bothered in past years to talk to her, and she didn't imagine they had anything to talk about now. But as she walked to her back steps, she realized he was right behind her.

Poppy swung around, staring up at him in the illumination of the porch light she'd left on, her mouth drying out at the vision of tall, dark, and dangerous that he presented.

Jack was dressed in leather riding chaps, jeans, a T-shirt, and a leather vest. His hair was windblown, his expression subtly predatory. She should have been scared out of her wits. But evidently, she didn't have the common sense for that.

"Can I help you, Jack?" She couldn't convince herself that he could possibly be dangerous.

She proved it when she turned on her heel and hurried up the steps to the back door. It didn't even occur to her that he'd follow her.

"You damn sure can," he muttered as she unlocked the door.

He sounded dangerous, his voice growly, with a rasp she found far too sexy.

She paused then, and was about to turn to him when his hands suddenly gripped her waist and he urged her into the house, following her closely. The door shut firmly behind them, the dead bolt clicking locked.

"Are you insane?" she snapped, slapping at his hands as she pulled away from him, turning on him furiously and staring up at him in the dim light of the kitchen.

"I have no doubt," he growled, and before she realized his intent, she found herself up against the wall, one big hand in the back of her hair as he pulled her head, the other at her waist to hold her in place, and his lips covering hers.

Poppy gasped, her lips parting, and he took instant advantage of it, his tongue pushing past her lips, licking, stroking against hers as instant, heated pleasure wiped everything but his kiss from her mind.

Her hands were in his hair, the cool, silken strands caressing her sensitive flesh as she let the pleasure surge through her, wiping away the fact that she was certain she didn't know this man. What she did know at the moment was every fantasy she'd ever had of him, every whisper of his name, as she fought to pleasure herself.

Just as she knew with every beat of her heart that a part of her belonged to him. A part that she could never reclaim.

Damn her.

This wasn't how he'd intended to kiss her the first time. He'd meant to go slow, easy. To explore rather than ravish. But she'd slapped his hands away from her as though he were some upstart kid.

As though he hadn't belonged to her from the day she found him hiding in the fucking garbage, shivering with pain and cold, starving for food and desperate for just a moment's respite from the certainty that his father was going to kill him.

Slow and easy would have been good, he thought hazily, but damn if this wasn't as good as it got too. Her kiss was hot and sweet, almost innocent as he nipped and sipped from her lips before his tongue drew from the endless heat of hers.

Before he realized her intent, she nipped his tongue, causing him to jerk back and stare into her defiant little face in surprise.

"Say no," he dared her, holding her still as she squirmed against him. "Say it, Poppy," he growled as her chin lifted, breathing hard, her breasts rising and falling in panting breaths against his chest. "Say it and I'll walk away."

He'd probably sit down and fucking cry worse than a five-year-old girl after being denied a treat. That realization just pissed him off. At himself. Because he hadn't realized just how much he needed her touch until now.

"You're acting like a possessive lover . . ."

"I am a possessive lover," he assured her, jaw tight as jerked her closer, one hand moving to the softly rounded curve of her ass. "Accept another date, baby girl," he suggested as he clenched his fingers in the curve. "You'll find out how possessive I can be."

Her eyes widened, surprise and excitement vying for dominance in her face.

"You don't have that right," she gasped as he pulled the skirt of her dress higher and caressed the back of her thighs.

Damn, her skin was fine.

"I don't even know you, Jack . . ." Her voice trailed off as the hand that had been tangled in her hair curved around her breast, then stilled.

Jack couldn't believe those words had left her lips.

"Well, baby, just let me introduce myself . . ." he growled, his hand moving from her breast to her jaw, his lips covering hers again.

Didn't know him, did she? Well, he'd take care of that.

Poppy moaned in rising excitement, the sound uncontrolled as Jack held her jaw open while he kissed her deeper, hotter than ever. His tongue thrust against hers, one arm curving beneath her rear and lifting her closer, causing the snug skirt to slide higher on her thighs, nearly to her hips.

As he kissed her, Jack's hand roved over her rear, slid beneath the silk thong she wore, and met the thick moisture easing from her vagina. The caresses had her arching closer to him, sensations whipping through her body with a speed impossible to process.

Any ability to think, to make sense of the mesmerizing eroticism of touch, was obliterated within seconds.

Stroking the plump, bare folds of flesh between her thighs, he stroked around her swollen clit, the entrance to her body, then eased back, his lips moving to her neck as she gasped for air and found herself with her feet on the floor once again.

And she needed more.

She needed so much more.

As his lips smoothed over the sensitive flesh of her neck, she lowered her hands, pulling at the material of his T-shirt, dragging it out of the way and pushing it to his chest.

He wasn't the only one who needed to touch, to taste. She'd waited so long for this, for his kiss, for the pleasure she sensed awaited her. She'd fantasized, plotted, and imagined exactly what she wanted to do, exactly how she wanted to pleasure him.

Before he could stop her, her head bent, her lips going to his wide chest. She touched her tongue to his flesh, moaning at the hint of salt and male heat that met her taste buds and made her even hungrier for him.

She'd waited so long for this. For his touch, for the chance to touch him.

She'd worry about the rest of it when she had to. For now, Jack was here, and rather than stopping her, as she licked over one hard male nipple, he slapped his hands flat to the wall and just stared down at her.

"Go ahead, baby." He flashed her a hard smile. "Do your worst. I dare you."

CHAPTER SIX

It was dark, the kitchen heavily shadowed with only the fragile illumination of an under-counter light on the other side of the room. Poppy couldn't see Jack's expression, but she could see the intent gleam in his eyes, feel the waiting tension in his body.

Did he think she didn't have the nerve?

Did she have the nerve?

She let her nails rasp from his chest to those hard abs, feeling the muscles flex and tighten beneath her touch. As her lips wandered over his chest, her tongue licking, stroking, she grew more curious, more aroused.

He was allowing her touch, however she wanted to touch him. Her fingers trailed to the band of jeans.

"God, yes," he muttered, the sound a hard rasp as her fingers trailed lower, feeling the iron-hard erection beneath his jeans.

She'd fantasized so many times about touching him like this, tasting him.

Her fingers met at the wide buckle of his belt, shaking as she loosened the leather, knowing she was reaching a point of no return.

"That's it, sugar," he encouraged her, his voice low, mesmerizing.

The snap released and she eased the zipper down, certain she was going to burn alive in the flames building through her senses.

Pushing aside the denim material, she couldn't help but moan as the fingers of one hand curled around the rigid flesh rising from between his thighs. Iron-hard, thick, and long, the power she could feel pounding beneath his flesh had her breath catching.

"Fuck, you're gonna make me crazy," he groaned, moving back before he turned her and pushed her into a chair at the table sitting to the side of the cooking area.

Then one strong hand gripped the back of her head, the other wrapped around the base of his cock, and staring down at her with a savage gleam in his eyes, he held her in place as he brushed her lips with the head of his cock.

Poppy's hands gripped the riding leather that still covered his thighs, her nails digging into the material as a breathless gasp parted her lips. And a breath later, the silk over iron flesh parted them further as she heard the rumbled groan that left his chest.

Oh God. She had never done this.

Read it. Watched it.

Her lips parted further, allowing him to fill her mouth with the swollen crest as she tasted it, licked it.

"Oh, fuck yeah," he whispered, his groan encouraging her, easing the nerves threatening to spoil this first venture into sensuality with the man she'd always dreamed of taking it with.

Jack swore he was going to lose his fucking mind. That was all there was to it.

Innocence filled every caress of her tongue over the head of his cock, every draw of her mouth around it.

There was no wrong way for her to take him like this, but what she was doing was destroying his senses. His knowledge that he was likely the first to ever fill her mouth with a hard dick added to the sensual, heated pull, testing his control.

"Fuck, that's it, Poppy," he groaned as her mouth tightened around the head of his cock and her tongue flickered over it. When she rubbed that hot little tongue against the underside, right there where it was most sensitive, and she moaned in rising pleasure, he nearly lost it.

He could feel her pleasure in the act just as well as his own. She was sucking his dick like it was a favored treat. One she'd never had before, but one she'd longed for. Silken hands caressed the shaft, stroking in tandem to the rubbing caresses of her tongue and the firm draws of her heated mouth.

Little moans left her throat, sounds filled with hunger and her need for him, as the moist caresses sent his senses reeling.

Staring down at her in the shadows, the combination of moonlight spearing through the window over the sink and the under-counter lights she'd left on gave him just enough illumination to see her face. Sweet innocence and feminine need, pleasure and the need to pleasure.

He could feel his balls tightening, drawing beneath the base of his cock as he fought to hold back his release. Hard-driven and intense, his sexuality demanded he bury as deep as possible, mark her senses with the taste of his release and ensure she never forgot him. Never forgot his hold on her.

A groan ripped from his chest as the hardened flesh spasmed, spilling a pulse of pre-come to her mouth and causing her to pause.

Jack clenched his teeth, fought to pull back his release and ease the hold he had on her hair when her ragged moan filled the air and her mouth tightened around him, drawing, her tongue licking, searching for more.

He was within seconds of giving her more when a knock at her front door shattered the eroticism weaving around them.

"Come on, Poppy, I know you're home," a male voice called out in irritability.

Her head jerked back, eyes widening in sudden apprehension.

"Oh my God," she whispered. "John David."

Her brother?

Jack eased back, realizing that the hunger he had to fill her mouth wasn't going to be sated.

"Ignore him," he growled.

"Ignore him?" she hissed. "He has a key, and he'll use it."

Fuck.

Forcing his erection back into his jeans, Jack secured the material and eased the zipper over his furious hard-on.

"You have to leave." She was on her feet and at the back door next to him in a second, fumbling for the doorknob. "Now."

His brows lifted.

Not that he wanted to see her asshole brother, but why didn't she want her brother to know he was there?

The door swung open.

"You have to leave," she demanded.

"Ashamed of me, baby?" he drawled, watching the little flush that crawled under her skin.

"I've never been ashamed of you," she whispered back, though her tone was imperative. "But he can't see you here tonight. Now please, leave."

Oh, he was getting to the bottom of this one fast.

He gripped her arm lightly as she moved to turn away from him. "This time," he told her. "But you better get a handle on that brother of yours if he has a problem with me. Or I will."

Releasing her, he slipped out the back door as he heard the dead bolt releasing in the front door, then went down the steps and strode to the alley without haste, hoping John David had the nerve to confront him with whatever problem Poppy seemed to think her brother had with him.

He let his lips curl into a slow, anticipatory smile. As he heard the sound of Harleys nearing and mentally prepared for the meeting ahead, he knew exactly how he'd handle Poppy, and her brother as well.

By the time he passed Poppy's gate and stepped into the alley, three of the powerful machines had eased up to his back drive, the riders backing them into the parking area next to his bike with quick, well-practiced movements.

"Hey, boss," the oldest of the three—recently dishonorably discharged SEAL Lucas Royce—greeted him. Six-two, thirty-three years old, his hair already salt-and-pepper gray in contrast to the single gray streak Jack had along the right side of his head. Jack had had his badge of horror since he was fourteen.

Lucas had spent twelve years in the SEALs. Purple Heart recipient, Medal of Honor recipient, multiple Distinguished Service Medals. All wiped away when he'd taken out a military contractor who had leaked intel on an operation that caused the deaths of the two youngest members of Lucas's team.

Next to him was Hayes Granger. Hayes was a fighting machine. The fucker would get up and keep charging when normal men would have been dead. Dishonorably discharged for not just one but multiple violent occurrences against civilian assholes. Which he'd have gotten away with, if he hadn't decided to punch a commander whose bad decision on an op resulted in the death of Granger's mentor and team leader. He'd broken the commander's jaw and put him in intensive care.

Thirty years old, six-two like Lucas, his dark blond hair still military-short, his left cheek bisected by a scar he'd received in a bar fight as a teenager. Hard-drinking, always up for a fight, and a grinning fool if someone made the mistake of pulling a knife or gun. He was merciless then.

Sitting at the end of the line, more in shadow than not, was thirty-year-old Hank Brady. Jack knew Hank from several missions they'd participated in, and knew that he had a very low tolerance for bullshit or fuckups.

Like Jack, he was quiet, antisocial, and worked well only within his own team. Until that team had fucked up and caused the slaughter of several innocent women and children. Then he'd gone on a rampage that put three other SEALs in the hospital and the team's leader on medical discharge.

At six-three, he was tall enough to be imposing, with a natural musculature similar to Jack's. He was damned strong, and smart enough to make his way back to a team if he could control his anger issues, once this mission was over.

All four of them had their asses on the line. They fuck this up, the dishonorable discharges were for real, for all of them. No matter which one of them caused the fuckup.

The Navy had informed Jack fast that this was his one and only chance to keep that early retirement package they'd given him for taking this assignment. With the pension would come an added bonus from sources unknown for fixing whatever the hell was broke in this area of the country.

The others had their own financial packages to think of. Jack didn't give a shit what they were getting, and he guessed that, as for him, the financial end of things was the least of their worries. What was going on in their backyards was another matter.

"Hope you have beer and pizza," Hayes drawled, dismounting from his bike and staring around the alley with narrowed eyes. "We goin' in or what?"

"Didn't you just eat pizza a few hours ago?" Lucas quizzed him with an edge of surprise.

"I'm still a growin' boy," Hayes retorted, his smile tight and cold. "I need fuel to work at peak capacity, and pizza gives me the biggest bang for my buck."

That was something Jack understood. For the time being, their funds went from Jack's extremely limited to the others' nonexistent. They were still a few weeks away from those first checks arriving. Hopefully they'd walk away from tonight's meeting with operating funds.

"Beer and pizza inside," he promised. "Come on in."

He led the way into the house, the men moving behind him, watchful, suspicious.

"Who's watchin' us, boss?" Hank asked, his voice low as the door closed behind them. "I can feel it, but can't place it enough to decipher whether it's friend or foe."

Jack glanced upward, wondering if God had just a minute to help him keep his head in the game and his dick out of Poppy for at least one more night.

"Neither," he told Hank as he flicked a finger at the four large pizzas stacked on the kitchen table. "Beers in the fridge."

"Everyone is either friend or foe," Hank informed him, grabbing the top box and propping himself against the counter as he pulled a slice free. "Though mostly just foe. In any case, it can't be neither."

"House across the street. That hot little redhead . . ." That was all the man next to Hank, Hayes, got past his lips before his feet were swept out from under him and his ass landed on the floor.

He stared up at Jack in surprise.

"That redhead doesn't concern you," he told the other man with icy fury. Because he knew, to his soul, that Hank had intended some real disrespect to spew from his lips.

Lucas clicked his tongue at the other man chidingly. "You smart-assed young'uns never learn. She wasn't watching us. She was keeping her eye on Bridger as he walked away from her house. You don't pay attention real well, do ya, son?"

Carefully, Hayes swallowed as he rose slowly to his feet again. "I got ya, man. Won't happen again."

"It happens again, you won't get a chance to 'get me,'" Jack promised him with a tight smile. "The redhead is off limits, period. No discussion." He glanced around the room, then turned back to Hayes and sneered, "You got me?"

"Loud and clear, boss," Hayes promised, pulling a pizza box to himself and flipping it open. "Damn, I'm hungry."

Jack made eye contact first with Lucas, who besides Jack was the strongest of the group, then with Hank, and finally with Hayes.

"We're operating within a tight window," he warned them. "We have four to six weeks to find out who's involved and who's not, and to eliminate the threats before securing the target."

"Anyone know what the target is yet?" Lucas questioned, all business now.

"There's someone here to apprise you of the details." Jack held his hand up as the door to the guest bedroom opened and Ian Richards, Kira, and former SEAL team leader Reno Chavez stepped into the room.

Tall, still powerful, with black hair and piercing blue eyes, Reno looked every inch the fine, incredibly instinctive SEAL he was. Retired or not.

"Damn. Royalty in the house," Lucas murmured around a bite of pizza, the sincerity in his tone apparent despite the muffled delivery.

Stepping forward, Ian and Reno greeted each man, then sat down at the kitchen table with Kira and Jack.

"The target is this." Reno opened a hard-copy file and laid it out on the table.

The three other men gathered around it, going through it slowly. There wasn't a lot there. A few images of a scientist, the outline of a female skeleton with notes and notations, and behind that, a schematic of sorts filled with a computronic diagram.

"AI," Lucas said, his voice low as the other two continued to read. "Android or bot?"

"Not just AI," Hayes whispered in disbelief a second later, his gaze rising to meet Reno's. "Fuck me. That's a human duplicate. How the fuck . . . ?"

"It's being slipped in a piece at a time, according to our intel, to preserve the secrecy of the project in the case of an unexpected inspection of computer or digital shipments. And they're being real careful, because they're aware information on it was leaked to a contact at the CIA. It's to be assembled somewhere close by, the location provided by someone within Crossfield-Dawson, with possibly several high-ranking employees participating.

"This, gentlemen"—he tapped the diagram—"is a human duplicate prototype, programmed to carry out its assignment, go into hiding, and shut down until remotely activated to perform again. It's a sniper and explosives expert, equipped with all known hand-to-hand combat styles, proficient with knife, sword, or claw hammer if need be. It has no individual scent; animals will sense only the electronics and won't sound an alarm. It automatically jams security systems and can move virtually undetected. It has a carbon-based lead internal structure that messes with X-rays and gives all appearances of basic human build.

"It's the perfect weapon. And potentially, the end of life as we know it, if we don't find it, disable it, and disassemble it in time. We have no clue to its mission, or its full capabilities. The only way to learn those things is to find the AI itself."

Jack stared at the image just as he had the first time Kira and Ian showed it to him, after he'd signed his agreement to the mission.

This was what the world was coming to, he thought. It was no longer armies, teams, or, hopefully, a few men with consciences. It was this. Unfeeling, undetectable, and nearly unstoppable.

And if they didn't find it and disassemble it in time, only God knew the ramifications.

"This ain't possible," Hank muttered. "Shipped in pieces? That would indicate bot, not replicant."·

"Who?" Lucas asked, the meaning obvious.

Who had created this abomination?

Sliding several photos from another file, Reno answered, "That's one of the things we need to know, but we suspect it's this man— Chinese-American, based in Bangkok. Orin Chin. Billionaire and close associate of China's president—along with the owner of a French biotech research firm, Oswald Renier." Reno sighed. "You need to get in place, because intel says whoever within Crossfield-Dawson is involved will be looking for men they trust to back her and provide interference once she's activated, if she's detected, to complete her mission. So far, we have reason to highly suspect Crossfield, but we're not certain if Dawson is involved in the transportation or not."

"Why Crossfield and Dawson?" Lucas asked. "Their reputations in the area are solid. Former SF, no records. What makes you think it's them? And why ship it here? Barboursville? Really? Hell, we're like the back of beyond compared to other places."

"CIA has been tracking Crossfield for several years now. Weapons shipments, drugs, and human trafficking shipments, just to name a few, have been going through the area to an unknown location, then shipped from there to other areas. He's careful—only his men oversee the transport into and out of the area, and he chooses his cargo wisely. In this case, though, he was specifically named by our contact as being involved."

"Why does the AI need any form of protection if it's that well programmed?" Hayes questioned. "Seems well able to protect itself if you ask me."

"According to our contact, it will need backup and possible

oversight of some sort. That's information we believe only Crossfield and those controlling the unit will have."

"And they just had to make it female," Hayes whispered mournfully. "Motherfuckers. Pardon my French, ma'am," he said to Kira, his voice low. "But it took pure black evil to do that shit."

"A pretty, fragile-looking little blonde," Reno amended. "And, there's reason to suspect she's capable of operating beyond her original programming. We have evidence she may have the ability to not just understand but to portray emotion. She could be capable of evolving intelligence with the possibility of becoming self-sufficient."

"Fuck." Lucas made the word sound like a prayer.

"Exactly," Kira assured the SEAL. "Once it's found, Ian, myself, and Reno will bring in a team with the know-how to disable the power source and ensure activation can't occur. If it does occur, then we're screwed if it goes into protection mode."

"The four of you, with your backgrounds, psych profiles, and history of authority issues will be perfectly suited as far as Crossfield is concerned. But on the off chance you're not, your ability to make certain other teams consider you too much of a risk to face will put you in the exact position to be chosen. And Jack's connection to one of Crossfield-Dawson's employees will ensure they don't overlook him."

"We already have a hit on Jack's background," Reno stated, his gaze musing as Jack met it. "John David Porter, Ms. Porter's brother. He has access to certain Homeland Security files through his position as DA, and he's investigating Jack. He's already received the background we put in place. Expect problems."

Expect them? He had a feeling they were already there.

"I suspect he's already begun pressuring Poppy," Jack reported.

"She's the only one that can get you where you need to be, Jack," Ian stated. "She's part of upper management and close to the owners. And, she has access to every single property they own. We checked Tessalon, by the way. He's clear. Poppy's meeting was observed by several other parties who overheard Ms. Porter effectively putting him in his place before she left."

Jack nodded at the information.

"Clear her and bring her into the op? If she agrees to help us, she could get us into the properties without all the deception," Lucas mused.

That would be the perfect answer. Except . . .

Jack shook his head. "She was raised with them. Known them all her life. Besides, she doesn't lie worth shit in most cases. She'll have to believe whatever she's told, and I have to be damned careful there. She's smart. Intuitive. And she's careful about where she places her trust. That's what Crossfield-Dawson's group has. Implicit trust."

"She has access to the properties. You have access to her," Kira stated regretfully. "Unfortunately, no one can run interference with her brother, because your cover depends on everyone believing you're the self-serving little fucker it details."

"I am that self-serving fucker," he assured her, glancing up at her in unconcern.

"Whoever we're after has to believe it. No matter what. And making John David Porter a believer is especially important. He's even closer to the two men than his sister is. He can make the believable the Holy Grail."

Jack stared at the diagram, then gave an unconcerned shrug.

"I'll handle Junior. And I'll handle Poppy. No worries."

And he knew he would do exactly that.

What other choice did he have?

God knew he had too much blood on his hands to deserve her, but he wasn't about to allow that to stand in his way.

"She's a good woman," Reno stated then. "Everything we found on her points to that. And a woman like that, she can hate with the same depth of emotion as she loves, once she's been betrayed."

Jack's gaze met the other man's, flat, hard. He had known the second he saw the file what he'd end up doing to her. And decided the cost was worth it.

He was just praying that her belief that hiding certain things to protect those she loved would extend to understanding that there were times that he had to do the same.

"I killed my own father when I was fourteen years old," he reminded Reno, the subtle growl in his voice a reminder of the lethal predator he could be. "With zero remorse. I have twenty justifiable kills to my record, and trust me when I tell you there are some whose bodies will never be found. And I have zero remorse. When I'm done here, that single weakness you claim I have will still be living, breathing, and a part of this world. And I'll have zero remorse."

At the end of the day, Poppy's safety was really all that mattered.

CHAPTER SEVEN

The next evening Poppy bypassed stopping by the house after work to change clothes, choosing instead to go straight to the small bar she and her friends met at most nights for drinks and a light dinner.

Several meetings in South Point, Ohio, with potential lessees for commercial offices she managed had ran much longer than she'd anticipated, and she knew that if she made the detour to the house to change she'd be more than an hour late.

She entered the bar ten minutes late as it was, thankful she and her friends had a standing agreement for them to order for her if she wasn't there by the time the others arrived.

She'd been friends with the four women since grade school, and they'd stayed close where other friendships hadn't survived. Sasha Crossfield and Saige Dawson were sisters to her bosses Caine Crossfield and River Dawson and worked at Crossfield-Dawson Commercial and Residential Properties and Storage as well. Erika Boone was a teacher at the local high school and Lilith Preston owned a clothing boutique in town.

They were all as different as night from day. Sasha was a cool,

sophisticated blonde whom others often saw as stuck-up or supe-
rior, but she had a heart of gold. Saige was the quiet one of the
small group, usually watching and listening rather than being an
active contributor to the hilarity, though when she did join in,
things could get hysterical. Erika was the instigator of the group
and had been the one behind some of their more outrageous
pranks growing up. She still managed to cause chaos and mayhem
at odd times.

Lilith was their oddball. Her hair could be any color at any
time, though it had been several colors at once lately. She was prone
to wearing colored contacts, to dress with a flair for the outrageous
that actually worked for her, and to come running, no matter the
time, if one of them needed help.

She was also the niece of the bar's owner and kept them in free
beer and food whenever they were there.

The four women were waiting at their usual table close to the bar,
drinks in front of them, a plate of sliders and wings in the center of
the table.

"There she is," Sasha drawled as Poppy slid into her seat, pushing her purse beneath the table along with four others. "You're late
again, girlfriend."

"Blame your brother." Poppy grimaced. "The majority of my
meetings were in Ohio today. The one in South Point was a killer."

"Oh . . ." Sasha murmured in interest, her blue eyes sparkling
in anticipation. "The commercial offices? Did you actually manage
to lease one of them? I told Caine they were wasted effort when he
bought them."

Poppy grinned in triumph. "All five empty suites are now leased
with first and last month plus security deposits. The leasing agent
outdid herself selling the offices, but they demanded a face-to-
face meeting for information. I didn't think I'd ever get away from
them."

"No wonder, Miss Career Barbie," Saige laughed, her brown eyes teasing. "You look hot. Hell, they were probably mentally jacking off the whole time. I know damned near every man here was doing just that when you strolled in."

Poppy flushed, looking around quickly to make certain no one had heard her friend.

"Would you shut up," she hissed, barely hiding her own laughter. "I didn't have time to go home and change."

The slim black skirt, three-inch heels, and sleeveless white chiffon blouse with golden yellow geometric print and pearl buttons was great for a meeting. Not so much for a jeans-and-beer bar.

"Hey, the dudes are lovin' it," Lilith agreed, her purple, pink, and blue highlighted shoulder-length hair a good complement to the violet-colored contacts she wore.

Erika grinned. "I bet everyone one of their G.I. Joes fucked good ole Barbie when they were boys. I know my Barbies disappeared every time my brothers got a new version of that Army nut job."

Erika hated Barbies as a girl and refused to participate when the rest of them had one of their Barbie dress-up parties. She'd actually bring her brothers' Army figures and cause chaos.

"Hmm, too bad they didn't have a Navy SEAL version of G.I. Joe," Lilith murmured, her gaze moving to the bar entrance. "I bet he'd have looked something like that. My Barbies would have been ecstatic."

Poppy knew even before her head turned who her friend was talking about.

He strolled in like a beast, an overgrown tiger or wolf. Like a predator, not really on the hunt but damned sure ready for trouble.

"Bridger," the bartender and owner, Mike Preston, Lilith's uncle, called out in pleased surprise. "Hey, man, heard you were home."

Jack lifted his hand and headed for the bar, but not before his gaze connected with Poppy's and he shot her a shocking, playful little wink.

No expression, no grin, just that sexy-as-hell gesture that reminded her of the night before and had heat working from her toenails up.

She jerked around quickly, almost groaning at the wide-eyed surprise on her friends' faces.

"Oh my," Sasha breathed out, curiosity filling the sound. "What have we here? Even Poppy's freckles are blushing, right to the roots of her red hair. Honey, haven't I warned you that the colors actually clash?"

Poppy laughed and tossed one of the rolls sitting in the middle of the table at her friend before sitting back and looking around.

When she'd driven up, she'd noticed the three Harleys parked at the front of the building. None had been Jack's, but she'd recognized them as the bikes that had arrived at his house that morning as she was leaving for work.

According to what her brother had told her the night before, Jack had met with three other men, former SEALs as well, who had moved into the tristate area in recent days, which was unusual enough, she thought, and all discharged under suspicious circumstances. The three men, according to John David, had all been held in the same secure lockup as Jack, and at least one of them was known to have been on a team that worked closely with Jack's overseas.

They weren't native to the tristate, but they were known to Jack.

She found three men sitting in a shadowed corner with none other than Ian Richards and his bodyguard.

Resignation washed through her. It seemed John David was more right than wrong. If Jack wasn't aligned with the man rumored to be running the Fuentes Cartel, then why were his men all chummy with Diego Fuentes's bastard son?

"My, my, isn't our little town attracting some worldwide attention," Sasha remarked, her lowered tone mocking as Poppy turned to her. "That's Ian Fuentes . . ."

"Richards," Poppy reminded her, though she didn't know why.

"Whatever." Sasha rolled her eyes. "Might as well be 'Fuentes.' As soon as he left the SEALs years ago, he spent over a year running the cartel before his father resumed the throne. Doesn't mean he's out of it."

"Diego Fuentes likes having an heir that's a former SEAL, according to the news," Saige pointed out. "Wonder what he's doing in our little town."

"His wife was in the shop yesterday," Lilith said, glancing around the table at them. "She's a very nice lady, actually. We had coffee and she bought several dresses. She even gave me the names of some suppliers of vintage clothes that I didn't know about."

"Clothes or drugs," Saige harrumphed. "I'd be careful if I were you."

Lilith shrugged at the suggestion. "I like her. And it's only rumored and suspected that her husband is part of his father's illegal activities, because of their blood connection. The Richardses have denied it on several occasions."

"She's an heiress in her own right," Erika pointed out. "She's her uncle's only living relative and his heir, according to the press. Everyone in those reports swears she wouldn't have married a cartel member. Until her marriage to Ian Richards, Kira Richards had been a very upstanding, law-abiding member of high society. Who knows what the truth is."

Yeah, who knew.

Jack took a seat at the bar, forcing himself not to look over at Poppy again. But damned if she didn't look good. Her long, curl-heavy, fiery red hair had been tamed in a French braid, but he was pleased to see that that errant curl had escaped and fallen over her brow.

And that blush. He knew it had gone from her breasts to her hairline, causing her emerald eyes to appear that much brighter.

He hadn't had a chance to talk to her since he'd left her the night before, but he'd been busy going through her electronic files whenever her phone, laptop, or tablet connected with the small device attached to her home internet.

Her phone messages had been real interesting. Especially the numerous texts warning her to stay away from him.

From her brother to a cousin as far away as Ashland, Kentucky, there had been clear, strict instructions to stay away from Bridger because of his association with Ian Richards and suspected involvement with the Fuentes Cartel. The rest of the messages concerning him had been mostly gossip. They had reminded him of gossipy little teenage notes. Not that Poppy had participated; she hadn't. She'd acknowledged the messages, changed the subject when she could, and ignored them when she couldn't.

Only two had stood out besides her brother John David's, both of those from her bosses, Caine Crossfield and River Dawson. Crossfield had inquired if it was true Jack was back in town to stay and to see if "Bridger" would be interested in selling the small farm his mother had owned and died on. Dawson, though, had known that Jack owned the house in Barboursville and instructed Poppy to acquire it "at any price."

The house across the alley from Poppy had been owned by the cousin who had fostered Jack after his mother's death. That cousin had sold it to Jack just before his death the year before. The paperwork hadn't even been filed in Barboursville until the week before Jack returned.

The information wouldn't be hard to find, but it would take a little work. And the fact that Dawson had done that work worried Jack.

Neither the farm nor the house was for sale, not at any price.

The messages had been interesting, all things considered. Jack had managed to slip into Tessalon's warehouse, not that he'd found anything. But he'd known going in that the chances of that had been slim. The setup Tessalon had would make it damned handy to receive the items Ian was looking for, though.

"Was wondering when you'd show up," Mike said, sliding a bottle of Jack's favorite whiskey and a shot glass across the bar. "Knew it was about time. How long you staying?"

"Back for good," Jack told him, tossing enough cash to the bar to cover the bottle as he ignored Mike's surprised look.

"About time," Mike told him with a quick nod. "I was wondering if you'd come back." He glanced over at the table where Poppy sat with his niece and their friends. "That little girl still can't keep her eyes off you, can she?"

"She's not a little girl anymore," Jack pointed out as he let a half smile tug at the edge of his lips.

Mike sighed heavily, his look warning now. "There's talk, Jack, about some people you're associating with. Worrisome things."

Damn, he was going to have to end up counseling Poppy's brother to keep his damned mouth shut, and that would only end up pissing Poppy off.

"Gossip, Mike," he said with a hint of censure.

Mike glanced to the back of the room where Jack's men sat with Ian and his bodyguard.

"Is it?" Mike asked softly.

"If there's no proof," Jack suggested icily, "then what more could it be?"

Taking the bottle and the glass, he strolled to the back of the bar where Ian and his bodyguard sat at a corner table that was mostly in the shadows with Lucas, Hayes, and Hank. As he approached, his three men stood and eased to a nearby booth while Jack slid into one of the vacated chairs.

"Did you know she'd be here?" Jack asked Ian as he tipped the bottle and filled his glass while glancing across the room at Poppy.

"I did." Ian nodded shortly. "Seems her brother has found more information to crucify your reputation with. Something about an operation in Germany and missing drugs last year."

They weren't missing. They'd been consumed in the fire started in the crude warehouse where they'd been stored. Jack and his team had made certain of it.

Jack tossed back the shot, placed the glass back on the table, and leveled a hard look at Ian. "Her employers, no doubt. Crossfield and Dawson still have contacts in the community."

"And those contacts have let it slip that the information is accurate. We didn't anticipate the brother's interference to this degree . . ."

"You didn't. I did," Jack assured him. "I know her and her family and friends. I'd have been more surprised if it hadn't happened." He was aware of the subtle glances in his direction and the hint of suspicion and concern on Poppy's and her friends' faces.

He could have used a few more days before giving her reason to suspect him, but the fact that it would happen hadn't been in doubt.

"He could become a problem," Ian warned him. "He intends to keep his sister away from you."

There was no doubt of that, and Jack had already figured it into his plans.

He gave Ian a mocking look before pouring himself another drink. "Is this all it took for you to become such a worrywart or some sort of micromanager? Or are you becoming a babysitter in your old age?"

Ian's lips quirked with an edge of amusement as he acknowledged that accusation.

"Operating funds came in earlier," Ian informed him, his voice low. "As we meet, said funds are being slipped into the saddlebags of your bike. Weapons and other needed supplies will be delivered as agreed on tonight."

Jack gave a slow nod. No doubt the weapons were procured from the Fuentes Cartel, one of Ian's favorite suppliers, it seemed.

No one was certain who the Richardses worked for, the Fuentes Cartel or Homeland Security; Ian showed up occasionally with agents from both sides. There was rumor that his father, Diego, was dead, but Jack doubted it. It was also rumored that Ian was the actual head of the cartel while the supposed leader, a distant cousin of Diego's, was merely a figurehead.

Who the hell knew what was the truth. Jack didn't really care. The man didn't mess with drugs, neither selling them nor attempting to use agents to transport them. Until he did, Jack was prone to trust him.

"Have you managed to contact Mac Porter yet?" Jack asked, aware that Poppy's brother could become a nail in his coffin if he returned before Ian had a chance to meet with him.

"I talked to him personally," Ian reported. "He's not happy with any of us, mind you. Sent you a message, though. If she gets so much as a scratch, he'll kill you."

Jack expected nothing less.

"Now I'd like to know how your message to him convinced him to hold back?" The query was more a demand. "What do you have on him, Jack?"

What did he have on him? Jack didn't have shit on Mac. They just had an understanding based on their mutual determination to keep one little redhead out of trouble, living and laughing.

"I don't have a damned thing on him." Jack shrugged. "He knows me, and I know him. That's enough for both of us."

They both knew exactly the extremes they'd go to for Poppy.

"Talk to him in a while?" Ian asked.

Jack gave a brief shake of his head. "Year ago maybe."

"He's on medical discharge. He's taking care of some family business in Ohio and expects to be back in a week. If she calls him, he'll answer the call, but says he doubts she will. She'll wait on his return to come to him."

She'd handle it herself.

Yeah, that was Poppy. She'd made a horrible decision eight years ago, choosing to remain silent about what had happened to Wayne Trencher rather than have him face charges in connection to Trencher's death.

And he would have, Jack knew. There wasn't a person alive that would have believed Poppy killed Trencher. Especially once that knife was identified. Jack had bought it in Barboursville and hadn't mentioned to a soul that he'd given it to Poppy.

He would have lost his commission, and he would have faced prison time. He'd known it, Poppy had known it. But he would have done it rather than see her face such a thing.

"He know what's going on?" Jack asked.

Ian sighed heavily before a tight grimace pulled at his expression and he rubbed at his jaw. "That's need-to-know, Jack. You think he needs to know?"

Medical discharge, friends with Crossfield and Dawson, and incredibly protective of Poppy. No, he didn't think Mac Porter needed to know any more than was absolutely necessary.

"He's going to shoot both of us, though," Jack warned him.

"He won't be the first to try," Ian grunted, sliding his chair back before extending his hand to Jack. "Give me a call if you need me."

Jack rose as well, accepting the brief handshake before nodding to the bodyguard, then stepped away from the table and made his way to where his men sat.

The damage had been done, though. He caught the look of suspicion on Poppy's face as she glanced at him. It wasn't the first time her gaze had slid to him. Along with the suspicion was a stubborn intention of interrogating him at the first opportunity.

He flashed her another wicked grin and watched the flush race over her creamy expression again as her friends laughed and teased her. What they said he wasn't certain, but it deepened the flush and caused her to flash him a look promising retribution.

And he was looking forward to it.

CHAPTER EIGHT

Poppy had hoped to be on her way home before John David arrived at the bar.

She'd seen the speculative looks from several of his friends after Jack left and knew it wouldn't be long before he showed up.

And she had almost made it. She was sliding into the driver's seat of her vehicle when he pulled in beside her and jumped from the latest version of the Jeep he was so fond of.

She rolled her window down, knowing there was no way out of talking to him now.

"I'm on my way home," she told him, noting his dark expression with resignation.

"I heard Bridger was here with Ian Richards," he stated, his jaw tight as he stepped to her car door. "While he was with Richards, someone slipped a package into the saddlebag on his Harley. Money or drugs, I'm not sure which. Still think he's so innocent?"

Innocent? Perhaps not. Guilty of a crime? Possibly. Of dealing with drugs? That was a definitive no. She couldn't believe it. The man she had known, the one willing to take the blame for killing

Trencher to save her, would never put her in danger with drug dealers.

"I don't know, John David," she snapped, gripping the steering wheel tightly as she stared back at him. "It looked like two men who knew each other just visiting for a minute. Nothing more. I didn't see anything else, and evidently neither did you."

No, she wasn't nearly that naïve, but she needed her brother to let this alone. Whatever Jack was doing, she would never believe he was involved with a drug cartel. He hated drugs. His father had murdered his mother and tried to kill Jack while high on drugs. Jack would never become involved with them, nor would he sell them.

"You'd defend him no matter what he did, wouldn't you?" he growled back at her. "You've never seen him for what he is, Poppy."

"John David, stop . . ." She clutched the steering wheel, forcing back an unfamiliar surge of anger. "I'm trying to be objective here, but I can't do that while you're harping at me."

"Are you sleeping with him, Poppy?" he demanded. "He lives right behind you. Who would know if he was sneaking over like he did last night before I arrived."

Poppy stared back at her brother in disbelief, though she knew she shouldn't be surprised.

"Jack's a friend if nothing else," she told him, desperate to end the confrontation before it went further. "What do you want me to do, John David? I'm not encouraging anything . . ."

"Why did he slip out of your house last night like a thief?" he demanded. "There were no lights on and you lied to me, Poppy. You said you'd just come in the back door. I know you'd been home quite awhile, with Bridger following you in when you arrived."

"Are you spying on me?" She glared back at him.

This was crazy. It was outrageous that he would do that.

"Every time he touches you, he stains you with the blood on his hands," he suddenly bit out, his tone angry. "Is that what you want? You're smarter than this."

She jerked as if his words had slapped her and stared at him, almost shocked.

"Any blood he spilled he did as a SEAL," she reminded him as she punched the push start on her small crossover SUV and glared at him. "He spilled blood he was ordered to spill."

"He killed at fourteen," he snarled. "Do you really believe it's the only time he killed outside of his orders? Ask him about his discharge. Ask him about the missing drugs in Germany. The agents trying to question that terrorist cell were murdered. Ask him about that."

Poppy fought her harsh breathing, and the furious words trembling on her lips.

"Poppy, he's trash—"

"Enough!" Her voice rose, so demanding and angry that her brother stepped back from the vehicle. "Jack has never been trash, John David. How dare you! God, how dare you say something like that when that man would give his life to protect me."

She was yelling at him, Poppy realized, her voice loud enough that anyone outside the bar could hear her. And she was only seconds from crying.

She took a deep breath. "Get off my back!" she ordered him. "And leave me alone about Jack before I stop talking to you entirely. Jack is my business from here on out. Period."

She reversed from out of her parking spot, leaving John David standing silently, watching her leave.

Jack had protected her, cared for her, and made certain she didn't suffer anyone's knowing what had happened that summer. No matter how humiliating it would be, she'd protect Jack from her brother now, even if it meant exposing her own secret to him to make him understand just why she trusted him.

Poppy was still furious when she pulled in behind her house. She was still shaking and almost crying, she was so damned mad.

There had been less than a handful of times that she'd been this furious with one of her siblings, and now she could add tonight at the top of the list. Slamming the door of her SUV closed, she fumbled with the key fob for a minute, locked the car doors, and had turned toward her house when a sudden, dark shadow rushed for her.

She screamed, cowering back against the vehicle, her hands lifting to protect her face as she saw hands coming for her.

She swore she heard an animal's snarl at the same time she heard her timid neighbor, Ross Jenkins, give a frightened cry just before a hulk-sized shadow slammed into him.

"No. Jack . . ." she cried out.

She knew who it was, and she knew what was coming. As his fist prepared to strike, she clamped onto his arm with all her strength and was jerked off her feet and into his back before he paused.

Ross Jenkins was cowering, on the ground, his hands over his face, little frightened whimpers squeaking from behind his fingers.

"It was my fault," she claimed breathlessly, refusing to let go of Jack's arm. "I was startled. It was my fault."

"Let go of my arm, Poppy," he ordered, his voice sounding calm, reasonable. But she knew the tone didn't matter. He was tense, muscles bunched to drive his fist into the puny little man he still held by the neck.

"I'm sorry," Jenkins was all but blubbering. "Please. Please . . . a package was left for her . . . I'm sorry . . ."

"Let him go, Jack," she ordered. "Take your hand off his neck right now and let him go."

In the dim light, she watched his fingers uncurl, felt him ease back by inches, his body still prepared to fight.

"A package . . ." her neighbor gasped again. "They left it at my door . . . I was just gonna give it to you . . . that's all."

Sure enough, a package lay scant inches from his head.

"Let go of me, Poppy, and I'll stand up," Jack offered then. "Or you can dangle off my wrist, your choice."

She let go of him hastily and watched in surprise as Jack rose and extended his hand to the still cowering neighbor.

Ross took the proffered hand cautiously, his breath expelling audibly as Jack pulled him to his feet.

"Sorry about that," he apologized. "Poppy doesn't usually panic easily."

"Oh. Oh. Yeah . . ." Ross stared back at them dazed, the whites of his eyes showing, his thin hair standing on end. "She screamed really loud . . . I didn't mean . . . I mean . . . the package . . ." He looked on the ground around him, still shaken, just as Poppy was.

"This is my fault, Mr. Jenkins." Her voice was still shaking, and she just knew she was going to start crying at any minute. "I'm so very sorry."

It had been a shit day, and wasn't this just the perfect ending for it.

"Oh well . . . No harm done, I guess." He still sounded confused and as frightened as Poppy felt. "Your package . . ." He looked around again.

"I have it," Jack assured him. "You sure you're okay?"

"Oh . . . yes . . . fine." He swallowed tightly. "I should have announced myself sooner . . . Thought she saw me . . . The headlights, you know."

But somehow, she had missed him.

She'd been too angry, too focused on getting into the house where she could finally cry in peace.

"I'm going to go in . . ." The slight man turned, looked to his house, then turned back to Jack. "Home . . . I'm going to go home."

He sounded as though he were asking permission.

"Be careful," Jack said pleasantly.

"Yes . . . yes . . ." He wandered off, glancing back at them every few seconds as though terrified Jack would follow.

A second later calloused fingers curled around Poppy's upper arm and Jack was all but dragging her to her back door.

"My arm is not a leash, and I am not a recalcitrant pet," she snarled, jerking from his hold. Well aware he only released her because he chose to.

"In the house, Poppy," he ordered. "You don't want this to happen outside where anyone can see us."

"Why not?" she cried out furiously. "Whoever's watching us could just report the full truth then."

Thankfully, she'd managed to hold on to her keys, she thought, almost shocked that she'd done so.

Gripping the house key, she tried to fit it into the lock, but even with the back porch light on she couldn't seem to shove the key into place, her hands were shaking so bad.

Which only made her madder.

"Here." Jack took the key from her fingers, slid it into the door lock and then the dead bolt, and within seconds was pushing the door open and stepping in ahead of her.

Poppy all but stomped into the house, went straight for the cabinet, and drew a bottle of her favorite bourbon and a glass from the cabinet.

Uncapping it, she poured a healthy drink, took it all in one swallow, and grimaced at the fiery sensation that washed down her throat.

And still, she just wanted to cry.

Behind her, Jack closed the door, set the locks, and waited silently.

It was more nerve-racking than all her brothers in a rage at once.

"Someone's watching me," she whispered tearfully, refusing to look at him. "Watching me and telling my brother, as though I'm some teenager who needs to be grounded. And he's convinced you're a traitor. A drug dealer. Someone's feeding him information I can't fight, Jack."

She moved to pour another drink when she suddenly found the bottle lifted from her hand. Jack capped it and put it away before turning back to her.

"John David?" he asked carefully.

She turned to look at him, still feeling the anger John David had pulled to the surface with his questions and determination to somehow control her. But feeling anger at Jack as well.

He was dressed in riding gear again. Jeans, leather chaps, boots, T-shirt. He looked wicked and wild. The ultimate bad boy.

He was staring back at her somberly, his gray-and-blue eyes dark, stormy. Only his eyes ever gave away the fact that he actually felt anything at any given time.

"I would guess that since John David couldn't find me tonight, he found you instead." He sounded certain of that fact. "I felt it best to talk to you before letting him find me, but maybe I should have just stayed at the house, waited for him, and dealt with that first."

"By hitting him?" she burst out, the tears gathering in her eyes again. "You are not allowed to hit my brothers, Jack." She pointed a shaky finger at him imperiously.

"Well, see, that's why I waited," he said, completely deadpan. "Before I busted his pretty face, I wanted to make sure if a little chitchat wouldn't suffice instead. So, tell me what I need to know, or I go find him tonight."

And he would.

She knew he would.

And if he did, they'd fight.

She felt her lips tremble, felt the tears that filled her eyes.

"He heard about your meeting with Ian Richards," she whispered. "Someone told him a package was slipped into your bike at the bar. He thinks you're involved with the cartel and refuses to believe otherwise. We argued, and I yelled at him. I told him you were none of his business. I hate it when they make me mad enough to yell, and it always makes me cry."

She glared back at him. "I didn't lie to him. I know you wouldn't be involved with drugs. That's not you."

His lips thinned for a moment, then pursed wryly. "No, Poppy, I would never mess with drugs. Not take them, sell them, or facilitate anyone else's use of them."

But he'd still met with a man suspected to be the head of a drug cartel. Why would he do that?

"What's going on, Jack?" she whispered, frightened for him, knowing he wouldn't just stop in to chat with someone involved in a drug cartel. "Ian Richards is dangerous. He's always in the news, suspected of some crime or meeting with people who are criminals. Why is he here, in Barboursville? What does he want with you?"

Men like Ian Richards didn't make friends with someone who didn't benefit them.

"He's the son of a former cartel leader, not part of any cartel," he promised her. "Ian and his wife are rich and influential. Their money didn't come from drugs but inheritances and investments. But because of his biological father, he's always going to be suspected of being involved with something criminal."

"How do you know him?" she asked, certain there was something he wasn't telling her. "Why did one of his men slip a package onto your bike?"

"We've met several times." He shrugged. "He's a former SEAL. He's advised on a few missions I was on, and we got along. As for what John David might have heard, the package was from a friend. And I promise you, there were no drugs included."

He moved to her as he spoke, his hand reaching up, fingers gripping her chin as his thumb brushed over her parted lips.

"As for John David. He knows what you have never wanted to see. I'm not a nice man. Most days, I'm probably not even a good man, and no doubt I don't deserve so much as a minute of your time. But I think I should warn you, Poppy, I'm going to demand far more than that. And it won't be wine and roses and pretty phrases." The warning stole her breath, had her lips parting farther apart, her mind shutting down as his lips lowered.

Anything else she wanted to ask, and there was more, dissipated as his lips met hers.

She'd fantasized about him over the years; sometimes she even cried out his name when she masturbated. And when his lips covered hers now, it wasn't the gentle kiss of the day before. This kiss was lust-driven and hungry, and Poppy knew it was far more than she was experienced enough to handle.

No apology, no experimental rubbing of his lips against hers, and damned sure no excuses. His hand held her head still by spanning the side of her neck and gripping it firmly; his mouth slanted over her lips and his tongue slipped easily past them.

One hand gripping the wrist at her neck, the other locked onto the hand that gripped her hip, Poppy whimpered. Not certain if she should give in to the heat suddenly pouring into her or to the rapid-fire impulses that urged caution.

Jack wasn't a man a woman could ever be cautious with and still be close to. Especially with his lips covering hers, his tongue licking, stroking in wicked, sensual patterns only to pull back to allow his lips to sip at hers, his teeth to nip.

Sensations rocked her nervous system, flushing heat, racing chills of warning, eagerness for more, uncertainty. Years of fantasy and dreams, and they all collided in that kiss until she felt rocked by a wild, erotic surge of need so swift, so overwhelming she instinctively fought against it.

"Jack . . . Jack, please . . ." she protested, her voice weak, her whole body weak as she fought to make sense of it. "Please . . . wait . . . I can't . . ."

She couldn't explain, couldn't process the flood of sensations, wants, and needs that she knew were wholly hers, but only brought to life by his.

When his hold at her neck loosened, she jerked back instinctively, stumbling from him, and staring at him in shock.

Oh God. How could she have ever thought he was safe in any way, shape, or form.

His gaze burned with lust, his cheekbones flushed, his lips swollen from their kiss. He stood stock-still. His body seemed taller somehow, wider. His breathing was hard, heavy, but hell, hers was too.

"Don't you dare pretend to be scared of me, Poppy," he demanded, his voice harsher.

Scared of him? She was terrified of herself.

"You don't understand," she whispered, fighting for breath. "I can't . . ."

"The hell you can't," he growled. "You don't have to tonight, don't have to tomorrow night, but eventually you will, and we both know it."

She shook her head.

"Yes, Poppy." Despite the rough, guttural, growly sound of his voice, it still felt like a croon. Of sorts.

"Jack, you don't understand . . ." She couldn't make sense of it, couldn't figure out the words to explain.

"What's there to understand, baby girl?" he demanded. "Something besides me in that bed of yours, fucking us both crazy?"

Her knees went weak. Something clenched, flexed in her lower belly with such a surge of pleasure it nearly stole her breath as she hurriedly pressed her hand over it. As though she could contain the sensation or the rush of liquid heat between her thighs.

His gaze shot to her hand, paused, his eyes narrowing before he looked back up into her eyes.

"I've never . . ." She swallowed tightly, shaking, shuddering in reaction. "God, Jack. I haven't . . . with a man . . ." She shook her head desperately. "I didn't want . . . Damn you," she exploded, furious with herself now, and with him, because she simply had no idea how to handle this. "I've never had a lover."

He tilted his head to the side, his eyes narrowing on her before he shocked her yet again with a hint of a glare.

"Did you at least think about me when you masturbated?" he growled.

She blinked back at him. "What?"

He was all she'd thought about when she masturbated.

"Did. You. Think. About. Me," he enunciated the words. "While you masturbated."

Sheer, overwhelming disbelief.

Her mouth dropped open a second before she felt heat rush from her neck to her hairline.

Fucker.

Who the hell else had she ever thought of when she did that? It was always Jack. She probably wouldn't even know how to fantasize about anyone else. Especially after tonight . . .

"You're crazy," she declared. "Get the hell out of my house."

"How do you do it?" His voice low, it took a minute for the words to register.

She swallowed tightly, refusing to answer him. She didn't dare even try to form words yet.

"God, Poppy. Did you take your sweet cherry with a vibrator?" he whispered at her ear, not touching her, but so close now she could feel the heat of his body stroking over hers.

"If I had a gun, I swear I'd shoot you," she whispered, completely mortified.

"You're wondering what the hell I needed the vibrator for? Well, it wasn't like you seemed interested in me, Jack," she informed him furiously. "You were too busy ignoring me."

She couldn't breathe.

God help her.

She felt his hand cup her hip, then move slowly upward, beneath her top, to a swollen breast, a pebble-hard nipple.

She stood there, unable to voice the words that would make him stop.

She felt her pussy pulse, her womb contract, and as she stood there, felt a wave of weakening sensation wash through her body.

"Oh baby, you did use a vibrator to lose your virginity." His teeth raked over her neck. "Since you denied me that little sweet, why not let me watch while you show me how you did it?"

"What?" The little squeak was so pathetic, but she couldn't seem to catch her breath.

"Let me watch, Poppy." His lips delivered a burning kiss to her neck as her head tilted to the side like a sacrifice to his lust and she shuddered at the sensations attacking her. "What kind of vibrator do you have? I bet you're a really smart girl when it comes to your body. A nice, round little toy with a clitoral stimulator? I bet all you have to do is hold it in place and let it do the work for you."

She felt drunk. Drugged.

What was he doing to her?

As he played with her nipple, she felt his other hand move to the band of her pants.

"Jack. Please . . . I don't know what to do," she whispered, held in place by the rush of pleasure washing over her in gathering waves and the need to know the pleasure she sensed awaiting her.

She'd promised herself she wasn't going to allow this to happen. That she would not let him make her weak.

His hand slid lower.

"Oh my, baby shaves. Or do you wax?" He rubbed his fingers against the soft flesh, slid them lower, rubbed the suddenly swollen lips and inner folds. "You wax, don't you, sweetheart? You lie back, spread those pretty legs, and let someone wax you? Lie back on your bed, spread them for me, and let me fuck you with your toy."

A cry tore from her as she felt her moisture spill, saturating his fingers as he rubbed against the sensitive opening.

"Goddamn, Poppy," he groaned. "That's it, baby. Get slick and wet for me. Get wild, sugar girl."

She felt his finger slip inside, then retreat, then another rush of her juices falling to his touch.

A low, ragged wail tore from her lips as she went on her tiptoes, the sudden thick intrusion of his finger nearly sending her tumbling into a pleasure she didn't know if she'd survive.

Then the finger was gone and before she could stop herself, she drove her flesh against his fingers, desperate for more.

"Oh no, not yet," he crooned. "Naked Poppy. You all sweet and naked. I'll watch you fuck yourself. Wouldn't that be so good? I promise, when you come it will be like no orgasm you've ever had. I'll even suck those pretty nipples for you until you get off. I swear, you'll love it. God help me, I'll love it."

She felt him lift her against his chest, knew he was carrying her to her bedroom, but all she could do was stare at him.

She'd never seen so many emotions straining his expression. His eyes were such a dark blue gray they were almost black, and heavy-lidded with a look of drowsy sensuality.

She could feel her nipples rasping against his chest and realized he must have taken her shirt off at some point.

"Jack," she whispered, fighting to find an anchor as she felt herself drowning beneath the waves of need and erotic intensity.

"Here, baby." He lowered her to the bed and leaned over her, his lips covering hers.

It wasn't like the night before, all raw, jagged lust. This time, he savored her lips, stroked them, sipped at them as she arched to him, her desperate fingers gripping his shoulders.

"Here we go." He eased back and tore his T-shirt off before turning his attention back to her.

Those diabolical lips went to her neck, spreading kisses to her swollen breasts, then to the violently sensitive peaks of her nipples.

Shudders tore through her, racing from her nipple to her womb, creating such a firestorm along her nerve endings that she was buried beneath it.

She was barely aware of him removing her clothing as his lips went to the neglected nipple. As he worked the needy point, his groan was like an added dose of a narcotic, drugging her with the knowledge of his pleasure as well as her own.

As his head lifted, he moved, pushing her legs apart gently and kneeling between them as he pressed the heavy vibrator into her hands.

She looked down at the thick shaft and attached ears that embraced the clit. All she had to do was turn it on and the thrusting action of the device would work itself inside her. Once her senses were going crazy with the pleasure, she'd turn the vibration of the ears on . . .

As he pressed the head of the device between the slick lips between her thighs, she watched, mesmerized, as his big hand gripped the hard length of his cock and slowly stroked upward.

He was big. Thick.

A whimper escaped her lips as the vibrator turned on, the slow thrust of the device's mechanics working itself inside her. Slowly. So slowly.

She was dying. This had to be a dream. Some incredible fantasy.

"Here, baby, let me help," he whispered as a wave of rich, electric heat raced through her. "I'll do this." He gripped the base of the erotic toy. "You play with your nipples until I come up there and suck them. Show me what you like."

Releasing his cock, he pushed her hands to her breasts with his free hand, and as she cupped them, he pushed the shaft inside her in one long, slow thrust.

Her back arched. The resistance her inner muscles created caused a slight pinch of sensation that drove her crazy. Why hadn't it ever done that for her?

"Jack. Oh God, Jack. It's so good." Her thighs spread wider, hips lifting and working against each movement of the device as it moved inside her.

"Fuck, that's goddamned hot," he groaned. "Your pussy is so wet and wild, Poppy. Your hard little clit standing to attention, begging for my lips and tongue. Or this . . ."

She jerked, crying out as the firm, silicone extensions on each side of her clit began vibrating, a setting that created a pattern that was more a tease than an orgasm.

Her head tossed on the blankets, her fingers working her nipples now, pinching and rubbing them, the flames building in her body, threatening to steal her mind.

"Please," she whispered, insensate, drugged with lust, riding a high she had no idea how to control. "Oh God, Jack." She was nearly sobbing with need now. "Please. It's not enough. It's not enough."

Sometimes, it was never enough. No matter how hard she tried, she couldn't peak, couldn't slip over that edge.

Her hips worked against the movement inside her pussy as she gasped for air. The need for orgasm rose by the second, until it tortured her senses.

"That's it, sugar girl," he crooned. "You gonna come for me? Is that toy enough, Poppy? You gonna come on it?"

She wanted to. Oh God, she needed to.

"Look at me," he demanded, his voice soft. "Open your eyes. Look at me."

She forced her eyes open as he moved, then quickly flipped her to her stomach.

Firmly, he dragged her to her knees, gripped the base of the vibrator, and began to work it inside her. Once. Twice.

She nearly, almost dissolved.

"Jack," she cried out in protest, lips parting to drag in oxygen when she found the thick, throbbing head of his cock at her lips.

Thickly veined, impossibly wide and imposing. It was much bigger than her vibrator, but unlike the toy it was hot, blood pounding just beneath the tight flesh and more than ready to take her.

And rather than pushing it away, her lips closed over the ruddy crest, her tongue tasting him, salt and male lust exploding against her taste buds and sending her searching for more.

The vibrator thrust inside her, hard and fast, then stilled again. She cried around the heavily veined shaft, sucking at it now, desperate for him. Growing increasingly wild and determined to have him.

His fingers tunneled into her hair, clenching on the strands, and the next second, she felt a heavy, heated tap to her ass.

She stilled. Felt the next heavy caress again, sharper this time, and sucked his cock deeper as she lifted for him. It came again on the opposite curve of her ass, then the vibrator was thrust hard inside her, the heavy buzzing indicating he'd turned the power up.

And still, it wasn't enough.

His hand landed on her again, the heat it created flushing through her. Again.

She moaned around his cockhead. Suckling at it, licking over it as desperate cries filled the air around her.

"I'm going to fuck you, Poppy," he promised her. "Do you hear me, baby? I'm going to slide right behind you and show you why that toy is a piss-poor substitute for what you really need."

He thrust against her tongue, pulled the vibrator free of her, then pulled back, taking his cock from her mouth and moving behind her before she could get her bearings.

She felt him position himself behind her, angling her hips higher, then shifting closer.

Iron-hard and hot, the head of his cock began pushing inside her as he held her hips with one hand, the other delivering another heavy caress to her ass.

Her pussy clenched, spasmed as though to draw him deeper as he pulled back.

When he returned, he pressed farther inside her, the shaft separating the fisted tissue in ways it had never been taken before. The pinch became more a pleasure that bordered pain and drew her deeper into the chaos gathering inside her.

She pushed back, crying out as she took more of him, felt that borderline pain building, mixing with a burning pleasure that obliterated thought.

"That's it, baby, work that sweet pussy on me. Fuck me back." She thrust back, feeling his hand connect with her flesh again as he thrust inside her once more, harder. Deeper.

Her head went back, her fingers fisting in the blankets.

"More?" Insidious, tempting, his voice teased her, urged her to demand whatever she wanted.

"More," she moaned, feeling perspiration along her hairline, between her breasts.

It was so hot, the ecstatic sensations striking so deep she wondered if she'd die from it.

He pulled away, and when he returned, she screamed. Her back arched, her pussy clenched and worked around the thick intruder, fighting to accommodate the girth. There was no chance to catch her breath this time.

His hands tightened on her hips, holding her in place, and he began moving. The drag and searing impalements had more of her moisture flowing, slickening her, but doing nothing to ease the pleasure-pain of her flesh stretching around him, clenching, shuddering.

Tension suddenly snapped through the muscles of her body, drawing her tight, a wail fighting to get breath as she felt a starburst inside her expanding, then exploding.

Her pussy clamped down on his shaft as she felt her juices spilling furiously along the thick flesh when he thrust deep, hard, and seemed to swell thicker inside her.

She clawed at the sheets, the explosion rocking through her until the final, violent tidal wave of pure ecstasy swamped her senses.

Poppy collapsed beneath him, nearly unconscious from the strength of the orgasm and the flames that seared her senses.

She heard Jack groaning behind her, jerking against her, and realized he was locked in his own release.

In a distant part of her mind, she could feel the shadow she always sensed around him easing closer now, as though in warning. But she was just too tired to make sense of it. Too tired to think about it.

She'd fought to ease the need that had only been building since the morning she glimpsed him outside her window. The erotic hunger and need for his touch drifted to the edge of her consciousness, ready to come alive again with the slightest encouragement, but appeased for the moment.

At least long enough to allow her to finally slip into sleep.

Dangerous.

As Jack carefully, gently cleaned the moisture from between Poppy's thighs and covered them both with a spare sheet he found in her closet, he couldn't help but curse himself and glare into the dimly lit room.

Never, not one time, had he ever known anything so fucking

hot and wild as what he'd felt from the moment he touched Poppy in the kitchen and realized how her body was humming with need.

Pulling her against him, he held her loosely, noticing how she settled against his chest, all those red curls tumbling around her back and shoulders.

Her skin was soft as silk.

Fuck.

Her pussy was pure paradise, gripping and milking his cock until he couldn't hold back. It had been all he could do to work a condom over his swollen cock before pushing inside her.

He wanted her on birth control, he thought irrationally. He wanted to fuck her bare, fill that tight, gripping little pussy with his come and know he'd marked her as no other man had ever dared.

Satisfaction raced through him.

His Poppy. His talisman against the darkness growing inside him, and he'd made certain she waited for him.

Only to come back to betray her.

He was going to break her heart, and he knew it. He felt it and fought to ignore it.

No, he wasn't a good man, but what he was doing now made him even worse.

He was betraying the sunlight.

And even God couldn't forgive him for that.

CHAPTER NINE

Poppy awoke to the most amazing sensations.

Like thick, heavy waves of nothing but pure, unadulterated pleasure, and she was drifting in the very center of it. Every molecule of those waves was intent on nothing but her pleasure and that slow, sliding climb to the explosion she could feel building by incremental degrees.

As she came awake, she was aware first of the sensations. The way the drugging pleasure had invaded her sleeping senses and spread throughout her body. She moved with the undulating waves, lifting and falling, her breathing erratic as adrenaline added fuel to the building heat and sent it accelerating through her.

Then, she became aware of the brush of hair against her thighs, calloused fingers cupping and gripping her rear as they held her in place, and heated lips and tongue and the warmth of a mouth eating her pussy with growing male greed.

Her thighs were parted wide for him, feet planted in the mattress, her hands tied . . . tied? . . . to the headboard.

He'd restrained her hands, making certain she couldn't touch him, couldn't dig her hands into his hair and hold on when the pleasure became so extreme she was buffeted by it.

It should have scared her. Should have terrified her. Instead, the knowledge that nothing was expected of her but her participation in this mind-destroying ecstasy made her hotter.

It was wicked. Decadent. So extreme and utterly sexually dominating that it completely laid waste to any thoughts of resistance.

She felt the hard wash of her juices meeting his tongue as that knowledge filtered through her, and gave a low, ecstasy-building moan as erratic pulses of sensation attacked her vagina and spread to her womb.

His tongue pressed inside her, slowly, so slowly, spreading the tissue apart and licking at her like a man starved for the taste of a woman. His groan vibrated into her flesh, causing her clit to swell further.

Breathing was instinct at this point; she knew hers was fast and hard, interrupted only by the involuntary groans and mewls of pleasure pulled from her.

His fingers slid into the crease of her rear, separating her cheeks, parting them. A tug of sensation where she would have never expected added to the sensory overload.

She wouldn't have expected it, but there was no thought of protesting it. At this point, her body belonged to him, to do with as he wanted.

And what he wanted, it seemed, was every taste of her he could get.

That diabolical tongue slid from her pussy, licked lower, found an area she would have considered forbidden at any other time, and sent a shocked cry spilling from her lips as it drove inside the tight little hole.

Before she could struggle against the caress—if she'd had enough brainpower to consider it—he caught her below her knees and lifted her legs farther, his tongue intent on washing away any inhibitions.

As though her shocked response made him even more intent to ensure she knew, he had no limits where her body was concerned.

Once her response to that penetration went from shock to participation, and the juices started spilling heavier from her, his tongue returned to her pussy, but his fingers lingered.

The slowly building chaos stepped up, swirling faster, hotter through her mind as the waves of sensation intensified and burned brighter.

"That's it, baby girl," he crooned as that forbidden entrance parted for the tip of his finger. "Give it to me just like that."

His finger slid back, gathered the juices spilling from her pussy, and sank inside her again, this time deeper. That heated pinch of her flesh separating mixed with the pleasure pouring through her as his tongue slid to her clit, leaving and applying just enough pressure to have her desperate for release.

His fingers continued their decadent penetration at her rear, working inside the tiny entrance as his lips and tongue tormented her clit, pushing her closer, so close . . .

He pulled back, ignoring the desperate arch of her body a breath before his other hand slid up her thigh, two fingers tucking at the entrance of her pussy as she felt a thicker intrusion at her rear.

Her eyes flew open, staring back at him as the need to orgasm built to a near-painful level.

"Please," she breathed out as he gathered more of the slick moisture to lubricate the tiny entrance he had possessed with a finger moments before.

"Please what?" he questioned, his voice gentle, demanding. "What do you want, sugar girl?"

She had no idea what she wanted—she only knew she needed it. Needed it so desperately her body was screaming for it.

"Jack . . . please . . ." she gasped as he continued working the building moisture back.

"Please what, my Poppy? What do you want? My fingers?" He stroked the entrance of her pussy. "Here?"

"Please, Jack," she cried out.

"What about here?" He pressed two fingers against her anal entrance.

"Jack . . . please . . . anything . . ." She wanted to sob, the need for orgasm, for sensation, was so extreme now.

Anything.

As his gaze held hers, his eyes narrowed, and before Poppy could even make sense of what was about to happen, two thick fingers pushed firmly into her rear, burrowing inside her until she tried to scream as the building sensations lashed her body and the pleasure-pain intensity of it blinded her gaze.

At the same time, two fingers worked inside her pussy in the same firm thrust, seating themselves inside her as his lips lowered to her swollen, agonized clitoris.

The dual penetrations were too much. They were decadent, bordering on deviant to her inexperienced mind. When he sucked her clit inside the moist heat of his mouth and began suckling at it as his tongue rubbed, pressed, she swore she was dying.

The detonation built through her senses, then imploded with such a fireworks effect that she became lost to it.

Over and over, the deep, body-clenching explosions of her orgasm laid waste to shock or disbelief as she gave herself over to a response so violent and extreme that all she could do was let it throw her where it willed.

And just when she thought it would ease, that she could catch her breath, she felt Jack's cock working through the clenching muscles of her pussy, separating them, stretching them, forcing them to relent and reveal nerve endings so sensitized by her release that it sent out shock waves of additional fiery explosions to destroy her senses.

She was left helpless against his possession, against the hard, powerful thrusts of his hips as he fucked her with pure, dedicated intent on forever marking not just her body, but her soul.

She lay beneath him, her neck exposed to his hungry lips and tongue, perspiration coating her flesh, her moans broken, growing weaker with each peak of release she was pushed to. He drove inside her full length in a series of fast, blinding strokes before he tensed, growling her name as she felt the flexing and brutal throb of his cock with each expulsion of his release.

She had no idea what time it was, and she didn't care. Exhaustion swamped her, pulling her into the dark comfort of sleep even as she tried to force it back.

"Rest, baby," he breathed against her lips as he moved, lifting from her, his cock retreating from her body as she gave a little moan of protest.

She felt the blanket he spread over her and told herself she could nap, just for a minute. Then she'd get up. Shower. Try to figure out what had happened.

Though she had a feeling she knew, no matter how she shied from the answer and tried to deny it.

She'd deal with it later. Much later.

CHAPTER TEN

Jack had left Poppy in an exhausted heap, fully expecting to find her at her house waiting for him when he came in that night.

The day had been spent tracking down a small mercenary team reported to have arrived in Barboursville. A five-man, efficient, highly effective team led by a former British Special Forces agent.

This was fucking crazy, he thought when he'd learned the team was there to check into a job being offered in the area for just such a team. For one minute he'd actually wondered if just killing Caine Crossfield and River Dawson would stop whatever the hell was going on in his hometown.

It wouldn't, though. Considering the stakes, it would only make things more dangerous.

Word was, once a team arrived in town for the job in question, they were to send a message to a secured, online site, then arrive at the bar and chill a few hours before they were contacted.

Ian had received word that this particular team had arrived that morning and were checking out the town. Jack had sent Hayes to watch the bar, then began scouting town for them, hoping to catch the commander of the group before the message was sent and the team arrived at the bar.

They hadn't caught sight of them until Hayes had called in thirty minutes before and reported their arrival at the bar.

The Friday night band was blasting a current country tune at the bar, the female singer's sultry voice drawing dancers to the dance floor, where they whirled and twirled in differing levels of alcohol-induced pleasure.

Jack stepped into the building, his gaze moving slowly over the inhabitants, searching for his quarry.

He found Poppy instantly at the same table she'd sat at with her friends the first time he'd come into the bar. With them were two of her brothers, John David and Evan, and her two bosses. The men had brought their dates, all but River Dawson.

But Jack knew why River appeared dateless. The former Ranger had been fucking his partner's sister for the past two months. It would be kind of poor taste to bring another woman to the gathering.

Lilith Preston, Erika Boone, and Saige Dawson had dates. Jack knew who the men were, knew their families though he'd never interacted much with them. The three men were no more than minor bookmarks in the women's lives, from what he guessed, three of a small crowd of casual dates.

Standing behind Poppy, laughing with her brothers, was another familiar face. A friend of John David Porter's, and obviously there to attempt to charm Poppy. The other man placed his hand on Poppy's shoulder with a bit more familiarity than Jack liked and leaned down to whisper something in her ear.

"Let him live, boss," Lucas murmured at his side.

Jack grunted at the advice, his gaze meeting Poppy's as she turned quickly to him. His eyes narrowed on her unblemished neck as he swore he could feel his back teeth ready to crack, he clenched them so hard.

He'd take care of that in a bit, he promised himself. First, he had a job to do.

A slow sweep of the room and his gaze found the commander of the mercenary team. Violet-blue eyes set in a square, imposing face narrowed on his as Jack gave his head a short jerk to the door, then turned and walked out.

Mick Candless was a damned good soldier and a hell of a commander. His second, a bastard half brother, Coye Booker, was former Army Special Forces and no slouch either. The other three team members were just as hard-fighting and efficient as the brothers, but with few leadership skills.

It didn't take long to arrange a meeting with the commander. Jack had met him several times before while in the SEALs. His team had coordinated with the British Spec Ops team Mick fought with at the time, in several operations.

"The job's rumored to have a large payout," Mick told him as they discussed his reasons for being in town. "No details, though, and I don't care much for that part. The message I received from an unknown source just before you arrived informed me that it was possible those behind the job were looking for sacrificial lambs rather than a successful team."

The message was sent from an encrypted number, the sender unidentified, but no one had known they were arriving to check into the job, either, according to Candless.

"We're walking away from this one," Candless informed him. "We stopped in for dinner while the pilots prepped our plane. There are large payouts with far fewer complications elsewhere. This one has my balls itching. And I don't like it when my balls itch."

Jack stared around the darkened, vehicle-filled parking lot, the sound of the music easily heard, giving added cover to the conversation.

"How did you hear about the job?" he asked the other man. "Nothing's come through any of my channels concerning it."

They'd known word had gone out that there was a paying op in the area, but where it had gone, Ian hadn't managed to learn. So far, they'd found no avenue for Jack and his team to apply for it.

And it was pissing him off, he admitted.

Mick stared back at him for long minutes, his expression bland, though his eyes were intent, watchful.

"Through our booking agent. I'll have Coye send you the details," he stated. "A message was sent to our board and he made a query into it. We were in the States and rather at loose ends, so we thought we'd check it out." He crossed his arms over his chest and tilted his head a bit to the side as he watched Jack. "Funny there, Bridger. Hadn't heard you'd placed yourself out for jobs. Did I miss something?"

Jack let a mocking smile tug at his lips. An icy curl no one could mistake. "You didn't miss a thing," he responded. "This is my town, and I figure if we're careful, there's just enough work here for my team. And I'm possessive. Territorial, so to speak."

Mick actually chuckled at that one. "I'd never imagine you were otherwise. But I get what you're saying. Your town, your job. But how do you intend to make that hold when lower, less business-minded groups show up?"

Effectively, Jack thought. Very effectively.

"I'm sure you'll hear about it if anyone's that intent on playing in my territory," he drawled. "You know me. How do you think I'll handle it?"

It was no secret that Jack didn't mind playing dirty if playing fair didn't work.

"Understood." Mick nodded. "I have my own territory I keep an eye on. I don't tolerate poachers either." He looked back at where his men waited in a small group not far from Jack's.

When he turned back to Jack, his expression was warning. "Be careful. As I said, this job doesn't feel right once you're contacted. And I've learned to walk away when that happens."

Jack reached out his hand. "Warning taken. It was good to see you again."

Mick gripped his hand and nodded to him. "Watch your ass, Bridger," he warned again. "And your woman's. I hear there's a bit of interest in her."

He turned and strode back to his team before Jack could question him on that one. But it didn't surprise him that in what little time the man had spent in the bar he'd heard of Poppy and the fact that Jack was claiming her as well.

Jack allowed that possessiveness he tried to keep bottled up to slip a bit. Poppy thought it was okay to cover the marks he'd left on her, the ones that would warn any other male that she was claimed, and let some bastard attempt to charm her while he was away?

Evidently, he'd been far too subtle in letting everyone know how unacceptable he might feel that was.

Especially Poppy.

Giving his men the signal to follow him, he entered the bar again and strode to the table with determined strides. He rounded it until he stood directly across from Poppy but behind Dawson, crossed his arms over his chest, and met her wary gaze as it lifted to him.

Next to her, Mark Fieldman, a lawyer with the DA's office, shot him a nervous look.

"Bridger, that's my six," Dawson sighed, not bothering to turn. "It's a bar, not a war zone. It doesn't need protection."

"Yet," Jack drawled, his smile tight, a show of teeth and little more.

It was enough to have his men moving to strategic positions, though.

"You weren't invited, Bridger." John David Porter rose halfway from his seat, his hazel eyes sparking with anger as he glared at Jack.

"I invited him," Dawson told the other man without looking at him.

Surprising, because it was a bald-faced lie told with all apparent honesty. He'd have to find out why Dawson thought he needed to protect the little fucker.

Jack ignored them both, his gaze flicking first to Poppy's neck, then to the other man's hand on her shoulder. As his gaze lifted to meet Fieldman's eyes, he saw the concern that shadowed them.

Oh, the bastard knew why he was there. He'd probably got the warning from her brothers.

"How ya doin', Fieldman?" he asked the man brave enough to touch Poppy in his presence.

From the corner of his eye, he saw the owner, Mike, watching the gathering with a worried expression.

"Bridger. Didn't expect to see you back in town." Fieldman almost sneered the words.

Jack couldn't help but smile.

"Well surprise, surprise, here I am." Jack held his hands out slightly away from his body as he let his lips curl in anticipation. He did enjoy a good fight; unfortunately, he doubted he was going to find one here.

"I'm leaving." Poppy came to her feet quickly, barely evading Fieldman as he moved to grip her wrist. "Jack." She stared at him coolly.

"Like hell," John David burst out. "You don't have to leave because of him, Poppy. He can leave."

Jack chuckled, staring back at her brother as he would a toddler displaying a temper. Which was pretty much how he saw the other man.

He returned his gaze to Poppy and caught her giving a little roll of her eyes.

"I've had enough for the night," she informed her brother.

"Fiascoes rarely interest me, and this began heading there once he showed up." She waved her hand toward Fieldman. "You should have given him hazard pay for what you put him up to."

Poppy knew exactly what her brother was doing. He wanted to push Jack into a fight, believing Poppy would be able to walk away from him if fists started flying.

"I'm tired." She looked at Jack once again. "And I rode in with Sasha, if you'd like to give me a ride home?"

It was as though the better part of the tension eased from Jack's body. His expression didn't change, but his gaze softened, going from gleaming with battle to warming in a way she had no idea how to describe.

"I insist," he told her, his voice still hard, cool as he stepped around the table to her.

She'd expected him to grip her arm and tug her after him; men liked to do that where women were concerned. Instead, he surprised her again by holding out his hand to her.

She placed her hand on his, feeling his fingers curling protectively around her hand rather than gripping it.

How odd, she thought, something softening within her. Jack had never held her hand, but she found she liked it. His grip was warm and just slightly firm, as though he were consciously ensuring he didn't put too much pressure on her fingers.

"Poppy." John David pulled her gaze back to where he'd stood from his seat, his expression tightly pinched with disapproval. "I'll be by the house later."

"She won't be there," Jack stated. "You may want to stop by my place." Then he turned back to her. "Ready?"

"Might as well be," she sighed. "Before he does something stupid. Or you do."

She stepped beside him and let him lead her to the door.

"Stupidity is my preferred state of being," he told her in that dark, far-too-sexy voice. "Want me to teach him a few manners? I can help him out."

"As I said," she muttered. "You or him."

He was angry, and she knew it. He wasn't really hiding it. But he wasn't reacting with it, either. Whatever he was pissed over—and she had a feeling she knew—she'd hear about soon enough.

Whether she wanted to or not.

CHAPTER ELEVEN

Jack led Poppy into the house, through the kitchen, and into her bedroom. Once there, he surprised her by taking her into the bathroom, turning on the lights, and positioning her in front of the mirror over the sink.

"What do you see?" The snarl on his face had her eyes widening as their gazes met in the mirror.

She knew what he meant, and she wasn't going to waste both their time.

"I covered the marks," she told him defiantly. "Dammit, Jack, it wasn't just one little one. Or even two. You marked both sides of my neck, and the beard burn between them was almost as bad."

"My marks." Deep, rough, he almost, just almost, hid that undercurrent of some deeper, darker emotion than anger.

Had she somehow hurt him? Had she hurt his pride that she'd hid the marks?

"Jack, the marks were too dark, too deep. It would have offended my brothers, and my daddy would have a stroke if he saw it," she whispered. "They know the marks are there, but I wasn't going to rub their noses in it. Besides, to me, that was private. I loved it. The pleasure was incredible. But I can't flash them like some brand of ownership."

His expression tightened.

"Jack, you don't own me," she told him firmly, ignoring the determined look that deepened in his face. "You wouldn't own me if we were married with a dozen children. And I don't care what you think, I will not brandish my private sex life for the world to see."

His hand came up, crossed her breasts, and before she knew his intent, his fingers circled her throat, exerting just enough pressure to drag her head back against his chest.

She kept her gaze on his in the mirror. She wasn't frightened of him or of any hold he had on her. It was sexy, that dominance, and it called to some part of her that challenged her to match it, to dare him. So far, she'd kept it under control.

"I left those marks for a reason, just the way I left them," he snapped, his gaze darkening. "Fieldman would have never put his hands on you if he'd seen them."

"And my brothers? My father?" she snapped, anger rising inside her now. "You have no right to act this way."

"You gave me this right," he informed her. "When you leaned your head to the side and begged for more, you signed that little contract, sweetheart; now live with it. Because the next time I have to challenge a man over you, I'll break his fucking bones."

"Are you crazy?" She knew he'd carry out that threat.

"I'm fucking tired of this argument." He dropped his hand from her neck. "Wash that crap off. I don't want to taste makeup while I'm burying my dick inside you."

He turned and stalked from the bathroom, leaving Poppy to stare into the mirror where he had stood.

He was lucky she wanted to wash it off, she thought in irritation. Otherwise, he could kiss her ass.

Jack stalked back into the kitchen, pulled Poppy's bourbon from the cabinet along with a glass, and poured a healthy measure.

Damn her.

When he'd shown up at the bar she'd tensed, remaining quiet, watchful, as though she didn't want it known who was sleeping in her bed. Hell, maybe he should have just walked away, but he'd never have been able to just walk away from her, and she was too important to the operation. She was the only reason he had for being anywhere near the two men suspected of being involved with the AI.

He was aware of it when she entered the room, quiet, watching him. Turning to her, he met her somber green gaze and he knew, just knew, he was not going to like what she was getting ready to say.

"You left my bed and walked out of the house without leaving your phone number, asking for mine, or dropping so much as a hint as to when you'd be back," she said quietly. "Everyone knows I spend most Friday and Saturday nights with my brothers and friends at that bar. Had I known how to reach you, I would have invited you. Had you been with me, the message that we're together would have been much clearer than any mark on my neck. Clearer to me, and to everyone there. I'm not a side piece, or a whore, Jack, and I won't be treated as such. If you want to claim me, then do so properly."

She stared at him silently for long moments, but hell if he knew what to say to her. "Now, I'm sore and I'm tired. I'm taking a hot bath, a couple of aspirins, and I'm going to bed." Pulling a drawer out from the cabinet next to the door, she reached out, retrieved a key, and laid it on the counter. "So you don't have to pick my locks again. Alarm code is my birth date. If you can't remember that, then don't come when I'm not home. Lock up when you leave."

She looked tired, he thought.

He remained silent as she left the room even though everything inside him demanded that he go after her and ensure his control over her. The fact that she was right shouldn't have mattered. He had a role to play, and she was part of that role.

He'd seen her eyes, though, heard her tone of voice. And something warned him that pushing her right now was not in his best interests. Or in the best interests of the operation.

She might not have a temper to match that red hair, but he knew for a fact she had the stubbornness. She'd cut her nose off to spite her face if she thought she was being forced into anything she didn't want herself.

Running his fingers through his hair, he was almost about to let a curse slip past his lips when the vibration of the phone inside his vest demanded his attention.

Pulling it free, he stared at the message. Ice shot through his veins as he saw Ian's text.

Candless has been struck! Directions to follow!

Candless's team had left only minutes after they'd reentered the bar. They'd laid a tip on the table and hadn't even bothered finishing their meal before they'd slipped away.

The directions Ian sent were to a deserted, private airfield about twenty minutes away.

Resetting Poppy's alarm, he left the house, locked the door behind him, and met the other members of the team where they waited on their bikes in the back drive.

"Hayes, you're staying here," he ordered, and pointed to Poppy's house. "Don't let anything happen to that woman. Understand me?"

Hayes glanced to Poppy's house, then returned his gaze to Jack as he nodded. "Nothing will happen, boss."

Swinging his leg over the Harley, Jack started it, put it in gear, and shot from the alley, the others following close behind him.

How the hell had anyone managed to strike at Candless's team? They were careful, always armed, always prepared. Based on where they'd been hit, they'd been prepared to board their plane and head out. Why strike at them then?

But as the night passed by, it wasn't Candless that filled his thoughts. It was Poppy.

"I'm not a side piece, or a whore, Jack, and I won't be treated as such. If you want to claim me, then do so properly."

Is that how she believed he saw her? Without enough worth to claim? That's what he thought he'd been doing when he'd marked her: claiming her. Did other men think that just because he couldn't constantly be at her side they could slip in on the only softness in his world?

But for eight years, despite the fact that he'd stayed away from her, she hadn't allowed another man in her bed, another part of his brain argued. Other than that damned vibrator and her own fingers, nothing had touched her sweet flesh, especially some bastard who thought her sweetness was up for grabs.

She'd waited for him.

Despite that fact that he'd never indicated that he'd claim her, had shown no interest in doing so, still, she'd waited.

When he would have taken the blame for Trencher's death, she'd refused to allow it. She'd demanded he hide the body instead. Get rid of it somehow. And when Mac had burst into that cabin and aimed that gun at Jack's chest, she had jumped in front of him before he could stop her.

She had tried to save him when she was just seven years old, and because she'd cried when she'd learned he was in a juvenile facility until the authorities could figure out what had happened, her father had found a distant cousin to foster him. A retired Navy SEAL. A man who had taught Jack what honor was.

Because of Poppy.

And she felt that in payment, he was treating her as though she didn't matter, as though the gifts she'd given him were of no value, because he didn't stand by her side and claim her.

God help him. If she walked away from him after he did that, it would strip his soul from his body. He couldn't imagine a hell greater than to have Poppy turn away from him after he showed the world that someone meant something to him after all.

What was he going to do when this was over? When she realized that lies of omission were still lies, and he had used her love to destroy her friends?

Friends who had been there when he hadn't been through the years.

Would her hatred go as deep as her love then?

As he neared the location Ian had directed him to, he had to force those thoughts away. He had to let the ice back in when all he wanted to do was warm himself with the knowledge that Poppy loved him. That she needed to be claimed by him. Even if he couldn't say the words, she needed him to show that she was of value.

As he and his men entered the valley Candless's team had flown into, he eased the Harley to a stop just past the EMS vans and stared around the area, almost disbelieving.

He'd seen worse, but that was in the heat of battle, where he expected to see worse. Not here in this lush green valley, where scattered plane debris and body parts littered the field. In places, blood seemed to bedew the grass. Tattered remains of clothes and Mick's men were like broken, disassembled toys thrown by a child's careless hand.

The carnage showed that no mercy had been given when the explosion had occurred, however it had occurred.

Lowering the kickstand and turning off the engine, he dismounted slowly, wondering if there was even a chance of a survivor.

"Jack. Over here." Ian stepped from behind the ambulance and waved him over imperatively.

There, lying on a gurney, its white sheets stained with too much blood, lay Candless. Shrapnel from the plane had buried itself in his legs, slicing at flesh, tearing it to the bone and ripping through veins.

He was conscious as the medics worked to stabilize the bleeding, his violet eyes burning in the bloodied, torn flesh of his face.

Several feet from him, medics worked to save his brother, Coye, though Jack was afraid it was in vain. A piece of metal had shoved itself into his chest, larger and thicker than the other debris that had flown into him.

He was unconscious, near death.

Jack stepped to Candless, staring down at him as the other man fought to swallow and speak.

"Coye?" The name finally slipped past his lips.

Jack glanced over his shoulder again at the brother, then turned back to Mick.

"It's bad, Mick," he told him. "Real bad. I don't know . . ."

Jack didn't know how the younger man could survive his injuries.

"What the hell happened here?" Jack demanded. "Why were you hit?"

". . . were getting ready to board," Mick groaned as he shuddered in pain. ". . . Didn't feel right . . . grabbed Coye . . . told him run . . ." He seemed to wheeze the words. "Didn't make it . . ."

His teeth clenched as his body jerked in what had to be agony. "The others? My men?"

He stared up at Jack, desperation gleaming in his gaze. He knew the truth.

Jack shook his head anyway. "I'm sorry, Mick . . ."

"Fuckers . . ." Mick wheezed, blood dripping from his face to the sheet beneath him. Or was it blood mixed with tears? "Told you . . . didn't feel right . . . saw shadows . . . another team maybe." He fought to swallow again, to breathe for long seconds. "Get the fuckers . . . Jack," he groaned. "For my men . . . Fuck . . ." His back bowed, then suddenly he crashed back to the gurney.

"Move! Move!" The medic pushed past Jack, lifted the bed, and, once the retractable legs and wheels were in place, all but threw it into the back of the ambulance.

The bed carrying Coye had already raced away, and before the doors had even closed on Mick, that one was tearing from the clearing as well.

Jack ran his fingers through his hair and turned back to the wreckage, staring around again in disbelief.

A pilot and three men had died here, and he doubted they even knew what had hit them.

"Explosives or missile?" Jack asked, turning to Ian as the other man stepped to him.

Where Kira was, Jack didn't have a clue. He was damned glad she wasn't here, though.

"We think it was explosives," Ian told him. "One of my bodyguards has explosives training, and that's his guess anyway . . . Fuck, didn't expect this tonight," he sighed.

Who could have expected this?

Except Mick. He'd said his balls were itching and he didn't like it. Something was off about the op being offered, he'd said.

"He has enough enemies—it could have been personal," one of the men standing behind Ian said, though Jack could hear the doubt in his voice.

"Mick said there were shadows. Perhaps another team," Jack muttered.

"Another team?" Ian questioned him.

"Could this be connected to the cartel?" Jack asked. "I know he uses mercs for transport sometimes." He couldn't see Mick transporting drugs, but sometimes the Fuentes Cartel moved things other than drugs.

"I'll ask," Ian stated, but his tone was doubtful. "My contact messaged a warning that the team was going to be hit, but not why. I haven't heard anything further yet."

Were they hit because Mick had talked to Jack?

"What the fuck does Crossfield think he's doing ordering this?" Jack growled. "This team had friends. Loyal friends. If we're not damned careful we'll have half a dozen teams in the area ready to commit carnage on their behalf."

"Only if Mick dies," Ian stated, but Jack could hear the worry in his voice. "Let's pray my people can keep him alive."

"Why order this hit?" Jack could feel the icy bite of rage threatening to overwhelm him. "What was in it for them?"

"I don't think they did." Ian's answer had Jack staring at him in disbelief.

"Why?"

Ian grimaced. "Neither sent a message, made a call, or received one. They didn't slip off to the men's room or talk to anyone that wasn't at the table. They didn't show signs of recognition when the team either entered or left. We can't trace where, how, or why the order went out to strike this team."

Mick had seen shadows, he said. Possibly another team.

Was another group hedging their bets on being picked for whatever operation Crossfield needed a team for? But still, why hit Mick's team? They were leaving.

"Lucas." He turned to his second. "Contact Hayes. Tell him to make certain no one gets in that goddamned house, even if it means slipping in himself and hiding in a corner."

"Already taken care of," Lucas assured him. "Your woman's fast asleep and Hayes is currently in position should anyone attempt to get in."

Jack hated the thought of another man in her home, a stranger who could frighten her if she came up on him in the dark. It would fucking terrify her. Hayes was no amateur, though, and if he was in the shadows, he'd stay there if Poppy awakened and began moving around.

"There's another team somewhere," he told Lucas softly, feeling the certainty in his bones. "Doesn't make sense to hit Mick as he was leaving, but they did." He looked around the area again.

His hunter's instincts weren't crawling, but he could feel the disquiet, the certainty that Mick had seen something to convince him someone was out there before the explosion.

"Looks like someone doesn't want competition, boss," Lucas suggested, his voice low, hard.

Which meant Jack and his men were likely marks now.

As well as Poppy.

"Find that team," he ordered Lucas. "And find them fast. Before our body parts are scattered over some field."

Lucas grimaced. "Thanks for an image that I could have done without, but I'm already on it, boss . . ."

Hayes had slipped from Poppy's house before Jack's arrival hours later. Night was beginning to edge into dawn when he stripped, showered to wash the stench of death from his body, then after drying crawled into bed beside her.

She turned to him, still asleep, snuggling against him as though she had been cold, when Jack knew he was the one who needed warmth. Needed her body next to his, sheltered against him and protected.

There had been a woman on that fucking plane, as well as the pilot, Ian had informed him just before they left the site. One of his men had found her body, mostly intact. A petite blonde who'd been wearing a wedding band.

God, he prayed she hadn't been Mick's or Coye's woman. Losing a wife like that could kill a man with no wounds. Shatter his heart right in his chest.

As he inhaled Poppy's scent, he knew he'd never survive losing her.

"Okay?" she whispered sleepily, causing him to realize just how tight he was holding her.

"I'm fine," he promised, loosening his grip on her only marginally. "Go back to sleep, baby."

She settled into him once again, slipping back into slumber as he stared into the dimly light room.

He and his men went out daily riding through town, looking at faces, watching people. They hadn't seen anyone from a team other than Mick's, hadn't heard from any of the contacts they were slowly pulling in of anyone who appeared dangerous skulking around.

That didn't mean they weren't there. They just hadn't been seen yet.

Not a lot of teams would have risked trying to take Mick out like that. If he survived, he'd learn who it was, and he'd make damned sure they paid. And if Coye survived to help him, those other men would beg for death long before they found it.

They were still fighting to live. Both men were still in surgery, and the last report Ian had relayed to Jack was that though it was still touch and go, they were alive.

If they'd made it this long, then Jack had hope they'd survive.

He'd get some rest now, just as his men were now sleeping in the house across from him. At least, that was what he'd told them to do. They needed a few hours' rest, a chance to catch a breath before they went looking for the shadows Mick had seen.

Finding that team and eliminating them was imperative now. Not just for Mick, but for their own safety.

CHAPTER TWELVE

Mick and Coye were still holding on the next afternoon when Jack and his team met with Ian and Kira at the house the Richardses had taken for the summer. Ian's contact didn't know why the team had been hit, but was still checking into it; all that was known for sure was that it had to do with the job they'd turned down in Barboursville. A job Mick had decided he didn't like the feel of.

Ian's people hadn't located any of the AI's components coming into the country, despite their best attempts. They were tracking what they thought was a suspicious shipment heading for West Virginia but were trying to get more intel on it.

According to their informant, half of the AI had been shipped first, and whoever had it was tracking the progress of the second shipment, waiting to see if further information had been leaked.

Once the first half of the AI was in its designated location in Barboursville, the second half would arrive in a short amount of time.

"It's possible we can add a week to the mission," Ian told them somberly. "Word is, the shipments left later than expected and had to be delayed. But expect that to change."

Their informant was careful, cautious.

"We might have some information on the team that hit Mick," Jack said, leaning back in his chair, his gaze locking with Ian's. "There's another merc team in town. A bastard named Chet Rollins and his team. Hayes caught sight of one of them in town just before we headed here. I'm not a big believer in coincidence, and I know at one time there was word Mick and Rollins were gunnin' for each other."

Ian's gaze swung to Kira.

"Don't look at me." She held her hands up as though to stop whatever he was about to say. "I haven't heard even a whisper of that."

"Your job to know, sweetheart," he grunted, but Jack could hear an undertone of the emotion Ian's voice always carried when he spoke to his wife.

"Who are they?" Kira asked then, frowning back at Jack.

"Small four-man team. Originated in South Africa, but they work mainly in South America. Chet Rollins is commander," Jack answered.

"Second is Rodrigo Sanchez." Ian grimaced. "His father was part of the Fuentes Cartel when Homeland took it down. Augusto Sanchez was killed in a mission to rescue three senators' daughters in Colombia. We've had some chatter the last couple of years that the team was moving into higher circles."

"I don't know about higher circles." Jack frowned. "The circles he works within haven't exactly given him great word of mouth. They're brutal, if that's what you're looking for. Within the first week girls will start disappearing, and if they show up alive, they're either too traumatized to identify their attackers or too damned terrified."

Ian's gaze sharpened at the information.

"My team dealt with them in Honduras several years back. We

knew they'd killed two young women they'd kidnapped from their homes. We were ordered to stand down. We were getting ready to hit them anyway when the team disappeared. I suspected one of our team members warned them we were coming." Jack still held that order against the commander that had given it.

"Suggestions?" Ian asked him softly.

"Take them out as quickly as possible," Jack stated. "I'm still trying to locate their nest. Once I have it, I suggest we go in, hit fast and hard, and leave the bodies to be found by local LEOs. Crossfield and Dawson will get the message."

The local law enforcement officers would make certain the news of a team of mercenaries dying in the county circulated fast.

"And what message is that?" Kira asked.

Jack's lips curled in anticipation. "My territory. Once word gets around, whoever's behind this will have to come to us, or pay a hell of a lot more than any other team is worth to get them to take the risk. Rollins is brutal, and known for it. Most teams would have a hard time getting the drop on him. I won't. He'll expect me to come knocking to find out why he's here and demand my cut of whatever work he has or will get. This is a small, tight-knit community, not a major metropolis where he can sneak in and out. He knows that. And he knows I'm here."

Unwritten rules.

It would also send a message to anyone else in that seedy little area of the underworld of cutthroats and soldiers for hire, that someone in the area didn't like poachers.

Ian gave a quick, hard nod.

"Your op, your team," he stated. "I can't provide backup . . ."

"We got this." Jack shrugged, unconcerned. "If we don't, then we deserve to be taken out. Rollins is small game, not one of the big dogs."

The "big dogs," as he called the more professional, high-end groups, would have checked the area out thoroughly, made note of the discharged and/or retired Special Force members in the tristate area, and either sent an agent to discuss joining their team or taken a cut of the fee for standing down.

That was, if they took the job to begin with. Most mercs had no desire to get on the wrong side of Homeland Security or the CIA, which they would if they accepted a job such as this.

"Give me tonight to find them for you," Ian said then. "I have contacts in the area and resources you don't."

"Sat tracking," Lucas murmured.

Satellite tracking was a game changer.

"You have till daylight," Jack told him. "We need to hit no later than tomorrow night or girls are going to start coming up missing. And I do mean 'girls.' Then, I'll get pissed."

"I'll have something for you in about six hours, give or take a few extra minutes."

"If you saw Rollins, then you can bet he saw us," Lucas pointed out as they left the house. "And he could be thinking the same thing we are, in reverse. Take out the home team and set up here until they're needed. Finding your place would be easy enough."

Jack flicked him a mocking look. "Worried about me?"

"Covering bases," Lucas stated. "I say we bunk down at your place, Jack. You have the bed in the basement, the spare room, and the couch. Rollins gets nosy, he sees the four bikes outside, he won't consider it in his best interests to do something stupid. Besides, when it comes time to exterminate the roaches, I'd like to be there, if ya know what I'm sayin'."

Rollins wasn't above attacking if he thought Jack would be a future threat, just as Jack considered him and his team a threat. The other man wouldn't know that, but there was no doubt he'd consider Jack a future hindrance to whatever he was there to do.

"Plenty of hot water and towels," Jack offered. "Make use of the guest shower." Then he turned to the electronics guru, Hayes. "I want sensors around the house and coordinating alerts at Poppy's place that are jam-resistant. If you need funds let me know and I'll have them wired to you."

Hayes shook his head as he mounted his Harley. "Been working on that already. Hank and I have almost everything we need. Jam-resistant requires a mix of old and new components. Just a matter of finding what you need. I should have enough to go ahead and get started, though."

Jack mounted his Harley and within minutes they were riding along the scenic, winding mountain road leading away from the house.

He paid careful attention to those instincts that would warn him they were being targeted, but so far, nothing more than an odd disquiet about the mission blipped his hunter's radar.

That would change soon if this mission didn't wrap up quickly, and he knew it. Once he took out Rollins's team, word would circulate, and there were always those teams that would challenge them just for the hell of it.

Life would change. If they weren't careful, the danger level would change as well. If he wasn't careful.

Jack was a damned careful man.

Poppy hated waking up early on the days she didn't work. It never failed to irritate her and completely threw her off balance. But for some ungodly reason her mother thought it was a good idea for her and Poppy's father to stop by before she had time to shower or apply the cover-up to her neck.

She'd been as nervous as a cat in a roomful of rocking chairs when her father stared at her neck for long seconds. When he didn't say anything, just hugged her as he always did and headed for her coffeepot, she almost breathed a sigh of relief.

Her mother clucked her tongue at her, then flashed her a teasing smile.

"It's so good to know you're seeing someone, sweetheart," she said sweetly, then laid in the guilt trip with, "I'm sorry you didn't trust me and Daddy to tell us. You know I always liked Jack Bridger when he was a boy . . . Be sure he comes to the house with you tomorrow."

She had known her parents saw Jack whenever he came to town, but she'd fought not to question them over the years and reveal how much it had hurt her feelings that he hadn't sought her out as well.

"He sent the prettiest vase of flowers this year," her mother stated as she and Poppy moved into the kitchen. "I keep telling him I enjoyed feeding him all those years ago, but he just thanks me and brings more flowers the next year. And your daddy doesn't admit it, but he loves heading to the home supply store with those gift cards Jack leaves lying next to the door."

Jack left them on the tall stand next to the door because her daddy always waved him away, telling him he'd do the same for any kid. Which her father would have, but Poppy knew that over the years Jack had endeared himself to her parents.

Two hours of her parents' subtle nosiness had her gritting her teeth before she could finally usher them out the door and get her shower. So much for hiding those marks on her neck from her father. She should have known her brothers would blab. They never could keep a secret.

After that, there was no time to relax with her own coffee before starting her day. If she was going to make it to Lilith's birthday dinner that evening at the bar, she was going to have to complete certain things early.

One of those things was a trip to the store, which she hadn't managed to get to Friday. She grimaced as that thought had her knees going all jelly, and her vagina moistening further. She couldn't seem to convince that part of her body that she was upset with Jack.

He'd taken the house key she'd placed on the counter, but he hadn't left his phone number, or taken hers. So evidently, being included in her social life wasn't too damned important to him.

When she left the house and hurried to the SUV to make the much-needed trip to the store, she noticed that the bikes were gone; they hadn't returned yet from wherever they'd gone. One day soon she was going to have to find out what was going on, and she knew it. Making herself do that, though, was getting harder by the day.

She'd heard the bikes leave early that morning, before her parents arrived. Jack wasn't one to have overnight guests in the years he'd made his trips home. Not friends or women. From the gossip she'd heard, he didn't hang out with anyone, not until this summer with his biker buddies. He worked on the house, went out for a few beers at the Downtown Bar and Grill, then returned home. Always alone.

She drove to the end of the alley, came to a stop, and was about to pull out when a large, tan, super-duty pickup suddenly sped around the corner without stopping and almost slammed into her.

Hitting the gas at first sight of it, she barely avoided the crash with the larger vehicle. The fact that it would have slammed into her car door, and at the speed it was traveling sent her straight to the hospital, wasn't lost on her.

She'd glimpsed the driver and knew she hadn't seen him around. He wasn't a local. And he hadn't looked nice, as he appeared to be yelling at the man sitting next to him in the passenger seat.

Both were big, brawny, though the one in the passenger seat kind of resembled the South American she'd seen at the bar several nights ago, before Jack had arrived. He'd asked her to dance, but she didn't dance with men either she or her friends didn't know, and she'd politely declined.

Shaking her head at the driver, she checked the rearview mirror, just to make sure they hadn't followed her, then made the next turn and continued on her way to the grocery store.

She had to prepare stuffing casserole for family dinner the next day, as well as the yeast rolls she had bought frozen. Those took several hours to thaw and rise before going into the oven with the lasagna, which itself would take several hours to prepare.

There were her own groceries to buy, though her list was short. Coffee, a few fresh vegetables, odds and ends mostly, and she was considering a couple of steaks just in case Jack made his way to the house one evening that she was actually home in time to cook.

There were several meetings scheduled late in the day during the coming week. The prospective lessees were coming into town from New York and couldn't fit earlier meetings into their schedules. The properties in question were two of Crossfield-Dawson's highest-rent properties and had sat unused for months.

Caine was eager to see them signed, and River pressed Poppy to complete the deal as quickly as possible, while River's sister, Saige, was stressed thinking that just as the previous party interested in the property had backed out, the prospective ones probably would as well.

Poppy had expected Saige to take over the deal herself. It wouldn't have been the first time Saige asked Poppy to let her handle a property because of the high-dollar rent or an out-of-state client's financial status.

She hurried through the store, picking up the items she needed. Thankfully, Miss Martha, the older lady at checkout, wasn't too gossipy today, and, pushing one of the small carts filled with her bags, Poppy hurried to her car.

Hitting the key fob to unlock the back of the vehicle, she unloaded the groceries and pushed the hatchback down. She returned the cart to the front of the store and had just hurried back to her vehicle when a large blond man seemed to rush at her.

Letting out a startled squeak of fear, Poppy jumped back, almost running into an older-model pickup moving slowly along the parked vehicles. The truck came to a quick stop, the door opened, and Poppy, feeling herself beginning to panic, gathered herself to run.

"Poppy, is that you?" Calvin Hitchins, a friend of her brother's, Mac-Cole, stepped from his truck and quickly rounded the door as he stared at her in surprise. "Did I hit you? You okay, girl?"

"I'm fine. Fine." She shook her head, but she didn't move for her car. And Calvin made note of it.

His sharp, intelligent brown eyes slashed to the man still standing at the back of her car, and he moved next to Poppy protectively.

"I'm sorry I frightened you, ma'am," the stranger apologized, his accented voice and charming smile somehow at odds with his eyes. "I'm visiting, and just thought to ask directions. I was going to go inside, but then there you were."

His smile was cold and hard, reminding her of the smiles that could cross Caine's face when he was patently lying to a client.

Poppy couldn't convince the adrenaline in her body to ease, couldn't convince herself there was no danger. He looked genuine enough, but she knew how deceptive that could be.

"Get in your car and get home, Poppy," Calvin told her firmly. "I'll give him directions."

Poppy nodded quickly. "Thank you, Cal." She turned to the stranger, who watched her, a smile still curling his lips, and she tried to smile in return. "Calvin knows where everything is. He can help you far better than I can."

She hurried to her car as the man thanked her, then she got in and hit the door locks quickly. As Calvin eased his truck out of the way, she backed up and quickly turned to head home.

Unknown men always made her uncomfortable when they approached her or popped up in front of her like that. The memories of that night nine years ago had never really gone away.

The drifter that had showed up at the parties a few times that summer suddenly appeared as Poppy hurried home on foot one night. One minute she'd been alone, and the next he'd grabbed her.

Gritting her teeth, she pushed the memory back and checked her rearview mirror, surprised to see a Harley behind her. It wasn't Jack, but if she wasn't mistaken, it was one of the friends who'd been at the bar with him.

The bike stayed behind her, then pulled into the small parking area across from hers as she parked behind her house.

Maybe she should have parked out front.

Her hands were shaking as she watched through the rearview mirror. Lucas, she thought she'd heard him called. He wasn't as big and muscular as Jack, but not many men were. Still, he was a big man and in peak physical condition. And other than the two of them, the alley was deserted.

She watched as he dismounted the bike, glanced her way, then walked to Jack's back door. Seconds later he stepped into the house. Hurriedly, Poppy pushed her door open, hit the lock and hatch release, and when it opened enough grabbed her bags with shaking hands and all but ran into the house after slamming the hatchback closed.

Panic was like a ball in her throat, threatening to explode outward even after she was safely in the house, doors locked, and her security turned on.

She looked out the window. The alley was quiet, the bike across the street still in place, and evidently Jack's friend still in the house.

Turning to the kitchen island, she put the bags on the marble top and breathed in, deeply, slowly.

She was safe, she told herself. No one was after her. No one was going to hurt her. She wasn't a teenager anymore and she wasn't making her way back home along a tree-shrouded path.

She was grown.

She was going to be okay.

Jack glanced at the display of his mobile phone, recognized Lucas's number, and activated the call with a frown.

"Thought you had a meeting," he remarked, keeping his voice low, aware that Caine Crossfield was standing close enough to hear his side of the conversation.

The other man had approached him moments ago, seemingly just to say hello.

"Rescheduled." Lucas's tone was hard and layered with ice as Jack stepped farther away from Caine. "We have a problem."

"Go on," Jack directed him when Lucas paused.

"I was heading to the meeting when I passed the grocery store and glimpsed a stranger standing at the back of Poppy's SUV just as she jumped into the path of an oncoming truck in the parking lot. I pulled over just to watch, make sure she was okay. Driver must have known her. He hurried her into her vehicle and got her out of there. I don't know what was said, but she looked scared, boss. I followed her back to the house; I'm watching her place from your house now. I'm almost positive the fucker standing at the back of her car was Rollins's man Van Nyes. And I think I glimpsed his cousin, Alberts, in a car that pulled out behind me and followed us back to her street before moving on."

Fuck. He knew he should have found that bastard and his men the night before and taken care of them.

"I'm on my way." Jack disconnected the call and turned and strode quickly away from the conversation he'd been having with Caine Crossfield.

He pushed through the door as he slid on his sunglasses, his gaze raking over the area, searching for any of Rollins's men as he mounted the bike and hit the ignition before pulling out of the parking spot and accelerating away from the bar.

Ian had contacted him with the group's location earlier and the information that they were currently away from the small, unoccupied farmhouse several miles out of town. A secluded little place owned by Crossfield-Dawson.

Not that the information on the owner proved anything. The company owned many unoccupied homes, and he knew Poppy put a lot of effort into filling them. The acquisitions manager, Sasha Crossfield, put just as much effort into finding and acquiring even more commercial and residential properties.

From all appearances, Rollins and his men had simply taken advantage of the deserted house and its secluded location to crash.

They'd die there too, Jack decided. If he didn't get the chance to take them out before that.

He wasn't a stupid man. Rollins's men had every intention of grabbing Poppy.

The subtle beep of a text message came through. Lucas. He'd called Hayes and Hank back to the house. Something Jack would have done as soon as he pulled into his driveway.

Lucas was a hell of a second. He had no desire to lead, even while in the SEALs. But he was damned good operating as second in lead, as Jack was learning.

It didn't take long to get back to the house. Backing his bike in next to his truck, he sat silently, watching Poppy's kitchen window, saw her moving past it, then turning back to whatever she was doing.

Narrowing his eyes, he watched a few more minutes, catching sight of her every few seconds. Everything seemed okay, quiet. She didn't seem stressed or moving in agitated motions that might indicate she had unwanted company.

Confident she was safe for the moment, he strode quickly to the house.

Just inside the door, Lucas sat with one of the high-powered rifles he'd brought to the house earlier in the week, his closed, set expression unemotional, his dark gray eyes flat and hard.

"Alberts made a pass in the car earlier," Lucas said quietly as Jack stood silent, still, in front of the door. "That little security camera you connected to your system at the front of her house"—he nodded his salt-and-pepper head toward the display monitor—"showed the car making two more passes after that, Van Nyes and Alberts both inside. They haven't returned in the past few minutes, though."

"Where are Hayes and Hank?" Jack asked, keeping his voice low.

"They're holding in a little restaurant in Huntington awaiting further direction. They're on the bikes, but Hank has an SUV parked close if needed. Prepared little fucker, ain't he?"

Jack remained still.

From the moment he'd learned Poppy had been approached, ice had begun filling him. He hadn't experienced it since catching sight of her again. The cold had slowly eased, leaving him not exactly friendly and warm, but more . . . content maybe.

He wasn't content now.

"Go to the basement and pack the gear you need from the supply room, along with any ammo you need. Contact Hank and Hayes. If they don't have what they need in that SUV, then pack for them. We'll meet them in Huntington. I'll get ahold of Ian and have him apprise us on when all four men are back at the farm. We'll go in as soon as they return."

He already had his gear packed. Mission clothes, boots, weapons, and ammo. Not that he expected the mini-war he'd be able to engage in with everything he'd stored beneath the seats of the truck, but he was prepared.

"I have what I need in the bike's saddlebags," Lucas stated, the information not surprising Jack. "The others do as well."

"I'll contact Ian. We'll stay here and watch her until we know they're in place, then leave."

And when he was finished, Rollins's men would be dead, or he would be. Poppy was his, and she was off limits, period. If he hadn't intended to take them out, this move ensured it. Though he was certain Rollins had only meant to force a meet, not a killing.

Still, all indications pointed to the other man's intent to abduct Poppy to get the message to Jack that he wanted to talk. The mercenary had never understood subtlety.

And now Jack would forget the meaning of mercy.

CHAPTER THIRTEEN

The farmhouse sat back from I-64, sheltered by an acre or more of thickly growing trees around it. The dirt road in was the only vehicle access.

Hank and Hayes went in separately, the car they stole for the occasion hidden beneath pine trees where it probably wouldn't be found until the bodies were. From there, the two men made their way on foot, arriving in position, with clear sight of the house as Jack and Lucas pulled into it.

Rollins, Sanchez, Van Nyes, and Alberts were in the house, according to satellite. The stealth drone used to survey the area detected no electronic surveillance being used. The mercenaries were confident of their position and their strength to hold it until whatever they were there for was completed.

Evidently, they didn't intend to stay long at the deserted house, because Rollins was known for his insistence where his creature comforts were concerned—especially electric.

As Jack parked the truck, Rollins opened the front door and stared back at him, his gaze narrowed on Jack. At barely six feet, his head shaven and a bushy beard covering his face, he looked like the bush scavenger Jack had always considered him to be. The wary caution and hint of surprise on the mercenary's face assured Jack the other man had expected something far different than a daylight visit and that he wasn't certain what to expect from Jack now.

"Afternoon, Bridger," he greeted, his voice wary, nodding as Jack and Lucas stepped from the vehicle.

"Chet." Jack nodded. "It's been a while."

"Yep, a while," Chet agreed, his gaze scanning the area, searching for any threats.

Jack could feel the gun sights trained on him from inside the house and spread his arms away from his body carefully.

"I'm just here to talk," Jack assured him.

Chet looked around suspiciously once again, but seeing nothing, and his hunter's instincts assuring him there were no sights trained on him, he gave a short nod and a hand signal to the men inside.

"Didn't expect you so early today, I have to admit," Chet said. "We were actually going to head to your place this evening."

His, or Poppy's? Jack wondered.

"Let's say I got your message loud and clear when you approached my woman in town," Jack said, stepping to the porch, Lucas behind him.

"How did you find the place?" Rollins was clearly still suspicious.

"My territory," Jack informed him. "Not a lot of abandoned places that would suit your needs. I think this is the third place we checked."

Rollins chuckled as he stood back from the door.

"You armed?" the mercenary asked.

"Left it in the truck," Jack assured him.

Rollins and his men were armed.

Chet's gaze went over him and Lucas once again, and Jack knew their black pants, boots, and T-shirts would have revealed weapons to an experienced eye and they would have been taken before they made the porch.

"I wondered if you'd take the message seriously," Chet remarked as they entered the house. "You're not known for claiming a woman. Kind of surprised me when I heard those boys bitching at the bar over you claiming their sister."

"So, you thought you'd approach her and scare her a little bit," Jack stated coolly. "I'm not happy over that, Chet. Barboursville is a quiet little place, not a war zone."

"Yeah, Van Nyes said she was a skittish little thing." He laughed, closing the door to reveal the South African where he had stood out of sight.

Roland Van Nyes wasn't as big as Jack, but he was a big boy. Muscle-bound, blond, his hair cut close to his scalp, his hazel eyes cold. He carried a short, easily held automatic weapon, his finger close to the trigger.

"You mind?" Jack asked Chet, his gaze flicking to the weapon. "This is supposed to be a peaceful meet. Or we can leave and come back later."

The message was clear: When Jack returned, he'd be armed.

"Put it down, Van Nyes," Rollins drawled, a hint of South Texas still in his voice. "Alberts, put that coffee on." He turned to one of the doors across the room. "We got company, Sanchez, get your ass out here."

The door opened a few seconds later, and Sanchez strolled out.

Small black eyes, a bullish build. His South American features were actually rather nondescript, but the cruelty in his black gaze was clear.

"Bridger," Sanchez greeted him warily, his voice heavily accented, those black eyes gleaming as he eased into the kitchen. "Nice little setup you have in town. Pretty area."

Sanchez was like a pit viper, striking without warning if a man didn't watch him damned closely.

"It's home," Jack said with a shrug, accepting Rollins's silent invitation to sit at the table.

Lucas remained close behind Jack but didn't sit down. When the time came, they'd use the weapons the men had on them to take them out.

Carefully making note of the knives on both Sanchez and Rollins, Jack started mentally counting down his time to Hayes and Hank's entrance.

"There was a team taken out night before last," Jack told them as he sat back in his chair in feigned comfort. "Mick Candless's team. You hear anything 'bout that?"

Rollins's brows rose slowly. "All of them?" The speculative light in his gaze hinted at real interest rather than guilt.

"Got 'em all," Jack said with a nod, lying. "Even the pilot and an unidentified female."

"That be Coye's wife," Van Nyes spoke up. "Heard she had a little bun in the oven too."

Fucker. There was no compassion, no regret in the other man's expression or his gaze, but neither could Jack detect guilt.

He knew Rollins—if his team had taken Mick out, it would be hard to keep the pride out of his expression.

"One less group to compete with, I guess." Rollins shrugged with a sideways grin.

"Where are your other men?" Sanchez was holding on to his suspicion, despite Rollins's apparent lack of it.

"Waiting at the end of the road," Jack informed him. "We came to talk, not to fight." He gave the appearance of smiling with ease. "I appreciate you letting me know you were in town.

Some groups might think it okay to conduct business here with-out alerting us."

Rollins nodded with a grin. "Hadn't heard there was a local group in the area," he said. "We didn't know till we saw you in town and heard gossip 'bout your woman. It was real amusing. Heard you got fucked over real good with those SEALs you liked to play with. You done with them?"

"What do you think?" he asked Rollins, his tone hard as he met the other man's gaze with a flat stare.

Rollins chuckled ruefully. "Yeah, got wind you told 'em to get fucked."

Van Nyes chuckled from his position behind Rollins. Lucas would have that gun, quick, Jack knew.

"Pansy-assed fuckers," Van Nyes murmured. "Their command-ers tell 'em to bend over, and they pull their ass cheeks apart for them."

Just a few more minutes, and he promised himself he'd make Van Nyes suffer.

"You have a job here or just passing through?" Jack asked, tired of the bullshit. "Because now, if you have a job here, we need to discuss a few things. If you're just passing through, then we'll just go."

That wasn't going to happen, but Jack had planned for the an-swer he got.

"Rumor of a job, maybe," Rollins answered, leaning forward in his chair, his gaze turning more serious now. "We heard something might be coming up and thought we'd stop in, since we were head-ing through this way anyway."

Bullshit.

He had a contact, Jack thought, wondering who the hell it could be.

"You have an offer then?" Jack laid both hands on the table.

This was his territory; he couldn't stop anyone from plying their trade, so to speak, but it was understood that compensation would be due.

"If it pans out." Rollins nodded. "Might even be a need for a bigger group. If so, we'll call you in."

Jack nodded as though in agreement. "What's your offer?"

Sanchez sat forward.

"The normal ten percent," Sanchez offered, his accent a little slurred.

Jack tamped down his satisfaction. The overly bright eyes, the slight slurring. Whatever the other man was smoking or snorting, it wasn't anything high-grade or too stimulating.

Jack sat back in his chair as though thinking about it.

"Fifteen percent," Van Nyes suddenly offered before licking his lips with anticipation. "And you let me have a few hours with that little redhead pussy. She looked sweet . . ."

The icy rage was instant. It shot through his senses, tore through his bloodstream, and filled every inch of his body with adrenaline spiked with bloodlust.

Jack moved.

In a flash he had Rollins's Ka-Bar and Sanchez's long knife in hand. A swipe across the Colombian's neck and he was toppling to the floor. Jack threw the same blade and buried it in Alberts's chest as confusion rooted the man to the floor across the short distance to the sink.

He slashed out at Rollins's neck before the mercenary could make sense of the fact that he was already dead, nearly severing his head with the depth and force behind the blade. Van Nyes didn't even get a chance to lift his weapon and fire, let alone get his finger on the trigger. Jack buried the Ka-Bar in his throat and listened to him gurgle as he went to his knees and began drowning in his own blood.

His gray eyes lifted to Jack as though pleading as his hands gripped the blade's hilt in a weak attempt to pull it free. But it was too late. Lungs filling with blood, his heart pumping dry, he was seconds from death.

"No man touches what's mine," Jack murmured as Van Nyes's eyes glazed over and he toppled to the floor.

Kicking the weapon away from him, Jack began a quick search of the men, starting with Rollins.

"Call in Hayes and Hank," he ordered the silent Lucas, briefly sparing a glance at the other man. "I want this place searched top to bottom for information. Rollins has a contact somewhere, and I want to know who it is."

He pulled a wad of rolled and banded hundred-dollar bills from the side pocket of Rollins's pants, plus a small clear bag of what appeared to be cocaine.

The band on the bills was still neat, the bills reasonably unstained. Someone had paid them to make their appearance here, but Jack doubted it was for the job Rollins believed. They were there to test Jack and his team. Or to assassinate them.

Or that was what he had assumed until he found a picture of Poppy sitting with her friends at the bar, a red circle drawn around her.

She was sitting with her fist propped beneath her chin, smiling with a whimsical little curl to her bow-shaped lips.

This wasn't good.

Rollins and his men were there for Poppy.

Why?

Checking the other men, he pocketed the cash he found on them as well, replaced the various drugs for law enforcement to find, then began searching the kitchen.

The latex covering he'd applied to his hands ensured no prints would be found, not that he expected a very thorough investigation once Ian worked his magic. But better safe than sorry.

He'd divide the cash with the other men once they returned to the house and let Ian know this matter had been taken care of.

"Boss, what happened to the plan?" Hayes sounded outraged as he and Hank burst into the farmhouse. "Goddamn, you don't play fair. Thought you were sharing this kill."

Bloodthirsty little prick, Jack thought.

"The big boy there nixed the plan." Lucas flicked his fingers toward Van Nyes where he'd fallen to the floor, staring vacantly into death. As Jack turned away, Lucas turned to the other men and made a waving motion at his neck with his hand. "We don't talk about the redhead again. Do not . . ." he hissed.

Jack caught the movement, heard the words, but let it pass as he moved to Alberts's body. Best they be warned where Poppy was concerned.

"Check the rest of the house. You have three minutes, or I keep your share of the cash I've pulled from these bastards. And they were paid well. Probably half up front, half when they completed whatever job they were here to do. And that job involved Poppy. Move it."

They moved.

The three men rushed to the other rooms, the sounds of drawers falling to the floor and a general search filling the house for the required three minutes.

Before Jack was finished checking the bodies, the others were back. No information had been found, but to judge by the weapons dangling from their shoulders and shoved into the pockets and waistbands of their pants, they'd found plenty of weapons. Hank carried a pillowcase of what appeared to be boxes of ammo, the material bulging with the amount it held.

"There's still more up there." Lucas lifted the four automatic weapons he carried by the shoulder slings attached to them. "Thought we'd leave a few just for appearance's sake."

In other words, there were too many to carry them all down. Lucas was a weapon-hoarding motherfucker. He didn't leave any behind unless he just couldn't drag them to his ride.

"If they have a contact, he kept the information in his head." Lucas kicked at Rollins's body as he paused next to it. "No phones, no laptop. Just packing enough arms and ammo to start a war."

No phones, laptop, electric, or gas. No generator, just the two vehicles and weapons.

"They were looking to be supplied while here or didn't expect to be long in the area," Jack stated. "I'm going to say they were looking to be supplied. I found this on Rollins's body."

He showed the other men the picture of Poppy.

"This was taken a couple days before anyone knew I was in the area; I remember the outfit. They didn't just arrive—they've been here over a week, getting the lay of things and waiting for the job."

"They were here to snatch her," Lucas said, his gaze calculating now. "That's why Van Nyes came up on her in the grocery parking lot."

"They wouldn't have kept her here." Jack looked around the farmhouse. "At least not for long. Too much risk."

"Insurance?" Hayes questioned. "You two have history. Whoever hired them knew that, and knew taking her would affect you."

But insurance for what?

"Contact wouldn't wait long to bring what Rollins needed, yet they've been hanging out here with no electric? Don't sound like Rollins to me. He likes to be comfortable," Hank stated from the door.

"Let's clear out," Jack ordered, heading for the door. "We don't want to be caught here."

Not that the group's employers would have any doubt about

who had left the bodies lying here. But they didn't need anyone that could definitively ID them.

Packing the weapons beneath the seats with their own and the extras in the heavy metal utility box in the bed of the truck, they were headed out of the area within minutes.

The weapons and ammunition Jack would add to the safe room in the basement, the money would be divided between the four of them. There was no sense in leaving either with the dead bodies, not when they could put it to much better use.

The next order of business was to figure out why they were after Poppy.

"Hey, boss, can you slide me some of that cash and let me out at my bike?" Hank questioned as they were pulling back out onto the interstate. "I figure you're probably going to the party for Ms. Porter's friend Lilith after you clean all the blood and gore off you. I thought I'd stop and get her a card or something. Just to be polite, ya know?"

Silence filled the truck, and from his periphery Jack caught Lucas's confused look as the same disbelief worked through his own mind.

Jack's gaze shot to the rearview mirror, where he stared at the other man's expressionless face and hard eyes. Hank Brady was not a buy-her-a-card-type man. He wasn't a birthday-type man. He damned sure didn't care about being friendly.

What the fuck was he up to?

"You got a fever, man?" Hayes muttered. "Seriously?"

"Fuck you," Hank drawled, the tone borderline dangerous. "And yes, I'm dead damned serious. Rest of you better not show up empty-handed either. Man don't show up at a lady's party without a gift. Don't you know that, moron?"

As Jack's gaze moved back to the road, the words hit him.

Jack felt his jaw tighten.

Poppy was going to that damned bar again and hadn't even invited him?

They were definitely having a talk later. Likely a long one. One that included showing her exactly why it wouldn't happen again.

Friends and family were gathered around the tables sectioned off for the party at the bar. One table held a multitude of gaily printed bags and unwrapped presents, while another held a half-eaten two-tier birthday cake.

Laughter and general cheer filled the more than two dozen friends and family who had gathered for Lilith's birthday. Though it was mostly friends. A few cousins and two brothers were the only family who cared to show up.

Still, Lilith was laughing and having fun. Dressed in a short, snug, black lace skirt, vest, black netted print stockings, four-inch heels, and a wide belt at her hips, Lilith looked like the wild spirit she was.

Poppy laughed as one of their male friends tried to get her friend onto the dance floor and once again Lilith turned him down. She never danced with anyone. If she danced, she went out on the floor with Poppy, Sasha, Erika, or Saige, never alone and never with a man.

She knew them all far too well, Lilith would laugh when asked why she refused to dance with a man. And when she danced with a man, she wanted to at least entertain the idea of being sexually attracted to him.

Sitting at a table with Sasha, Erika, Lilith, and Lilith's brothers Sam and Bannon, Poppy sipped at the beer she'd ordered and discreetly checked the time on her phone.

She had to leave before it was too late. She had rolls to bake, a chicken stuffing casserole and lasagna to slip into the oven for dinner the next day at her parents', and a variety of other things to complete.

She still had no clue if Jack was actually going to join her the next day. A part of her was hesitant about it. Jack hadn't had family growing up; he might not understand a lot of the interaction and friendly fussing at one another.

Finishing the beer, she'd just sat the empty bottle on the table when a sudden silence descended over the tables around her. Glancing up, she turned in the direction everyone was staring, and just barely kept her mouth from falling open in shock.

Four men—in snug blue jeans, leather biker's chaps, snug T-shirts, and boots—entered the bar and headed for them, with a scowling Jack in the lead.

And they carried birthday bags. Gaily printed, pastel-tissue-paper-peeking-out birthday bags.

From her periphery, she watched Lilith slowly sit down in her chair as the four men moved toward her.

"Happy birthday." Jack shoved a bag at Lilith, then moved to Poppy, his gaze stormy.

The other three men were a little more graceful about it, but Hank, the last one, paused a minute.

He cleared his throat and handed Lilith his bag.

"I have a baby sister," he said quietly. "She said you never crash a girl's party without gifts. Happy birthday."

He sat the bag at her feet, then moved for the bar with the other two men.

Jack slid a chair over from another table and positioned it behind Poppy and a bit to the side before sitting in it. Propping his elbows on his knees, he shot her a glare.

"You didn't tell me about the party." It was a smoothly delivered accusation.

"You didn't leave me your cell number or bother to text me so I could get hold of you," she pointed out.

"Hmm," he murmured, though whether it was in agreement or protest she had no idea.

Damn, he looked hard and dangerous, she thought, trying to focus her gaze on Lilith, who, in her bemusement, was pushing the tissue paper aside to peek inside the bag Hank had given her.

"He doesn't seem like the birthday-present-buying type," she reflected as Lilith's expression softened as she pulled away the tissue paper, then tucked the bag under her chair.

"What did he get her?" Poppy turned to Jack, curious now.

"Fuck if I know," he growled. "I think Hayes got some kind of wind chime, though. Lucas started into a lingerie store, but Hank jerked him back and sent him into a candle store. It would have been laughable under any other circumstances."

"And what did you get?" she asked.

Suddenly Lilith laughed, with one of the most melodic sounds Poppy believed she'd ever heard, and Poppy turned in her direction.

She held up a slate plaque with the words "MY WINGS ARE OUT FOR REPAIR SO I'M RIDING MY FRIEND'S BROOM . . ." Beneath it dangled a shapely witch flying on a broom.

Poppy smiled and felt something melt in her heart at the fun-filled grin on her friend's face as she tucked the plaque back in its foam-lined box and replaced it in the bag.

"She used to have white-blond hair and the palest gray eyes I've ever seen on a person," Jack murmured. "I busted a few faces when y'all were kids, for laughing at her. They always made her cry."

Yes, they did, Poppy recalled.

"From which store did Hank buy her present?" she asked, curious, as Lilith seemed to be protecting the bag beneath her chair.

"Erotic toy store." There was a heavy sigh in his voice. "She needs to be careful of him. Hank isn't a forever kind of guy. He'll break her tender heart."

"That's what everyone keeps telling me about you," she said softly.

He was quiet as she turned back to him, watching him, seeing the cool, expressionless mask he wore and the way the gray and blue darkened in his eyes and seemed to rage.

"I will," he finally agreed, his hand lifting, his fingers brushing over her cheek. "I'll hate it. I'll hate myself for it. But that, baby girl, is inevitable."

CHAPTER FOURTEEN

She was beautiful.

The blouse she wore was soft and dark green. Its short sleeves covered the marks he knew still marred her shoulders, not to mention the tops of her breasts, which the blouse concealed while daringly conforming to them. Green enamel buttons held the blouse closed, then ended at the band of the skirt, with a flirty little hint of bare skin showing at the bottom where it slanted away from the last button.

The skirt was making him crazy. Ending halfway to her knees, it looked like it was put together with unevenly cut and hemmed panels of materials that layered over each other and threatened to play peekaboo with her flesh.

The subtle piecing of the material ensured it showed nothing it shouldn't, but watching her walk, seeing the shift of the material, the illusion of the panels sliding over each other, almost had him sweating.

Dark green, creamy white, with hints of pale blue, the material whispered over her pertly rounded ass and drew male gazes, much to Jack's dismay.

Two-inch, dark green heels covered her delicate feet and gave her a sexy-as-hell feminine strut that he loved to watch himself, but almost growled seeing that others were watching as well.

She was charming and playful with her friends, posing for selfies with them, making silly faces, laughing at their antics. And though she'd moved away from him to help her friends celebrate, her gaze touched him often, as did her smile.

She hadn't said anything at his promise to break her heart; she'd simply given a small, short nod as she lowered her head, watching as she smoothed a finger over a nail.

She was preparing herself to accept the pain, he thought with an edge of regret.

What the fuck did a man do about a woman like that? One willing to step into those flames to have him while she could?

It made no sense.

Her self-preservation instincts should have been better than that.

Standing at the bar with his men, he watched her have her fun while he kept an eye on the men who came around her. And he waited.

He ignored Lucas and Hayes as they poked at Hank over what he could have bought Poppy's friend, not that Hank was saying. He'd just give them that flat, hard stare that could mean nothing or be a warning of violence.

As he sipped on a beer, Jack was aware of River Dawson moving toward the bar. He stopped here and there to talk with friends for a minute, but there was no doubt he was heading Jack's way.

"Lucas, you and the others give us some space if he makes it over here," Jack murmured.

River was going to make it there. Jack could see the determination in the set of his jaw, the way his gaze kept track of Jack as though to ensure he was still there.

As River came closer, Jack was aware of Lucas and the others moving down the bar and talking to several of the women from the party who were ordering drinks. One of whom was the birthday girl. And Hank made a beeline for her.

What the fuck was up with that?

Dawson eased up and caught the bartender's attention. "Hey, Mike, bourbon," he ordered, then glanced at Jack's nearly empty beer. "Let me buy you a drink, Bridger," he offered. "Bourbon, right?"

Jack didn't betray his surprise. "Does a man ever stop drinking it?" he drawled, as though certain they didn't.

"Not the smart ones." Dawson sighed. "Two bourbons, Mike," he ordered.

The trouble with small towns was the fact that some people just knew too damned much about you.

"You lookin' for work yet?" Dawson asked as the bartender served the drinks.

"According to the job." Jack lifted his shoulder negligently.

"Living the dream, are you?" Dawson grunted.

"And what dream would that be?" Jack asked.

"That teenage fantasy of bikes, booze, women, and brawls." River shot him a mocking look. "Seems to be working for you."

"Seems to be," Jack agreed.

Dawson seemed pissed over something.

Shifting his gaze to where Poppy and Sasha Crossfield stood laughing, Jack leaned his elbow on the bar and slid a look at Dawson. Oh, he was keeping up with his woman, same as Jack was. The difference was, he wasn't publicly claiming her as he obviously wanted to.

"You know, a lot of people are going to be pissed if you break her heart," Dawson pointed out. "And Poppy might seem accepting of your lifestyle at the present, but she's going to expect you to get a job soon, to be an adult."

Jack scratched at his jaw and gave Dawson his full attention.

"You know, River, when I hit you, I'll break your face," he said conversationally.

River's dark green eyes narrowed as arrogance settled over his face like a shroud.

"Maybe, maybe not. Doesn't change the truth. Seems to me like a mature man would take things a little more seriously," Dawson warned him, his voice tightening as though offended.

"We'll see," Jack promised him, then turned back to find Poppy. "For now, I think I'll take my immature ass over and claim my woman. Maybe you should do the same."

Walking away from the bar, Jack headed for Poppy as he caught her gaze.

Those green eyes of hers heated as she smiled at him, a dimple flashing in her cheek.

"Time to go, sugar girl," he told her as he stopped next to her and lowered his head to nuzzle her ear. "You wanna ride with me? One of my men can drive your SUV."

He watched her face flush, but it was pleasure, not embarrassment, that curled at her lips.

"Not if you rode in on your bike," she murmured. "This skirt would become indecent fast."

He grunted at that. "Baby, I hate to tell you, that skirt is already indecent." He slid one hand over her thigh and found feminine flesh that grew heated awfully quickly.

"It's perfectly decent unless that hand of yours decides to get unruly." She tilted her head, smiling up at him teasingly.

"Well, now, that's always possible." He played with the jagged hem, making certain his fingers stroked the flesh just under it.

She caught his wrist, curling it around herself as she leaned back against his chest.

"Not here, it isn't," she told him firmly, though there was

amused pleasure in her voice. "But I do need to be going soon. I still have lasagna, my chicken stuffing casserole, and rolls to bake tonight for dinner tomorrow."

Chicken casserole? Lasagna and rolls? Real ones? The kind made at home?

Hell. He didn't think he'd ever eaten the real stuff.

"Say your goodbyes then," he told her. "I'll be at the car when you're ready."

She moved away but glanced back at him, another of those soft little smiles tugging at that dimple in her cheek as she moved to her group of friends.

Turning to the bar, Jack motioned Lucas over.

"We movin'?" Lucas asked.

"Follow me and Poppy out to the parking lot and take her keys. You can take her ride back to the house to pick up your bike," Jack told him.

They'd dropped Hayes and Hank off at their bikes earlier. The other two men had followed behind Lucas and Jack to the bar.

Lucas went on out while Jack waited by the exit, leaning casually against the wall and watching as the crowd enjoyed their Saturday night. He saw familiar faces, but they belonged. There were a lot of people he didn't know, but no one who stood out. No mercenaries or threats.

Ian would have LEOs notified sometime after daylight tomorrow of the bodies at the farmhouse. It would take another hour or two for the news and local gossips to start spreading the word. By noon, if they weren't already aware of it, both Crossfield and Dawson would hear about it.

"I'm ready," Poppy told him as she neared, strolling in that lazy way she had of walking.

All he could think about was fucking her when he watched her walk. His cock, unruly bastard, was fully erect, his balls tight with the hunger he couldn't seem to sate. He felt like a man who hadn't fucked in years and was dying to slam his cock into a sweet pussy.

Straightening from the wall, he pushed the door open ahead of her and stepped out first.

There was Lucas standing between her SUV and Jack's pickup, looking like the dangerous shadow he could become.

"You ridin' with me or not?" he asked Poppy as they neared the vehicles.

She handed him the key fob with the air of a woman choosing her battle.

Not that he knew why, but he had the key and that was all that mattered.

Tossing it to Lucas, Jack hit the electronic lock on his pickup and escorted Poppy to the passenger side as Lucas strode quickly back to the bar.

Opening the door, he gripped her waist and lifted her to the seat, and when she would have turned and drawn her legs into the vehicle, he stopped her.

They were at the edge of the parking lot, with her vehicle shielding them from the side, ensuring a measure of privacy.

"What?" She stared up at him in the dim light, the interior of the truck dark, the inner light disconnected.

He reached behind her and flipped the center console up, then gripped her head and pulled it back for a kiss.

He meant to be gentle; he was certain he knew how. She wasn't his first woman, or the first decent woman he'd fucked. But the second his lips touched hers, he was devouring her kiss like a fucking animal.

His tongue thrust past her lips, then pulled back, his head angling to part her lips for the deeper, savage lust that burned through his senses.

"Jack," she whispered as he pulled back, his hands pushing her skirt up her thighs, desperate to get to the sweet flesh beneath.

He remembered the taste of her, the sweetest summer taste, like heated ambrosia, potent enough to make a man drunk on her.

"I'm going to fuck you right here, Poppy," he growled. "I'm going to suck those pretty nipples, push you back in that seat, and spread your thighs. Then I'm going to watch that pretty pussy take every goddamned inch of my cock."

He watched her eyes widen, her breathing hitch, and hard, tight little nipples press beneath the thin material of her blouse.

"Now, are you going to unbutton that shirt and push your bra out of the way? Or do I just rip them off you." And he was fine ripping them off.

"It's not far to the house . . ." she began, but he heard the heat in her breathy little voice.

"Unbutton the blouse, and make it quick," he demanded. "My patience is thinner than that material, and my control even more so."

Graceful fingers moved quickly to her blouse, fumbling as she slid it free, but within seconds she was unclipping the front of her bra.

"Show me your tits, baby. Let me taste those sweet little nipples," he demanded.

She spread the material slowly, revealing the smooth, swollen perfection of her breasts.

Jack worked his belt loose, his cock straining beneath his pants.

"Come to the edge of the seat," he growled, his voice so rough it surprised him.

She scooted to the edge of the seat, her legs bracketing his thighs as he drew the hard length of his erection free of his jeans.

"Lean back on your hands." He could barely speak for the need to suck one of those pretty nipples.

She leaned back, and Jack leaned forward.

Cupping a breast with one hand, he lowered his lips and covered the hard little peak, sucking it into his mouth.

Poppy jerked, moaned, one hand coming up to grip the back of his head, her fingers threading through his hair.

Oh, she loved that, he thought, but so did he. Stroking the tight peak with his tongue, feeling her shudder when he raked it with his teeth and moan when he sucked her firmly. She arched against him when he moved to her other breast, cupped it, and loved it. And God, how he loved her responsive little nipples.

Almost as much as he loved her even more responsive little pussy.

So wet, fist-tight, and eager for his cock. She loved how he stretched her open, made her sweet pussy burn with the width of his dick.

And he loved it. She took everything he wanted to give her, blushing like the sweet innocent she was, and giving him every part of herself. Just as he'd known she would.

Just as he'd ensured she would.

Drawing back, he surveyed the moist points of her breasts, the little marks he'd left at the side of the swollen curves, and felt satisfaction raging through him.

She was his. And before he was finished, she might hate him forever, but she'd never be able to let another man fuck her without thinking of him.

He was making certain of it.

"Lay back." He was on the verge of panting. "All the way back."

He heard the little whimper that parted her lips, but she lay back, her blouse and the cups of her bra framing her breasts as the moonlight seemed to spear into the truck to shine over them.

His gaze went from those hard-tipped mounds down to the

minuscule material of her panties. Those, he ripped from her, the fragile elastic giving way easily to his strength.

Her hips jerked at the action, arching to him as arms stretched over her head, fingers curling against the leather seat. Stretched out for him like a sensual little feast.

Lifting her knees, he arched her hips, angling them as he pushed one knee back toward the dash, opening her fully for him. And just as he'd threatened, he watched as he guided the head of his cock to press between the glistening folds of flesh, where he immediately began to work inside her.

He was bare. Fuck. He'd forgotten to cover the stiffened flesh, and now he didn't know if he had the strength.

Her pussy was slick, heated. He felt her moisture washing over the sensitive crest, making her slicker, hotter. He didn't feel her like this with a condom. The way her inner flesh clenched and the subtle ripples caressed the head, then the shaft as he worked his cock back and forth, forcing it inside the fist-tight grip.

As he retreated, he watched as the heavy juices clung to his flesh, glistening in the moonlight, the way her clit now stood at attention, flushed a ruby red, aching and needing.

He thrust inside her, harder, deeper, giving her that lash of pleasure-pain that he knew she loved so much.

He was rewarded with a smothered cry as her head twisted against the seat, the lush waves of red hair framing her face like flames.

"Poppy . . ." he groaned, pulling back again, thrusting deeper, harder. "Baby. No condoms . . . in the truck . . ."

His nuts jerked at the thought of pulling out of her, of giving up the heated grip she had on his cock before he'd filled her with the hard ejaculation of his release.

"I'm protected," she moaned, stretching into the next, full thrust with a low, sensual groan that nearly had him spilling himself inside her then and there.

A warning pulse shot from the head of his dick, causing him to arch his back, which only drove him deeper. Buried to the hilt, he ground against her, his gaze caught by her swollen clit again.

Desperate for release now, he grabbed her arm, pulling it from over her head, and then, taking her hand, he drew her fingers to her clit as she stared up at him in surprise.

"Stroke yourself," he snarled. "Make that little clit explode, baby, and I'll make this sweet pussy come around my dick. Come on . . ." he ordered as she hesitated. "Fuck. I'll go crazy when I come."

Her fingers moved, stroking around her clit as he watched, felt the sweat trickle down his neck, and knew he was losing control.

Holding her thighs, fighting to keep his fingers from bruising her, he gave in to the need to drive inside her, to fuck her like the man possessed that he was becoming.

He groaned, feeling her pussy rippling around him, clenching as he retreated as though to hold him inside her. Her smothered moans only made him hotter, impossibly harder.

And when he felt her arch, her entire body tightening, her pussy spasming around his dick, he lost it. He slammed inside her, the need for release ripping past his control, and filled her body with each hard, furious ejaculation of his seed. Feeling her orgasm, the way it locked her inner muscles tight around him and sucked at him with eager ripples, was like nothing he could have imagined.

He'd never taken a woman bare, never thought to.

Until Poppy.

And now, he'd never be able to take her any other way.

Lying over her, he let his lips wander over hers, gently now. He pushed her damp hair back from her face, eased her as ripples of aftershock caused her to tremble beneath him.

Goddamn, she burned him alive, made him crazy for her, made him resent every fucking second that he had to spend away from her.

He wasn't going to have enough time with her. Not enough to sate himself, to walk away from her and not be tormented by the hunger for her.

He'd told her that he knew he'd break her heart when he left Barboursville. What he didn't tell her was that he knew she'd break that part of him that he hadn't even known he still possessed. She'd break his soul.

He'd never be the same after Poppy looked at him with hate in her eyes, and he knew it.

CHAPTER FIFTEEN

The Porter house was just as he remembered it, Jack thought the next morning after he parked in the back lot and grabbed the large box of food Poppy had packed that morning.

Opening the wide gate into a yard protected by a privacy fence, Poppy stood back and held the gate open for him to step through. The box wasn't that heavy, but he'd seen her try to lift it and had immediately taken it from her.

Lasagna, a couple of dozen yeast rolls, and a chicken stuffing casserole that had a good portion missing. Come to think of it, so did the lasagna. There were several rolls missing, too.

She'd been outraged before they left the house to learn he'd dug into the food after they'd gone to bed the night before. And she'd blushed so prettily when he told her it took food to fuel the energy needed to keep her orgasms coming through the night.

Which was exactly what he'd done. And still, he wanted her.

There had to be a point where a man sated his lust for a particular woman and finally had her out of his system, he'd told himself. But even as that thought had whispered through his mind, he'd known better. He'd wanted her when she was seventeen, and that need had only grown stronger over the years.

Even before Ian and Kira had come to him with this op, he'd known he'd be returning for her as soon as possible and that he was going to claim her. He hadn't thought past getting into her bed, multiple times, so he hadn't once thought about walking away from her.

"Mac, John David, and Evan are not going to be happy that you ate so much of the lasagna and casserole," she warned him, breaking into his thoughts as they approached the porch. "That and Momma's chicken and dumplings and fried chicken are their favorites."

"Sucks to be them," he grunted, not really caring how they reacted.

Was it possible to have a food orgasm? Jack wondered a little too seriously. He'd never tasted Mrs. Porter's chicken and dumplings or fried chicken, but he'd sure as hell heard about them from the brothers' friends—who were invited to the Porter house often for dinner.

He'd never been invited. The one time Poppy had forced him inside, it had been hot vegetable soup and homemade bread, but even that had been more of a meal than he usually had. School lunches were usually the best he could hope for during those years.

He followed her up the back porch, the food in the box almost forgotten at the thought of the delicacies that awaited him inside that house.

As they stepped into the large kitchen, chaos greeted them, but Poppy didn't seem to mind it.

"Aunt Poppy!" a child's voice cried out. "Aunt Poppy's here and there's a giant with her. A big giant."

Two pint-sized little boys tore from another room and raced into Poppy's arms as she bent down and wrapped her arms around both of them. On their heels, a little girl no more than two toddled behind them.

The little girl, her red curls surrounding her face, bright green eyes filled with excitement, sidestepped Poppy and made a beeline behind her to Jack.

Jack stared down at her as she raised her arms up to him, her chubby cheeks stretched wide in a grin.

He knew what she wanted, but damn, memories of the one and only time he'd been in this kitchen were like a splinter digging into him. He hadn't been welcome here then, he thought. What would make him think he would be welcome now.

"Best pick her up, Jack," Cole Porter advised him from the doorway. "If she starts her caterwauling, we're gonna blame you."

Jack looked back down at the little girl, whose smile had begun easing from her face.

Bending, he placed his hands under her arms and lifted her gingerly from the floor. She was light as a feather and so damned fragile he was almost terrified of breaking her.

Easing her to his chest, he was shocked when she wrapped her arms around his neck and laid her head on his shoulder.

"Wow! She doesn't like anyone but Aunt Poppy," one of the boys breathed. "Uncle John and Evan can't even hardly hold her."

The little girl seemed perfectly comfortable with her head on his shoulder and jabbering at him below his ear.

He looked at Poppy helplessly as she rose to her feet, obviously silently laughing at him.

"She's a very picky little girl," she agreed with the boy standing in front of her. "But Jack's very nice."

"Jack's very big," the boy breathed out. "Like a mountain or something."

She did laugh at that. "Jack, these two little heathens are Benton and Kenneth Myers, my sister Jackie and her husband Ted's boys. There's two more hiding around here somewhere. Alice and her husband Blake Thomas's sons, John and Mason. And that little sprite is Eliza Poppy Porter."

"And she's mine." Mac-Cole stepped into the room, shaking his head at the little girl lying so comfortably against Jack's shoulder.

He hadn't heard Mac had married, or that he had a daughter.

"Da . . ." the little girl jabbered happily as her head lifted and she stared back at her father with one of those bright smiles.

Thankfully, she held her arms out for him.

"Come on, squirt." He took the child from Jack's hold and cuddled her against his shoulder. "Nap time for you." To the others he explained, "When she starts wanting to be held, we know what time it is around here."

"It's the only time she stops moving." Poppy laughed, unpacking the box Jack had placed on the counter as he came in.

"Hello, Jack." Melissa Ann stepped into the room, her smile welcoming. "It's so nice to see you here today."

Poppy resembled her mother. Melissa Ann Porter's hair was more gray than red now, and her face was older, but there was no doubt the two were mother and daughter.

"Ma'am." He nodded his head, then grudgingly turned to Poppy's father. "Mr. Porter," he greeted.

"My name's Cole," her father informed him firmly. "I told you that more than once, Jack." He turned to Poppy. "Give us a hug, sweetie." He opened his arms to his daughter, hugging her tight before releasing her. "Your sisters are currently fussing at their husbands in the family room for forgetting the beer. You'd think boys their age would remember."

"There's beer in the ice chest in the truck, Dad," she told him. "Jack picked it up yesterday to bring, but he had his hands full of food coming in."

Jack didn't observe a lot of social rules, but the "bring beer where men and meals are concerned," his teammates' wives had taught him early on.

"I'll get it now." Jack turned for the door.

"Just bring it out front, Jack. We have a lack of giggling and girlish confidences out there. In other words, peace," Cole said.

Poppy's mother laughed at him. Cole Porter kissed his wife on the cheek, then looked back at Jack expectantly.

Jack glanced at Poppy to make sure she didn't need anything else from the truck.

"Go on," she told him, unwrapping the food she brought. "Jackie, Alice, and I will help Mom with the meal. It will be a while before everything's ready."

He felt as though she were sending him to his execution. What did he know about dealing with a woman's family?

He returned to the truck, hefted the filled ice chest from the back, and at the last minute grabbed the extra case from the back floorboard. Locking the truck, he carried everything around the house to the front porch, where Poppy's brothers, minus Mac, and her father sat waiting.

He knew them, though only superficially. He'd made a point when he came in over the years to be in position to "run into" members of her family, say hello, and ask about Poppy. A part of him had known he'd return for her one day, and he'd wanted her family to at least be familiar with him. A man didn't just form a relationship with his woman, but with her family as well. Her happiness was dependent on more than just his presence, and a smart man knew that.

A smart man also knew not to lie, even by omission, to that woman, he reminded himself. Something he was doing every day he was in her life. He was just praying that when the time came, she'd forgive him.

The backyard fight was filled with screams, tumbling bodies, and no small amount of childish giggles as four preteen boys wrestled with Jack, struggling to use their combined strength to take him down, as they'd informed him earlier that they were fully capable of doing.

Poppy stood in the kitchen window watching, aware of her sisters behind her, watching as well.

She paid attention to how Jack handled the boys, and had no doubt there wouldn't be a single scratch or scrape when he finished with them. He let them use their boyish strength and gave them just enough of his strength to make it hard for them without risking hurting them.

Dinner had come and gone, the kitchen and dining room had been put back to rights, and the rest of her male family had gone to the family room to watch a baseball game on TV when the boys had challenged Jack to a "fair fight" as he'd followed behind the others.

She grinned at the memory of it. Jack had stared down at their confident little faces, tilted his head, and watched them for a moment before asking them if they understood that he was trained to face short combatants and asking if they had their parents' permission to do battle.

"He's grown up," her mother said from behind her, her reflection joining Poppy's in the window. "When I first saw him all those years ago, I doubted he'd live out the winter. Seeing the change in him over the years has been good."

Poppy nodded at that. "He almost didn't."

To survive, he'd been forced to kill his father, then sent away to foster care. She wondered if anyone besides her had ever loved Jack.

"Do you know what you're doing, Poppy?" her mother asked, her voice compassionate, and concerned.

"No, not really," Poppy admitted with a small smile. "But I've decided I don't want to keep wondering what could have been, either. I don't want to keep waiting for him, watching for him. I've been doing that for too long."

She watched as Jack finally let the boys pin him for the required three seconds. That hard, muscular body was laid out flat on the grass, a grimace of defeat on his face that was clearly feigned.

The boys jumped to their feet, whooping in triumph, then all four of them reached out a hand to help him up.

Not that he availed himself of their assistance. With a surge of power, he vaulted to his feet, causing wide eyes and pure admiration in her nephews. Not to mention in Poppy.

She couldn't imagine the strength and training it must have taken to be able to move like that.

"I like him," her mother decided. "It takes a good man to be that patient for that long with four energetic boys when he was clearly interested in watching the Sunday game with the other men."

"He's damaged," her sister Alice murmured. "It won't be easy loving him, Poppy."

Poppy watched as he shook hands with the boys and congratulated them on a fair fight.

"Loving him is actually very easy," she said. "That, or I've just loved him for so long that it seems effortless."

Turning away from the window, she went back to stacking the bowls of leftovers she'd put aside in a box.

When her mother had learned Jack's friends were waiting at his house, she'd insisted on making extra food to send back to them. Especially after Evan had laughingly mentioned the amount of pizzas being delivered to Jack's front door.

Poppy's mother hadn't just prepared an extra skillet of the fried chicken for Jack's friends, but she'd put aside half of a chocolate fudge cake and a whole apple pie as well.

When Jack stepped back into the house, he eyed the box of food Poppy was just finishing packing and looked at her.

Poppy just smiled, went to the family room, and told everyone goodbye. She kissed her parents and hugged them back, then turned to Jack.

"Ready? Or do you need another bout with the boys?" She grinned. "I think they're pretty tired, though."

He grunted at the question.

Moving for the door, she looked up at him in confusion when she saw his empty hands.

"That's my box on the counter." She pointed to the box topped with the sealed plastic bowls and foil-wrapped items. "Could you get it for me?"

Carrying the box, he led the way to the gate, letting her open it and step back into the yard while he went out first. He hit the electronic door lock, put the food in the back, then helped her into the truck.

It wasn't quite dark when they pulled into the driveway, but the three men Jack seemed to be spending a lot of time with were waiting for him, propped on their bikes and watching as Jack parked.

As they got out of the truck and Jack went to lift the box of food from the truck, Poppy laid her hand on his arm.

"Mom sent that for you and your friends," she said softly. "Evan told Mom he'd heard about all the pizzas being delivered. She fried two extra chickens and everything. So, you can't refuse."

Jack stared at the food. He'd watched every serving he'd put on his plate to ensure he didn't seem as hungry as he was for the real, home-cooked food that had weighed down the table at the Porter home. There was more food here than her three brothers had eaten the whole day.

"There's half that double fudge cake and an apple pie as well," she whispered, looking up at him teasingly. "I saw those hungry eyes of yours trying to decide which dessert to have after dinner. So, make sure you get yours first."

A whole apple pie?

Those pies weren't normal-sized, either. They'd been about twice the size of a normal pie. And the cake had been a double sheet, according to her father.

"Come over whenever they leave," she told him, straightening and bracing herself on the truck, lifting to her tiptoes to kiss his cheek. "I'm going in. I have some paperwork for an early meeting to finish before I go to bed."

Stunned by the Porters' generosity, he watched her walk away, that cute little ass of hers making him consider if he wanted more food and dessert, or Poppy. Hell, he wanted both. The knowledge that he could have both was almost more than he could take in.

Hurrying after her, he saw her into the house, checked each room, and stole himself one of those hot little kisses at the door before returning to the truck.

He was aware of the men waiting expectantly. The fact that they were waiting for him rather than waiting for him to call meant they had information they considered important.

He lifted the box from the truck, closed the door with a bump of his hip, and strode across the alley.

"Hey, boss." Lucas uncoiled from the bike as the others followed suit.

No one paid much attention to the box in his arms, as Hayes moved ahead of him to open the back door and check the interior before giving the all clear.

Jack walked to the kitchen, and it wasn't until he began unpacking the dishes that three hardened, disillusioned, dishonored SEALs became excited, hungry little boys.

Hell, he hoped he hadn't acted like that at Poppy's parents' house.

"Oh my God." Hayes sounded delirious. "Is that fried chicken, boss? Real home-fried chicken?"

"Oh hell, stuffing casserole . . ." Lucas all but whispered.

"Come on, boss, just let us have a taste." Hank sounded like a man begging for one last breath before taking a fatal bullet.

"Get the plates," he told them. "Poppy's mother felt sorry for your scruffy asses . . ." He shook his head.

No one was listening after that, and three SEALs trained to move quietly sounded like a herd of buffaloes in his kitchen as they got plates and silverware and rushed to be first in line.

Thankfully, Lucas thought to get Jack a plate as well.

"Are you men or dogs?" Jack growled, more amused than he wanted to admit to.

"Starving junkyard dogs," Hayes hurried to assured him. "Now get yours and get out of the way . . . please," he tacked on as an afterthought.

Jack set the desserts aside without revealing what they were, filled his plate, and moved to the table. Within minutes the other three were there, and other than delirious moans of carnivorous ecstasy, nothing was said.

What, Jack wondered, was it about good food and a good woman that turned hardened killers into little boys? He'd seen it happen more than once, but he'd never seen it as clearly as he did with the men who made up his team.

There was enough food that each of them made it back for healthy seconds and cleaned their plates before sitting back replete, their expressions no longer those of disillusioned killers, but of men well satisfied with the world for a moment.

"So why were you waiting on me?" Jack questioned them, giving the food time to settle before revealing the dessert.

"Oh yeah." Lucas shook his head as though shocked he'd forgotten. "The local LEOs were tipped off about the bodies, but not by Ian. Anonymous tip came in early this morning. Ian contacted me, assured me he hadn't had time to get anyone on it. He was scrambling to make sure he had his guy on the investigation, though. We should be in the clear, but it's probably already hit the news. Ian's people have managed to cover the plane wreckage so far. Bodies are being prepped for burial, or whatever Mick decides to do—they figure he should be conscious in a day or two."

"We planned for Rollins to be found early," Jack reminded him. "They had a contact in the area for sure, supplying them information." Secrecy was more important than leaving someone to wait around and watch for the contact and risk being identified himself.

"Other than that, there's no new intel," Lucas assured him. "Ian says stay on course and he'll be in touch if anything changes."

"Poppy's friends, other than Ms. Crossfield, seemed to take to us while we were there. I hadn't expected that," Hank pointed out.

Yeah, Jack had seen Lilith Preston sneaking little looks at Hank several times. Whatever had been in that bag, the present must have impressed her. And he had a feeling it wasn't an erotic toy.

"Saige Dawson's an interesting little thing," Hayes stated. "Smart, wary."

"They all are," Hank murmured. "A little too wary for what's natural."

"Same with Erika Boone." Lucas nodded in agreement.

"Crossfield's sister wasn't interested at all," Hayes stated.

"She's too busy keeping River Dawson from claiming her," Jack pointed out. "I get the feeling he's straining at the bit where revealing that relationship is involved. And he's not too happy with the lingering secrecy."

"Yeah, that would suck." Lucas nodded seriously. "Lot of tangled webs here, boss. And they're all connected to Crossfield-Dawson. We"—he nodded toward the other two men—"learned last night that even Erika Boone and Lilith Preston work in some capacity for the company, mostly in a cleaning service capacity. Both of them work several hours on the weekends cleaning the offices. They've also been called in to clean residences or commercial suites before a showing."

That hadn't been in Ian's report.

"It's not unheard of." Jack rubbed at the back of his neck and stood. "I expected it."

Jack laid out four large paper plates for the desserts. As he unwrapped them, each man rose and approached him cautiously.

Jack cut a large square of cake and pie, placed each on a plate, and wrapped them and set them aside. Then he sliced another large piece of each to eat.

"Make yourselves at home." There was more than enough.

The little boys made another appearance as they dug into the decadent chocolate first, then the apple-and-cinnamon perfection.

Jack almost grinned at the delight in the faces of men whom the military had deemed to have antisocial personality disorder and to be borderline sociopaths.

They were just men, he thought. Too hardened and scarred, too distrusting and uncertain where anything good was concerned. Too certain they didn't want to risk losing anything that could become important to them. They'd been destroyed too many times to want to chance that destruction again.

Or at least, he had been.

But he'd walked into this with his eyes wide open, he thought, thinking of Poppy and his certainty of how she believed she felt about him. It was going to break him to walk away from her, but until then, he was going to relish it. Store every memory. Make certain they were as clear as possible.

It was all the comfort he'd have when he had to leave.

Still, it was a hell of a lot more than he'd had in his life to this point. He'd make it be enough.

CHAPTER SIXTEEN

Poppy admitted she wasn't one to follow local news. She kept up with the international scene, just because it wasn't as upsetting for some reason. But when she entered the office that evening to turn over the leases and checks from that day to Sasha, it was the local news that caught her attention.

The four men found "slaughtered," as the news anchor put it, in a local deserted farmhouse were identified as a team of international mercenaries wanted for questioning in several nations for a variety of crimes.

An American, a Colombian, and two South Africans.

According to the anchor, a local had reported having spoken to one of the men and giving him directions to a hardware store in town. In this age of Google Maps and online navigation, the local had scoffed over someone asking for directions, it was reported.

No one had mentioned Poppy, though, and the fact that the slain man had approached her and caused her to nearly be hit by said local. Thank God.

She recognized another man in the picture as well: Chet Rollins, the commander of the group. She'd barely glimpsed his face when he'd nearly run into her at the end of the alley as she was pulling out, but there was no doubt it was him.

The reporter said local law enforcement revealed it looked like the men had faced off against more than one person. No gunshots had been fired; each man had taken a knife blow to the heart or the neck.

Guns, ammunition, and drugs had been found in the house, and nothing more. It was suspected the deaths were the result of a drug deal gone bad, but there were no suspects at present.

Poppy had a horrible suspicion, though. She remembered seeing one of Jack's friends pulling into the store and backing his Harley between two large trucks. Then she'd glimpsed him behind her as she drove home. She hadn't thought much of it at the time. Just noticed him.

She remembered Jack and his friends leaving early that morning, and according to the news, the coroner placed the deaths just hours afterward. Not that it was proof, but suspicion was like a weight in her chest.

Turning the contracts and checks over to Sasha, she quickly made her excuses and headed home. Jack hadn't mentioned that morning if he'd be back, or what his plans were. But, she hadn't asked, either. Just as she tried excessively hard not to be possessive of his time, or curious about the time he spent away from her.

Unlike most women, she truly didn't believe her lover needed to live in her pocket, or her in his. But, she knew Jack in ways she would never tell anyone else, especially him. She knew him in ways that were frightening.

For instance, she'd known his men would make it to her home before they left and thank her for the food. They didn't praise her or compliment her mother. Quietly, they said, "Thank you for the food, ma'am," and went on their way.

His men.

She paused after deactivating her security and stared into the shadowed house.

Like a team leader or an employer.

They called him "boss"; she'd heard it several times, just as she'd heard him give them orders. Oh, nothing important, just little things.

They deferred to him.

They followed him.

There were times she wondered why they didn't just go ahead and salute him.

Jack had said he was retired. Her brothers said the others had been dishonorably discharged and that Jack had only missed a dishonorable discharge because he knew people. Evidently, he'd been very good at what he did.

Moving through the house, she went to her small office, opened her laptop, and sat down in front of it. There, she pulled up the news story and read it again, pushing back the stubborn curl that kept slipping over her forehead and over her eye.

Those men wouldn't have just accidentally slammed into her vehicle or just happened to have wanted directions from her.

They would have seen her with Jack at some point, she guessed. Or seen Jack coming to her house if they were watching him.

What was he doing in Barboursville that had four international mercenaries approaching her or willing to slam their vehicle into hers? That made absolutely no sense.

Biting her lip thoughtfully, she shut the laptop down, then returned to the living room, where she'd placed her leather carryall, and pulled out her phone.

She typed a quick message to Jack and pushed send.

Having dinner at the bar with Lilith and Erika.

Having done that she rushed to shower and change before leaving, wishing she had time to cancel, or to reschedule as Sasha and Saige had done that afternoon.

She needed to think about this, needed to consider it before she dared question Jack about it. Before she faced him with the suspicions that he and his friends had killed those men.

And she needed to know why.

Jack looked at the caller ID on the smartphone and activated the call.

"Yeah?" His tone was clipped.

"Your friend is curious about the deaths of the mercs," Kira told him quietly. "The search just popped up on her computer."

"We knew she'd recognize Van Nyes." Jack wasn't too worried about it. She was a smart girl; they'd known that all along.

"If she's as smart as you think she is, she's going to put two and two together and come up with four, my friend. I would have known the instant I saw the news story."

"You're part of this world—"

"She's not stupid, remember?" she broke in chidingly.

He paused, relieving the body at his feet of a substantial amount of cash as Lucas did the same with another man.

"I'm kind of busy right now," he told her, turning to begin a search of the small confines of the camper. "Is that all you needed?"

She gave a low, amused laugh. "He needs a report," she told him, speaking of Ian. "Did you find them?"

"Found. Taken care of. Searching the camper they were pulling now. So far nothing, but enough cash to keep them comfortable for a while and more guns than they needed."

Silence filled the other end of the conversation for long minutes.

"One of us will contact you later. He says you need to meet. New intel has come in as well."

Jack grimaced, his jaw tightening at the order.

He'd known when Ian caught chatter that another team was in the area for reasons unknown. Jack had a feeling he knew the reason. Someone wanted him either out of the way, too busy to get involved in what was coming, or too dead to care. And someone thought it was okay to use Poppy to achieve that.

Stepping aside, he nodded at Lucas, a silent signal to load the weapons and ammo.

"These two were paid more, or they came prepared to stay awhile and live extravagantly," he told her.

"Cash, guns, and ammo are yours and your men's," she assured him. "He said burn the rest."

"Will do."

He stepped outside as Lucas carried out the last of the haul.

"He says burn the evidence," he relayed the order, nodding to Hayes and Hank. "Take care of it."

They lifted the jugs of accelerant that had been placed at a pickup point earlier. Hayes went into the camper, Hank opened the doors of the truck. The accelerant Ian had provided burned fast and hot and would ensure the two men inside wouldn't show signs of the blades that had swiped across their necks. There would be nothing but teeth left.

No more than a minute later, the two men were dropping the fuses to the flares placed inside the camper and the truck. Once it was lit, the team would have sixty seconds to clear out of the small spot next to the river where they'd found the men camping.

At exactly seventy-five seconds, the truck exploded, then the camper. It would take a while for LEOs to be called in, considering the deserted area where the team had found the men.

"Second team, heavily armed and filled with cash," Lucas said from the passenger seat, his tone suspicious. "What the fuck is going on?"

"No doubt something that's going to piss us off," Jack grunted. "Ian has intel, though; let's hope it's something that will clue us in, because I'm going to get sick of this fast and question Crossfield myself. He needs to choose teams that aren't the dregs of an already rotten lot to offer jobs to. I'm getting tired of killing cockroaches."

He had a bad feeling in the pit of his stomach that this had been another team called in to grab Poppy, or something worse. He knew Rollins's crew; if they'd gotten their hands on her, she wouldn't have survived it.

He wasn't as familiar with the two-man team they'd just taken out, but he knew their reputations, and they weren't any gentler than Rollins and his men.

They were muscle, nothing more. And according to the answers they'd given Lucas when he questioned them, they were there on a rumor that a job was coming up. A big one. One with a high dollar payout and a guarantee to throw the United States into complete chaos.

When asked if part of their job was acquiring a redhead, they'd both smiled. That was all the answer Jack had needed.

There was always the chance the next team that made it to town would get lucky. These two had arrived in the area before Jack and his team had taken Rollins out, and they'd been looking to contact Rollins.

He was going to have to figure out what the hell to do about Poppy in all this. She was a way into the circle of friends she had, to ensure that Crossfield and Dawson had easy access to him and knew exactly how dangerous he could be.

As he and the team hit the Barboursville city limits, the smartphone he'd anchored on the bike lit up, showing a text message from Poppy.

He knew that woman could cook, but she was rarely home for dinner. How could she stomach the bar's food over her own? Hell, he was close to begging her to cook for him.

He'd join her at the bar after a shower and change of clothes. Not that any DNA stained him this time, but he didn't want to go to her with the stink of death in his nostrils, either.

Activating a call to Lucas, he used the sensitive Bluetooth communications set in his helmet.

"Yeah?" Lucas answered.

"I'm showering, then meeting Poppy at the bar. The three of you do the same and we'll meet up there."

"Copy that," Lucas agreed, and ended the call.

Making the turn to his house, he veered off from the other men, checked his rearview mirror, and, satisfied that he wasn't being followed, continued to the house.

He drove down the street in front of the house first and made note of the black Lexus parked about halfway up the block. He knew the vehicle, knew the man who drove it.

He rode to the alley, parked in the back lot, swung off the bike, and faced the man resting against his pickup.

Now, wasn't this unexpected.

"Can I help you, Crossfield?" he asked Poppy's boss, seeing the smug smile that threatened to curl the other man's lips.

Blond, still in good shape physically, still a threat, considering his background. Jack considered himself well able to match the other man in a fight, though. If it came to that.

With his hands resting comfortably in the pockets of his slacks, Crossfield straightened from the side of the truck and inclined his head toward the house.

"Can we talk?"

"Sure. Come on in." Jack led the way up the cement path to the back door, unlocked it, and stepped inside.

"Beer?" he questioned the other man as he stepped into the kitchen, catching Caine Crossfield's careful surveillance of the room.

Yeah, motherfucker, you're being recorded, he thought.

"Beer would be good," Crossfield said with a nod.

Pulling two bottles from the fridge, Jack handed one to Crossfield, then twisted the cap on his own.

"How can I help ya?" he drawled. "Or should I guess? Stay away from Poppy?"

Crossfield chuckled at the question, shaking his head. "No, I figure that ship's already sailed. Poppy's always been a stubborn little thing, and sweet on you for as long as I can remember." His head tilted and he watched Jack curiously. "How the hell did you manage that, anyway? Make her wait on you like that?"

Jack tipped the beer to his lips, never taking his eyes off Crossfield, and took a large swig before setting the bottle aside.

"So, if you're not here to warn me off, why are you here?" Jack asked, ignoring Crossfield's question.

If Poppy hadn't told the other man anything, then he sure wasn't. Besides, like Poppy, he'd always felt that what had happened between them that night was their memory alone. It had nothing to do with this man for sure.

Crossfield took a sip of his beer, turned, and paced the living room, looking around curiously.

What the fuck was he looking for?

"I sent you several letters over the years, offering to buy your farm," Crossfield remarked. "You never replied."

He turned back to Jack rather quickly, as though certain he'd catch Jack moving for him, or betray some emotion in his expression. Jack just continued to watch him questioningly.

Jack didn't say anything. He hadn't answered the queries; that should have been answer enough for Crossfield.

"Did you get the letters?" Crossfield was acting amused, but Jack sensed his frustration.

"I got 'em." Jack shrugged and said nothing more.

Crossfield was on a fishing expedition of some sort, and Jack was determined not to take the bait.

"Still not interested, huh?" Crossfield asked knowingly.

"Not today," Jack assured him. "Next month? Next year? Who knows?"

Surprise almost widened Crossfield's eyes, but he held the response back. He was out of practice, Jack thought. It was hard for a killer to maintain that ice when he stopped killing.

All shit aside, spec ops, including SEALs, killed. That was part of their job. They excused it as justified, and most of the time, it was. At least, in the sense that they went where they were ordered, accepted command's version of the conflict, and killed in completing their assignments.

Didn't change the fact that they were killers. That Crossfield too had been a killer. One out of practice, definitely, but still a threat.

"You don't think you'll stay in Barboursville?" he asked.

Jack shrugged. "Lot of memories here."

The memories were all but forgotten, deliberately so. Jack knew he'd never get rid of the farm or the house. The basement alone was worth more than any other house he'd seen in a long time. And he'd seen some really nice places.

"If that's all . . ." Jack took a step toward the door.

"Actually, no," Crossfield told him, his voice hardened.

Jack took a backward step, the weight of his weapon at his back, concealed beneath his shirt, inviting him to pull it and get the upper hand. He ignored the impulse.

And he waited.

Sometimes, it was best to just wait, let the other man wonder what you were thinking rather than the other way around.

Impatience wasn't something Jack had ever been known for, and he didn't display it now.

"It's hard to step out of the life, isn't it?" A smile tugged at Crossfield's lips. "Especially when you keep your hands bloody."

Blue eyes swept over Jack's hands. Jack didn't follow. He knew his hands were clean, just as he knew exactly what the other man was doing.

"Your hands bloody, Crossfield?" he asked softly, never taking his eyes off the man.

When dealing with a cobra, one didn't look away, or he found himself dead.

Crossfield's lips quirked at that. "Stained, perhaps. Fresh blood is another story. I learned it's best to let others do the dirty work."

Jack arched his brow slowly but didn't speak.

It was evident Crossfield was waiting for a response.

"I have a job for whoever took out that merc team the other day," Crossfield finally stated, and Jack had to admit, it surprised him. "I also heard there was an explosion by the river—another possible team. I'm going to bet the same men took them out. If you hear who they are, I'd like the courtesy of a meet."

"And I'm supposed to know who it is?" Jack guessed.

"I think we both know who's responsible," Crossfield said softly. "Like I said, I have a job, if they want it."

"And what kind of job should I let them know they're looking at?" He put just enough mockery in his voice that Crossfield was still forced to play the game.

"Nothing too taxing if they do the job right." The other man gave a negligent lift of a shoulder. "But I'd only be willing to discuss it with the team I'm looking for."

Jack let Crossfield turn and slowly make his way to the door. And there, just as Jack knew he would, he paused.

"Whether you have fresh blood on your hands or not, you'll

always be a risk to her," the man stated, keeping his back to Jack. "You'll always be the reason she's in danger."

He opened the door and left, closing it gently behind him.

Pursing his lips, Jack strode to the door and set the locks, thankful now that he'd spent years remodeling the inside of the house. A strong steel door, steel between the brick and drywall of the house. The window frames were reinforced, the glass bullet-resistant.

It had taken a decade to complete the work without anyone becoming suspicious.

The basement was even more secured. A hidden safe room, the door to the tunnel secured against anyone who might accidentally find it, or anyone searching for it.

If anyone made it into the basement, they wouldn't find anything of any value. And damned sure nothing they could use against him.

Even the man who'd fostered him and given him the place hadn't known about the tunnel, and until this mission had come up, Jack hadn't told another living soul about it.

Dawson had been trying to buy it for the past several years, though, just as Crossfield had been after the farm. Multiple letters, messages given to those they knew he was sure to see when he visited home.

He showered quickly and dressed in his normal evening wear: jeans, T-shirt, boots, and leather biker chaps. He pulled on his leather vest as well. Bending, he tucked a weapon in the holster built into the side of his boot. Small, compact, it hid easy but got the job done. He slid his Ka-Bar in the holster built into the inside of his vest, along his side and just under his arm.

The weapons wouldn't be detectable by the naked eye, but within easy reach. He was starting to suspect it would be best to stay armed at all times. Something he hadn't looked forward to.

He didn't wear jewelry; he wore nothing flashy. His size and his obvious strength were flashy enough. There was nothing he could do about it, so he'd learned to accept it instead.

Dark was just beginning to fall when he started the bike and pulled from the back of the house. Glancing along the narrow back road, he saw an unfamiliar gray pickup, its windows tinted, parked at the upper end.

Could be another resident's company car, he told himself. He'd check the bar parking lot before he and Poppy left.

If it was there, then he'd check it out.

CHAPTER SEVENTEEN

There were two things Jack noticed when he entered the bar. Well, three actually.

The first was Poppy sitting at the usual table with her friends, this time only two of them, the schoolteacher and the boutique owner.

She wore jeans and boots and a lacy white top, with all that fabulous hair pinned in a messy pile atop her head.

She looked good enough to eat. Something he intended to do once he got her back to her house.

Her expression was shadowed with suspicion as she watched him, her gaze dark with it. Yeah, he had to agree with Kira now: She knew. And he prayed she didn't ask him about it, because he wasn't going to lie to her. If she was smart enough to know, and courageous enough to ask, then she'd get the truth.

The second thing Jack noticed was the pair of SEALs from his former team in a shadowed booth, sipping beer and eating nachos.

They were in jeans and work shirts, the construction kind. A little ragged and unkempt, but unmistakable; he knew them like most people knew family. Hell, they'd been his family for years.

The little hand signal the one facing the door gave warned Jack to keep his distance. That told him they weren't there for him. At least, not yet.

The third thing he noticed was that Ian and Kira sat several booths down from the SEALs, their four cartel bodyguards in one of the booths between them and the SEALs.

Fuck.

So much for a meet later.

"Lucas, you and the others stay close," he warned the man who'd taken the unofficial second-lead position in their little group.

"Gotcha," Lucas muttered under his breath, and he and Hayes and Hank moved to the table between Poppy and her friends and the two SEALs.

Homeland Security made a show of keeping Ian and Kira under investigation, and Diego Fuentes was serious about ensuring his only son was protected at all times. It got crowded around Ian in public sometimes, Jack thought.

He strode across the bar to where Poppy sat, the remains of her dinner pushed to the center of the table.

The small group was more subdued than normal, though the other two women didn't seem suspicious, just following Poppy's lead perhaps.

"Hi, Jack," Lilith greeted him.

Tonight, her eyes were a navy blue, though her hair was still purple, blue, and pink. Dressed in a flowy soft dress and heels, she was pretty, but nothing compared to his Poppy.

The same could be said for Erika. The teacher's short-sleeved gray blouse was paired with jeans and sneakers. Casual, relaxed.

"You need to cheer Poppy up, Jack," Erika told him, her tone a little too sincere. "She's in a mood tonight."

"I'm not in a mood," Poppy informed her friend, her tone disgruntled. "I told you, I'm just tired."

And she didn't blush.

Poppy had just told a bald-faced lie without blushing.

Now how interesting was that?

He slid into the chair beside her and slouched back. Reaching up, he twirled around his finger a little loose curl of hair lying at her nape.

"Hard day, baby?" he asked, keeping his voice low.

She turned to him slowly, her gaze hooded, the green gleaming with a hint of fire.

"It was interesting," she answered him without so much as a smile. "How was your day?"

He inclined his head marginally. "Mine was interesting as well."

"Did you see the news this evening?" Erika leaned forward, staring past Poppy, concern creasing her face. "This morning, they reported that a mercenary group had been killed not far from town. This evening, a camper down by the river blew up with two men in it. Some men who were fishing when they showed up said the men were really rough-looking and sounded foreign. Something bad is going on . . ."

"I wonder if Jimmy's death is tied to this." Lilith turned to Jack. "Our friend Jimmy Stafford was killed last month just after he radioed in and told dispatch he was checking out some unusual activity between two box trucks he'd passed on a back road outside of town. When he didn't respond later, two officers when to check on him." She swallowed, distress showing clearly in her gaze. "Someone had shot him in the head and just left him on the side of the road."

Jack had seen the report, and he knew Ian believed the officer's death was connected to everything going on now.

As Lilith dropped her gaze sadly, Jack became aware of one of Ian's bodyguards moving from the table and coming his way.

Shit was getting ready to get real.

Fuck.

"I'm ready to go . . ." Poppy paused as the bodyguard stopped at their table.

"Excuse me, Mr. Bridger," Breck Harding, one of Ian's bodyguards, said as he stopped next to the table. "Mr. and Mrs. Richards would like a moment of your time." He paused. "If you don't mind."

The fact that it was more a demand than a request was clear.

"I'm going home." Poppy started to rise to her feet.

Jack gripped her leg, holding her in place, his gaze locked with the bodyguard's.

"I'll be there in a minute," he agreed.

"I'll wait." The bodyguard's smile was tight. "Again, if you don't mind."

"And if I do?" Jack growled.

"I'll wait anyway."

"I'm leaving," Poppy said again, her voice nearly a whisper as Jack straightened in the chair and leaned close to her ear.

"You'll remain right here, at this table, until I come back," he told her, hardening his tone until his voice sounded just as cruel as he meant it to. "Agreed?"

Those green eyes narrowed on him, anger licking at the brilliant color as he watched her consider defying him.

He didn't say anything else. He held her gaze another second, then motioned to Lucas at the bar.

"That is dirty," she hissed when Lucas rose from his stool and Jack straightened from his chair and began walking to the other table.

Hell. Now what the fuck was going on?

Poppy glared at Lucas, forcing herself not to speak, not to allow the anger burning in her chest free.

He began talking to Erika, and after a few minutes Hank made his way over to talk to Lilith. Hayes remained at the bar, his gaze on the meeting between Jack and the Richardses.

Poppy knew they had arrived in Barboursville more than a month before and that local police had questioned them when Jimmy's body had been found.

She, Lilith, Erika, Saige, and Sasha had gone to school with Jimmy. He'd been a year older, and he'd always wanted to be in law enforcement. The police believed Ian Richards was in town to negotiate with local gangs in the tristate area about cartel drugs. They believed Jimmy must have driven up on one of those gangs and ended up dead because of it.

She should have guessed the former disgraced SEAL would eventually reach out to the recently disgraced one.

"What is going on?" Erika whispered as she leaned closer to Poppy. "It's hard to believe the Richardses are who the news suspects, but with everything that's going on, it's hard not to wonder."

"I don't know," Poppy whispered back, sneaking another glance toward the group.

Jack did not look happy.

"He meets with them a lot," Lilith pointed out worriedly.

"I'm getting scared for you, Poppy," Erika said softly, and Poppy could hear that fear in her friend's voice. "All of a sudden Jack's home with those men, and now mercenaries are showing up and getting killed."

It wouldn't help for her to admit that today, she was kind of scared for herself.

He had burned his buddies.

Hell, he was the bad guy, right? Jack told himself. And Ian knew they were there, knew who they were, even if they weren't aware of it. Covers had to be maintained, and sometimes that required being the bastard.

Jack had always excelled at being the bastard.

So, he stopped at the booth where his former teammates sat, stared down at them, and informed them their cover was blown, that they needed to get their asses out of town while Richards was in a good mood and willing to let them go.

"Fuck, Jack," Garlin Sutton, a man who had called Jack his friend several times over the years, whispered in regret. "Man, I really didn't believe it until now . . ."

"Believe what, Sutton? That I got tired of the bullshit? Trust me, it's the truth," he assured the other man.

"Be watching for us, Bridger," Ward Baines, one of the few men in the world Jack really respected, snarled back at him.

"Always am," Jack drawled. "Trust me on that. Always am."

They rose from the booth, tossed some bills onto it, then strode from the bar. They might be waiting when he left, but he had no doubt Ian had already ensured they were ordered to stand down.

This was the really bad part about being the bad guy. Former friends, his lover, her friends. They believed the illusion. It was required.

He didn't have enough friends to give a fuck, but the suspicion and hint of fear in Poppy's eyes when he returned to the table did something to his chest.

Made it tight. Made it ache.

And he wondered if that was how it felt when the heart began to break.

Poppy rarely used Jack's expression to determine what he was thinking or feeling. She went by his eyes. A mix of gray and blue, they could darken to nearly all blue or lighten to almost a pure gray.

She remembered the day when she'd found him in the cold, hiding behind their garbage bins. His eyes had been blue. Anger had filled his expression, pride, determination. And she'd seen every one of those emotions clearly on his face.

He didn't carry the emotions on his face anymore. There was rarely any strong emotion on it at all. But it still showed in his eyes.

And right now, they were almost as blue as they had been that cold winter day so long ago.

Anger, pride, determination.

She'd heard the exchange with the two men in the booth several feet away. They must have been SEALs he knew. And they were there to watch the Richardses.

He'd burned them, he said.

He must have told the Richardses who they were, but he'd stopped and warned them, she told herself desperately. He'd given them a chance to escape.

"Let's go." He held his hand out to Poppy, his expression fierce as those eyes stared down at her, daring her to refuse.

She reached out and took his hand, and she knew she surprised him. He had his tells, just as she had hers. Hers were just more extreme, that was all.

Saying goodbye to her friends, she followed him out of the bar. Just because she didn't fight him in public didn't mean he wasn't going to hear an earful from her once she got home. She wasn't temper-prone, but on those rare occasions that her anger had blown past her laid-back psyche, it hadn't been pleasant.

And "laid-back" wasn't applying tonight.

"I'll follow you home," he told her as the three men who rode with him moved silently behind them. "Lucas and Hank will be in front of you, Hayes and I will be behind you."

The fear she'd managed to push back all evening suddenly rushed forward, and she could feel her heart racing in her chest, a sense of panic tightening her stomach.

"What's going on, Jack?" she whispered, aware that they were walking fast. "You're scaring me."

Jack's arm was behind her back, and she was almost running to keep up with his long stride.

"We'll talk when we get home," he told her, his voice barely more than a whisper. "Just do as I told you. Stay on Lucas's ass and I'll stay on yours. Hear me? Don't be scared, baby. I just don't have time to explain, that's all."

Trust was a bitch, she thought as she nodded.

Because it was impossible to get past that innate trust she had of him. She'd always trusted Jack, always seen the good in him, even when it wasn't apparent.

Like now.

He hurried her into her car and shut the door, then stepped to the Harley he'd parked beside it. When Lucas and Hank pulled out and stopped, obviously waiting for her, she backed out, slid the vehicle into drive, and followed them.

She should be racing to her parents, or to Mac's place, she told herself. Instead, she was following Lucas's bike as close as possible as he took several back streets and alleys rather than the most direct route to her home.

When she parked next to the fence surrounding her back-yard, Jack was there before she'd slid her seat belt free and opened the door.

"Come on. My place."

The other three men were waiting at the back of her SUV, and although they didn't surround her like a wall of muscle, she knew they'd taken protective positions around her and Jack as he rushed her across the alley and into his house.

And if she wasn't mistaken, they were trying their best to hide weapons they held ready in their hands.

"This is ridiculous!" She surprised herself, not to mention the four men who entered the house behind her, as she stopped, swung around to face them, and all but screamed the words up at Jack. "It's stupid and insane and I want it to fucking stop."

Jack didn't move back, but his head tilted as though uncertain whether or not she'd try to hit him.

"Oh, I just wish I were tall enough to smack that arrogance off your face," she snarled, and then, before she could stop herself, she planted the toe of her boot in his shin as hard as she could.

He just blinked.

Other than that single movement, he just stood there and stared at her.

"Boss, should I . . ." Lucas started to speak up.

"'Boss'? 'Boss'?" She swung on the other man, watching in satisfaction as he did back up. "Are you on his payroll? Did he hire you?"

Lucas looked at Jack, then at her, clearly uncertain as to whether or not to answer.

"Do you have to ask permission to speak?" She ground the words between her teeth as she glared at him. "I thought you used to be a SEAL? Don't they teach you how to talk in the SEALs?"

"Hell." Lucas wiped his hand over his face, then turned to the other two men before turning back to Jack. "Why don't we wait in the basement. Hayes has leftover pizza, there's a coffeepot and a TV. Give us a yell if you need us." Then he turned to Poppy. "See, I talk just fine, ma'am."

But before she could snap back at him, he, Hayes, and Hank had hurried into the kitchen and to the basement door. Within seconds, it closed quickly behind them.

That left Jack.

"You can't make me run in fear," he warned her, staring back at her, his eyes more gray than blue now.

"What have you done, Jack?" she cried out, feeling not just the anger but the hurt as well racing through her as she smacked his chest. She accomplished nothing but hurting her hand. "What have you done?"

"You have to be more specific, Poppy," he told her, his quiet voice holding an edge of regret.

Turning away from him, she put her hand on her forehead, fighting the tears she wanted to let free.

She breathed in hard, deep, then turned back to him.

"The men that were killed yesterday morning," she charged him. "The one they called Rollins would have slammed into my car as I came out of the alley if I hadn't accelerated when I saw him swing around the turn. The one they called Van Nyes, he came up on me suddenly outside the store. Both men scared the crap out of me. Is that why they're dead, Jack?" she whispered. "Did you—"

"Stop." His hand went over her lips, his eyes suddenly fierce, his expression demanding. "Be careful, Poppy. Be damned careful. Because I won't lie to you. Not to you. So, before you ask me a question, make damned sure you want the answer to it."

He stepped back, releasing her slowly, his expression smoothing out once again.

"Do you want a beer? Fuck, I need a beer." He moved for the kitchen.

"Bourbon," she corrected him, her voice rough, those tears not far behind. "I need bourbon. I want to go home, Jack."

She needed to go home. She needed her space, her shower. Her bed.

God, she needed that bottle of bourbon.

"You can't go home yet." He moved to the cabinet over the sink, opened a door, and pulled out a bottle of her favorite bourbon.

She couldn't go home?

She couldn't ask him questions unless she wanted the truth?

She wanted the truth—she assured herself that she did—but she wanted the truth to be far different than she knew it was.

And that was where the bourbon came in.

She could handle the truth after a couple of shots, she assured herself. She just had to steel herself for it, that was all.

She took the glass with the puny amount of liquor he poured, then silently demanded the bottle. When he handed it over, she doubled the amount before handing it back to him.

"You get drunk, then you're not getting fucked tonight," he warned her. "You can fuck me sober or do without."

She snorted at the statement and glanced at the erection straining his jeans, framed by those perfect fucking riding chaps, then stared back up at him.

"Bet me," she dared him furiously, leaning forward and narrowing her eyes on him as she made the challenge.

She tipped the bottle to her lips and swallowed a fiery, nerve-bracing mouthful of the bourbon. "I just have to stay sober enough to get my mouth on your dick, Jack Bridger, and you'll fuck all night."

Goddamn her.

Jack tipped the bottle to his lips and took a hard drink himself before shoving the cork stopper back into the bottle and replacing the bourbon in the cabinet.

And she was right; that was the part that pissed him off.

She'd just have to be sober enough to convince him she wanted him, and he'd be on her like a bee to honey. He'd strip her down, eat her until she was screaming for him, and fuck them both crazy.

"Like I said, I'm not a good man." He shrugged. He'd accepted that fact a long time ago.

A good man would make sure she stayed sober.

Hell, a good man would never have allowed her to be involved in this.

"Get that bottle back out." She pulled out a chair from beneath the table and sat down, reaching up to release her hair from the clip that held it.

His balls tightened as the curly mass fell around her shoulders, framing her face with the fiery silk.

"You used to puke when you got drunk," he reminded her, but he got the bottle out anyway.

"I won't get that drunk," she breathed out roughly. "Just enough that I can handle this shit without crying. You know I hate crying, Jack."

It only made her mad when she cried. The more the tears fell, the more furious she'd become with herself, as well as with the object of that anger.

"I know, Poppy." He set the bottle down, then sat across from her. "Just let me know when."

Let him know when she could handle it?

She didn't think there was that much bourbon in the world. So, she was going to have to go for the next best thing. She'd just drink enough that she got madder, rather than weepy. Then she'd ask her questions.

CHAPTER EIGHTEEN

Watching her closely as she sipped at the drink, his gaze narrowed on her, and yes, she could see the lust in his eyes. And she knew exactly what he was thinking about. Oh, she'd watched the way his eyes had gone all hot when she'd mentioned sucking his dick.

She'd only done it that once, and he hadn't given her much time to learn how to do it.

"You should have taught me to do it properly," she told him, sipping at her drink again. "You know, when you had the chance to."

His gaze flicked from the drink to her lips, and she watched the way he swallowed with a hard, tight movement.

"Meaning?" he asked her carefully.

Oh, he knew exactly what she meant. Damn him.

Damn him, she hated this. She hated hurting like this, and she hated that hint of blue in his eyes that she'd always equated with his inner hurt.

"Lilith said she learned watching movies and using a vibrator to practice on." And Lilith would completely kill her if she knew . . .

The basement door snapped closed behind her.

Poppy swung around but didn't see anyone.

She turned back to Jack and tilted her head questioningly.

"Hank," he murmured, lifting the beer to his lips. "He heard what you said. He's all hot and bothered for Lilith. The conversation was likely too much for him."

Poor Hank, she thought. Lilith would never trust a man enough to share that with him, she didn't think. Her father had made certain of that. She shrugged.

Hank wasn't her problem until he made a serious move on Lilith.

"So, back to what you were saying before that." He cleared his throat. "You thought I should do what?"

She let a grin tug at her lips, despite the hurt she could feel waiting to push forward.

She took another gulp.

The flames that shot through her senses pushed the hurt back further.

"I tried to practice it with the toys and movies. They weren't you, though, so I just felt silly," she sighed.

He finished half a beer in one swallow, turned in his chair, opened the fridge, and grabbed another.

"You did fine without instruction," he assured her.

Poppy shook her head. "That's very kind of you to say, Jack, but we both know better. I was just saying. You should have taught me how to do it the way you like it."

This was why she didn't drink the bourbon often. It wasn't that she didn't have wicked thoughts or wasn't brave enough to say what was on her mind. It was that, this was Jack. She was always so stressed out with emotions and a lack of confidence where he was concerned. He was her first lover. She hadn't exactly found her footing there yet.

"I like it fine the way you did it," he assured her again.

"You wanted to pull my hair and fuck my mouth," she told him, certain of that. "You wanted to make me take that big dick and you were too worried I'd get scared."

He seemed to stop breathing. His gaze shifted to a stormy gray, the color turbulent and hungry.

"Fuck. Goddamned Poppy," he cursed, his voice strained as he wiped his hand over his face and stared at her with so much lust she could feel the heat of it licking over her body.

She wasn't anywhere near drunk, but her inhibitions were more relaxed, and that false bravado she used to be so good at was able to step free.

"Really, Jack, you sound so shocked," she said, hearing the quiver in her voice that would tell him she wasn't quite as certain of herself as she pretended to be.

"Shocked?" Denial crossed his expression. "It's not shock, baby. But you're damned close to getting those clothes torn from you and my dick fucking that smart little mouth like you seem to want."

"Well, restrain yourself," she advised him, sipping at the drink again. "At least for a minute."

"Restrain myself?" She could hear the disbelief in his voice. "You put a lot of faith in my ability to do that, Poppy. Far more than I have."

She had a lot of faith in him, period. She'd always had a lot of faith in him.

"I want to make my memories," she admitted to him, staring at the liquid in the glass rather than at him. "I know something bad's coming, something I don't know if I can face, and I want just a little of the fantasies I've had, for when it's over."

For a man who rarely allowed emotion to show on his face, the hollow, aching regret she now saw on it nearly broke her heart.

"Poppy . . ." he whispered, his voice low, echoing with regret.

"You know I love you, don't you? That I've loved you since I was a teenager, loved you all these years . . ." She watched him, letting him see what she felt for him. "But I have a feeling, Jack, I'm going to be very, very angry with you very soon. Maybe I want to make a few more of those dreams I've had before reality destroys the chance for them."

Jack felt something shredding inside him. Not in his chest where his heart resided, but somewhere deeper, in that place that had once been a hard, icy core, devoid of conscience or emotion.

Yeah, he knew she loved him. Hell, she'd loved him since she was seventeen and casting him those flirty glances. When he'd held her as she cried, the horror of having a man attempt to force himself inside her tearing at her mind.

And now, she had no idea the danger she was in, or the type of men being paid to abduct her.

Why involve her? he wondered, because Ian didn't seem to have that answer.

"I'm sorry, Poppy . . ." he whispered. "Hurting you is the last thing I ever wanted."

Poppy promised herself she wasn't going to cry.

She knew he didn't love her, and that was okay, because at least he wasn't lying about it.

She could live with the rest of it, but he'd sworn to her, nine years ago, that he would never lie to her, that he would always tell her the truth.

"So." Lifting the glass, she finished what amounted to two shots of bourbon, then sat it down heavily. "How much time do I have to make a memory before the world explodes around me?"

Jack lifted that second beer to his lips and finished it before replacing it on the table.

How long to make a memory? he thought. Not long enough. And though every second with Poppy was a memory, he knew what she was asking.

"I don't know," he answered, letting his fingers form into a loose fist on the table. "A little over a week, maybe two, maybe three."

Resignation was evident in the curl of her lips. "Maybe a week, no more than three?" she whispered, playing with the glass in front of her.

She looked up at him then, and any illusion of liquid courage she may have presented moments before was dispelled by the look of sober, stubborn determination that came over her face.

"Well then, stud, looks like you have until daylight to see how effective you can be in making me accept the answers to the questions I'll be asking when the sun rises." Her head tilted, those green eyes suddenly so fucking sultry, sexy, that lust tightened his body to a breaking point. "So, Jack, do your worst."

He was out of his chair in the next breath, and he stalked to the basement door, jerked it open, and yelled down, "Come up here before daylight and I'll fucking shoot you."

He slammed the door closed, turned back to a far-too-amused Poppy, and let the reins he kept on himself where she was concerned slowly drop away.

She'd been sixteen when he realized the girl he'd tried to protect for so long was growing up. From the day he'd been shipped out of Barboursville to the foster home that actually saved his life, he'd threatened, bargained with, and bribed everyone he knew in Barboursville to keep her safe. Just keep her safe. Until she turned fifteen and he'd seen the first teenage Don Juan trying to charm her. After that, he threw all his efforts into keeping Poppy innocent.

She was a baby, he'd reasoned, too young for a broken heart or to have all her sweet innocence stolen before she knew what it was herself.

Then there was the summer she turned seventeen. When he'd burst into that run-down shack after hearing her screams to see that bastard collapsed over her, dead. Because he hadn't protected her properly. And she'd had to protect herself instead.

And he made certain that if any man seemed to be getting too close, he was quickly warned away.

Because he knew he'd come back for her. Inside, where a man can't lie to himself and can only hide from the truth for so long, Jack had known he hadn't watched over her because of her kindness that cold winter's day.

He'd watched over her because when that seven-year-old girl had put her hands on her hips and demanded he get his butt in the house right now, so he could get warm and her momma could feed him, he'd claimed her.

She had owned every part of him after that, even after her father had sent him to face the worst hell a child could face, still, Poppy Octavia Porter had owned him.

All the way to his broken, scarred, black soul.

He'd reined himself in to protect her. Her innocence, her inexperience, her dreams of a tender lover. He'd fought to hold back the dark, gnawing hunger he felt for this woman, to ensure she never knew a moment's hesitation with him.

She'd grown up. Matured. And maybe he'd forgotten that in his need to protect her. And if he knew to his soul he belonged to her, then every part of him belonged.

Even the hunger he had for her.

CHAPTER NINETEEN

Poppy watched the look that came over his face.

Sexual. Intense.

His look darkened to the color of thunderclouds, and a hint of red stained the sun-bronzed cheeks.

She was crazy to push him like that, and she knew it.

Jack wasn't a man to try to convince a woman to let him touch her. He would know if a woman wanted to be touched, and if he wanted her, then he'd touch.

He was confident. Secure in himself.

And he believed he wasn't a good man. Her heart ached with that knowledge.

As she sat in the chair, staring back at him, wondering what he'd do, she knew the moment he had made that decision.

He removed his leather vest and tossed it to the counter, then his T-shirt. Dressed in nothing but jeans and those black leather chaps, his hard, muscular body rippling, he released the button and zipper of his jeans.

Poppy lost her breath.

She lost her sanity.

As he stepped to her, he released his erection from his jeans, his fingers curling around it, stroking up to the crest, then down again.

She had to catch her breath, but she knew it wasn't going to happen.

The dark crest was swollen, plum-shaped, throbbing. Moisture gleamed on the broad tip, and as she watched, a bead of pre-come welled from the slit.

She could feel the heavy, sexual lassitude filling her. That feeling that even bourbon couldn't give her, invading her senses. It was like being drunk and being high at the same time as her body, her senses began preparing her for him.

Poppy drew in a hard, deep breath as he slid his hand into her hair, his fingers suddenly bunching in the curls, creating that luscious, sharp sensation in her scalp that she knew she'd always associate with Jack.

He didn't ask or tell her to part her lips for him. With his free hand he cupped her cheek, his thumb finding her jaw and exerting just enough pressure to make certain her lips parted for him. To ensure that when the heavy crest pressed against her lips it was able to push inside her, stretching her lips around the fierce, iron-hot flesh.

Poppy's hands jerked to his thighs, her nails digging into the leather chaps, her eyes widening as he pushed in deep.

"Suck me, Poppy," he growled even as her mouth tightened on him and her involuntary groan escaped her throat.

"Do you think I'll be slow and easy?" he demanded, moving against the grip her lips had on him. "That I'll make a single allowance for your inexperience now?"

God, she hoped not.

She wanted him. All of him. Every part of him in that short time that she had him.

"Get ready, baby, because when I'm done, you're going to be

swallowing that cock while I fill that tight little throat with my come."

Someone should have warned her, though, her eyes widening as he began to move against her lips, his hard voice darker, more sexual than she'd ever heard it as he demanded she suck him tighter, harder.

Her tongue swirled over the head as he thrust inside and retreated, pressed and rubbed against the underside when she couldn't lick. She felt the thick, heavy veins throbbing against her lips, the iron hardness of the head filling her mouth.

The hand in her hair held her still, kept her in place as his hips moved, pushing in and retreating as he demanded she give him exactly what he wanted. All of what he wanted.

When she felt he was pushing in too deep and tried to pull back, he held her still, and demanded to know if she'd changed her mind. He couldn't know that it was like striking a match to gasoline when that raw stubbornness she possessed was concerned.

Her eyes watered as she struggled to take him, her nails clenched into the leather covering his thighs, and she could hear her cries as though they were someone else's. Low, hungry sounds as that intoxicating sense of raw lust began to strengthen inside her.

Soon, his own moans covered hers. Low, ragged curses, his voice tortured, his thrusts increasing in intensity as he gripped his cock at that point where it wasn't possible for her to take more.

Poppy didn't just accept each thrust passively; she sucked, licked, her moans vibrating against his flesh as he pierced the back of her throat. She was lost in a dark, sensual world where his pleasure drove hers, filling her senses with that rush of powerful, drugging pleasure that made no sense but that she nonetheless accepted without protest.

"Fuck, Poppy . . ." he snarled, the thrusts changing rhythm now, becoming shorter, more intense. "Fuck yes, baby girl, suck it deep . . .

"Beautiful, baby . . .

"Ah fuck. Damn you, Poppy . . ."

His breathing was heavy, laborious, but so was hers as she struggled to draw enough air through her nostrils.

She could feel his thighs tightening, bunching beneath her fingers until they were like columns of steel. He thrust against her lips, her suckling mouth, as her own thighs tightened and she felt the whiplashes of sensations striking at her clit, her pussy.

She was lost in the sensations and the pure, raw need burning through her. He did that to her, laid waste to even her greatest fantasies of him. It was rawer and more intense than she could have dreamed.

"Take me, Poppy," he groaned, his hands tightening in her hair as he fucked her mouth, his cock shuttling back and forth between her lips before he buried it as deep as possible. "All of me . . ."

She felt the head of his cock swell further, and an instant later the first, hard pulse of semen exploded at the back of her throat.

Poppy fought to breathe, to swallow, to experience every moment, every sensation of having Jack completely, exactly as he was. Hard, unyielding, his sexual hunger as dark and focused as the man himself.

"Damn you, Poppy." He pulled away from her, his hand still in her hair, his still hard cock framed by his open jeans and those damned riding chaps.

And Poppy could have sworn she orgasmed at the sight of it.

The sensation was like a mini-starburst going off in her womb and radiating outward until she felt her pussy tighten and moisture spill furiously from the clenched, sensitive tissue.

She didn't have time to recover or to balance her senses. She barely had time to take a breath before he pulled her from her chair, lifted her in his arms, and joined her lips to his as he carried her from the kitchen through the house and into a bedroom.

The door cracked on the frame as he slammed it closed, and a heartbeat later she felt herself falling. Gasping as her back met a mattress, she stared up at Jack, the feeling of dazed intoxication still holding her in its grip as she watched him sit on the chair across from the bed and remove his boots as though he had all the time in the world.

"Get those clothes off," he demanded, his lips kiss-swollen, his gaze focused and intense. "Now."

Bending forward, he reached out, snagged one foot, and jerked a boot from her foot, then did the same with the other.

"Now, goddamn it," he barked.

Poppy jerked up, sitting on the bed, her fingers fumbling at the buttons of her shirt as her breathing became harder, faster. It seemed to take forever to unbutton it and hurriedly pull it from her shoulders.

Then she made the mistake of looking up at Jack.

His boots and socks were off and he was standing, releasing the chaps before sliding the zipper free along the sides of his legs. He tossed them aside, then slid the loosened jeans off his muscular legs. Defined, powerful, his legs were solid foundations for the rest of his body.

He looked up, his eyes narrowed.

"You're still dressed, baby girl," he pointed out, stepping to her. "I'll have to punish you for that."

Before she could do more than gasp, he broke the front clasp of her bra and pushed it from her, revealing the hard, swollen state of her breasts. Her back met the bed again, and two seconds later the jeans as well as her panties were sliding from her legs and Jack was tossing them aside before lifting her until she lay full-length on the bed.

From the table next to the bed, he drew a bottle of lubricant and a small vibrator and put them within easy reach before turning back to her.

She had no idea what to expect from him now, and that thought excited her far more than she liked to admit.

"I bought that little toy there just for you," he told her as he pushed her thighs apart with his, spreading them wide.

Poppy watched him, fighting to breathe as her fingers fisted in the blankets beneath her.

Her hips jerked when his fingers ran over the folds of her pussy, sliding easily over the heavy juices gathered there, then parting her folds to find the entrance he sought.

"Baby's so wet," he whispered with a tight curl of satisfaction tugging at his lips.

Then he pushed two fingers inside her, fast, deep, sending a burst of fiery sensation streaking through her senses.

Poppy cried out, her hips lifting, feet digging into the bed as the shock of the penetration nearly threw her instantly into an orgasm. Inside, waves of pressure began rushing through her, the overwhelming need for release amped up so fast and so hard it radiated like a flame through her.

As she trembled on the edge of orgasm, every cell in her body reaching desperately for it, he eased his fingers back, slowly, retreating from the clenched inner muscles as her hips arched desperately to hold him inside.

"Think it's going to be that easy?" he crooned, easing over her until his lips were touching hers, brushing over them teasingly.

His kiss, when it came, was deep, hungry. A mating of lips and tongues as he used it to hold her locked on that edge of desperate hunger. That place where she could sense her release, but couldn't quite reach it.

When she was panting, fighting for air, his lips slid from hers and moved to her neck. She could feel the rasp of his evening beard, the scrape of his teeth. Poppy arched her neck into the kiss as she felt pleasure exploding along her neck's nerve endings and pulsing through her body.

She moaned, her hands coming up to grip his shoulders as he

placed one of those burning caresses that left his brand on her neck and felt so damned good.

By the time his kisses moved to her breasts, she was shuddering with a need that was almost painful, poised as she was at the edge of an orgasm.

Then his mouth covered a hard, ultra-sensitive nipple, and she swore she would finally slip over the edge. The hard, pulsing strikes of sensation to her womb, her clit, had her back arching, thighs tightening, certain she'd slip over that edge, only to have it back away again.

"No . . ." she moaned, reaching for it, her nails biting at Jack's shoulders, her head thrashing against the bed.

She heard Jack chuckle, though the sound was strained.

Then he was drawing on her nipple, his tongue rasping over it as he slid his hand between her thighs, his fingers sliding through the excess of slick moisture gathered there.

He moved to the other nipple, treated it similarly, until Poppy felt her body was a mass of violent, sensitive nerve endings, each screaming for relief.

As he tormented the hard peaks, his fingers played between her thighs. Stroking, pressing, rubbing against the swollen folds and the tight nubbin of her clit.

She could hear the desperate mewls leaving her throat but couldn't stop them.

He was playing her body like a windup toy. Winding her up, backing off, pulling her from the edge only to push her back again, yet never allowing her to slip over.

His mouth drew harder on her nipples as her need for more sensation grew to an imperative level. She felt his fingers sliding along the ultra-slick folds between her thighs before finding the crease that led to the tinier, nerve-laden entrance below.

Then his touch shifted, moved. It returned, over and over again, spreading yet more slick moisture. Until she finally felt his fingers exerting pressure, separating delicate tissue, and slipping inside.

Her hips lifted, ground into the penetration. She would have begged, pleaded for more, but she couldn't find the breath. The pressure increased, sending white-hot, thrilling flares of intense sensation racing through her.

Then something harder, thicker.

Her eyes opened, focusing on his, staring up into the hot depths of his stormy gaze as he lifted her legs over one arm and she felt the tapered erotic toy slipping into place inside her rear.

A second later, it began to vibrate.

"Jack . . ." she wailed, her hips moving, not knowing if she was trying to escape the sensation or get closer to it.

"Now, baby," he groaned, spreading her thighs wide, using his knees to keep them apart.

Looking down his hard chest, the tight, rippling thighs, she watched as his hand stroked his cock, easing up and down the heavily veined flesh. The head was so tight, so hard, it appeared bruised, the dark shaft throbbing from the blood pumping through his veins.

The vibration in her rear was making her crazy. Her pussy wept with slick heat, the inner muscles clenching with the need to be stretched. To be filled.

"That's it, baby." His voice was a harsh, graveled purr. "Are you burning for me, Poppy?"

"Jack . . . Jack, please . . ." she whimpered, her fingers clenched in the blankets again, nails digging into them as she felt perspiration gathering on her flesh. "I'm burning. I swear."

"Remember this, Poppy," he crooned, though the sound was more of a silky warning. "Keep pushing me, baby. Keep daring me. I can keep you like this all night long. So certain that orgasm you're dying for is just a breath away." He smiled. A tight, satisfied curve of his lips. "But that breath won't come until I let it come."

She shook her head desperately.

"I won't . . . no more . . ." she panted. "Food . . . won't cook . . ."

His eyes narrowed.

"I swear . . . won't . . ." She was ready to cry, she needed to come so bad, but she'd be damned if she was going to beg him.

But she would cook for him. If he'd just let her orgasm.

"Oh baby," he whispered. "You're going to come so hard . . ."

He came over her, pulling one knee up with him and laying it against his hip as Poppy felt the wide crest of his cock pressing against her pussy.

The pleasure . . . Her neck arched, her back bowed as she felt him working the stiff erection inside her. Her pussy clenched, rippled with each inward stroke as the vibration farther back seemed to intensify, to send heated waves of extreme pleasure tearing through her.

She lost herself.

There was no control, no holding on. There was no reality, no sense of time. There were just her cries echoing around her, her hands at his shoulders, desperate to hold on to him, his lips at her neck as he sank to the hilt inside her. The waves of pleasure became rolling shudders of pure sensation. Rapture with an edge. It went beyond pleasure-pain and had her begging.

As he began to thrust inside her, working his cock through the ultra-tight grip she had on him, she felt her senses rushing, gathering at that edge she'd poised on forever.

Then he was holding her closer, groaning her name and fucking her as though the pleasure was as dark, as desperate for him as it had become for her. As the sensations raced and gathered inside her, tightened, and stole her breath, Poppy was certain she'd died.

No one could survive the explosion that imploded inside her.

So much ecstasy, such rapturous intensity couldn't be survivable. It wasn't possible.

She tightened, bucked against him, needing both to escape and to push closer to the fiery center of pure, overwhelming sensation. It tore through her body, her mind, her soul.

She was aware of Jack groaning, a low, fierce sound as he plunged deep, then gave in to his own release.

The heated ejaculations were an added stroke of rapture, extending, radiating the sensations through her.

It seemed to last forever.

When the shudders, the implosions, finally calmed to ripples of sensations rather than the melting, soul-deep rapture they had been, she felt Jack easing back, heard him groaning as her inner muscles continued to clench around his flesh.

The vibrations that had racked her body had ceased, but she couldn't stop the low, aching cry of added pleasure when he drew the toy free of her.

She just wanted to sleep.

Exhaustion edged at her mind, pulling her, threatening to drag her into a sleep deep enough, heavy enough to allow her to forget for a little while that a reckoning was coming.

She didn't want to face a reckoning. Not yet.

There was the feel of a damp cloth, then a dry towel moving over her, cleaning the sweat and their combined releases from her breasts, stomach, and thighs.

Gentleness echoed in every touch, and when she forced her eyes open it was to see his expression softer than she'd ever seen it before.

"Rest, baby," he whispered, leaning down to smooth a kiss over her lips. "Just sleep. There's plenty of time later for other things. Sleep for now."

He eased the sheet and blanket over them as he lay next to her, sharing the warmth of his body, satisfying her need for a touch that kept them connected. Nothing more. Just so she could feel him.

She loved him.

She loved him with her whole heart—she always had. But she wasn't a woman who could ignore the truth or allow herself to live in the darkness of ignorance. There were things she had to know.

Even if it destroyed both of them.

CHAPTER TWENTY

Jack slipped from the bed, careful to cover Poppy, before quickly dressing. Carrying his boots, he eased from the bedroom and closed the door quietly. He stepped into the living room, quickly pulled on his boots, then walked to the basement door, opening it and peering downstairs.

There, Lucas, Hayes, Hank, Ian, and Kira waited, all turning at the sound of the door opening.

Ian and Kira had obviously used the hidden entrance that connected to a drainage system beneath the street.

With a jerk of his head, Jack indicated that they join him.

He was sitting at the table finishing a cold beer as they stepped into the kitchen, looking around curiously.

"She's asleep," he said. "The room's soundproofed, and I can see the door from here. We shouldn't be disturbed."

He twisted the cap off a second beer and stared at Ian as he and Kira made their way to the table.

"Sutton and Baines?" he asked about the two SEALs from the bar.

"Right now, they're watching this place, waiting until you're alone, I presume." Ian grinned faintly. "They'll be gone within the hour. Reno and Clint are currently en route. We may need the two men from your former team, but we're unable to read them into the op just yet; they'll be told enough to keep them contained until they're needed."

Jack nodded.

"Crossfield showed up before I headed for the bar. He wants the name of the team that took out Rollins and the other two mercs. Said he had a job for them." He sneered. "I didn't reveal it was us, but he knew."

It was information Jack had been unable to give Ian while meeting at the bar. Ian's sole purpose had been to make a more public show of meeting with Jack. The decision had been made last minute when word had reached Ian through the Fuentes Cartel that they'd been approached to provide a competent team capable of abducting and holding a female from Barboursville.

Diego Fuentes, at Ian's request, had returned the call personally with a refusal to act against one of his new contractors in any way, and to inform the party requesting the service that Jack would be informed of the call.

"Diego received another call," Ian told him then. "They requested that he reach out to you in regards to a job they had, but they refused to provide details. Diego refused to pass along the information without them."

Jack nodded as he ran the information over in his mind.

"Any further word on the shipments?" he asked.

"All we know is that they're en route," Ian said.

"We did receive additional intel on the design concept of the AI," Kira told them, shaking her head as concern filled her eyes. "What we're getting in can't possibly be true, though. Either our contact is fucking with us, or someone's fucking with him. There's no proof to substantiate the claim, but according to everything coming in, if we can't acquire the AI, then it's unlikely we ever will. The nanoprocessors have what our contact called a 'Chameleon effect.'"

"Meaning?" Hank asked.

"It's not possible." Kira laughed, but the sound was tinged with a fear that maybe . . . "According to the contact, the AI isn't just fully functioning, but sentient. It has awareness. Its capabilities . . ." She shook her head. "If even half of the reports are true, if it possibly escapes, there's no way to identify it again. We'll have a weapon out there that's impossible to identify or to stop."

"Who's the contact?" Jack leaned forward and Hank moved closer to the table.

"Anonymous," she sighed. "So far, all the intel they've provided has completely panned out, though, until the last one. The AI was created and programmed by Gustav, just as we were told. He was a genius. When he disappeared, he left behind some very radical theories in the field of biotech, such as nanotechnology and a way to process electricity into a long-sustaining source of energy."

"They called him insane," Hank mused, glancing at Jack and Kira. "Before their deaths, my parents followed the field of biotechnology and nanotech carefully. They were fascinated by his theories, but they and those they collaborated with agreed the technology to produce it was a century or more away."

"That's right—your parents worked in experimental biotech," Kira seemed to remember.

"Nothing like that," Hank grunted. "They worked in the research and development of organ growth for humans. Biotech is something else entirely. And nanotech." He shook his head. "Sci-fi stuff. And trust me, if he followed his theories, then that AI wasn't shipped here in pieces. It made the drive itself."

"The Army's developed experimental bio-skin and nanotech," Ian stated, frowning at some thought. "Little-known labs in Virginia and Switzerland. They're supposedly at the programming stage of a technology that would enable the nanotech to perform surgeries on what would be fatal wounds in the field. They say it would stabilize soldiers at the very least, until they could reach surgery teams capable of completing the process."

Jack shook his head.

"But nothing like what you've heard. Right?" he asked, the possibilities terrifying.

"Nothing," Kira agreed. "Which makes the reports we're receiving impossible. There's no way AI could be that self-evolving. And no possible way a human consciousness could be transferred or contained in one. It makes a hell of a story, but no way is it realistic."

There was no doubt whatever that what was coming was dangerous, though.

"I'll give Crossfield a few days to a week, see what happens, then contact him." Jack turned to Ian with the plan. "Then I'll let him know we were the ones that made the hit. I'd like to get closer to your contact's deadline now that he knows that bringing another team in isn't going to happen."

"How are you going to explain this to Poppy?" Kira asked. "She didn't look happy with you to begin with."

"She'll have questions when she wakes." He shrugged. "I won't lie to her. But I won't volunteer anything, either. And if need be, I'll let her know it's not something I'm willing to discuss." He tapped a finger on the table as he leaned back in his chair and glanced to the bedroom door. "I would have preferred it to not come to this, though."

"I'll make sure she's covered when you're not with her," Ian promised. "She'll be protected, Jack."

Jack gave a hard nod. She'd better be protected, because he didn't know what he'd do if anything happened to her. It would kill him. Literally.

Poppy came awake slowly, the previous night's events rising in her mind instantly, as well as the questions she knew needed to be asked.

"Poppy," he whispered behind her, his chin brushing against her hair. "Don't ask questions you can't handle right now. Save them for when this is over. Right now, you're going to have a lot to deal with, and decisions to make. Don't make that harder."

"Because you won't lie to me?" she asked him quietly.

"No, not to you," he told her. "I could lie to anyone else, Poppy, and I have, many times. But not to you. Not ever."

He kissed her shoulder, his lips just brushing over her skin, more a comforting gesture than one meant to arouse.

"Why me?" she asked. "Why am I different?"

"Because when everyone else overlooked that scared fourteen-year-old boy, you protected him, ordered him into your home, and made certain he was warm and fed before he was sent back to hell. No one but you had ever done that," he told her. "From that moment on, you were always more to me than anyone else would ever be."

Not because he loved her.

Poppy blinked back her tears, and though she told herself she wasn't surprised, still, she was. And it hurt.

"You've been home over three weeks now," she whispered. "Those men call you 'boss,' like you hired them for some job when you don't seem to have one yourself. Do you have a job I'm unaware of, Jack?"

He was silent for long moments before he stroked her hip with a lingering caress as he pressed a kiss to the top of her head.

"I won't lie to you," he reassured her. "But some things just aren't explainable right now. That's one of them."

"Just as Ian Richards is unexplainable?" she asked him. "A drug cartel's son that you're far too friendly with?"

"Ian's a friend, Poppy. His father is the cartel, not Ian. And that's all I'll say on that," he answered her, and she heard the regret in his voice.

He wouldn't lie to her, he'd promised. Ian was a friend. His father was the cartel. But he didn't say Ian wasn't part of it or associated with it.

"Am I in danger, Jack? Is my family in danger?" To have her family in danger was unacceptable. She couldn't bear that.

"Your life isn't in danger as far as I know," he told her. "And I'm certain your family's aren't." And he believed that, she thought.

She licked her lips nervously and took a deep breath before continuing.

"I have to know about those men that were killed the other day." She swallowed tightly, forcing herself to say the words, despite his warning.

"Poppy . . ." he whispered warningly, but before he could say more, she continued.

"Did they die because of me?" she asked hurriedly before she could chicken out.

He sighed heavily. "I killed them because they were a vicious mercenary group that would have begun kidnapping and killing young girls soon. That's what they do wherever they have a job. When they approached you, I knew it was trouble. You were targeted. Rollins and his men had been hired to abduct you."

She jerked away from him, turning back quickly as she held the sheet to her breasts and staring at him in shock.

Jack rolled to his back, one arm bent and resting beneath his head, the other reaching out to lay against the side of her thigh. His gaze was somber in the dim light, his eyes dark.

"Me?" she whispered, fear causing her breathing to escalate, her heart to pump wildly. "You said I wasn't in danger."

"I took out another two-man team yesterday, mercs as well, with the same intention," he answered her next question, and she hadn't even asked it. "Someone wants leverage against me, we believe, and they've targeted you. I left the message that it was a very bad idea. That simple."

"'That simple'?" she demanded in disbelief. "Where the hell do you see that as simple, Jack?"

His jaw clenched, and his expression hardened.

"Because I took care of it," he informed her, staring up at her with such pure, hard determination that it simply amazed her.

"And if another team shows up?" she demanded.

"No one else is going to show up." And he sounded as though he was certain of that. "But, if another does, it will be taken care of. They know that now."

And she was sure he actually believed it.

Poppy stared back at him, not certain what to believe now or how to feel. She knew Jack would do everything in his power to protect her, and he was a powerful man. But eventually, he would have to blink.

"Jack . . ."

"It's over, Poppy. No one will come after you again. Trust me. I believe the attempt to take you was to hold you in exchange for my agreement to do a job for them, or to stand down while someone else did it. I know who's behind it, and they know I know. And they know I'll kill them if another attempt is made. That simple."

It was that simple? Nothing was that simple.

"And what was last night all about? Is Ian Richards part of this somehow?" She felt like pulling her hair out.

None of this made sense, and he was only confusing her more.

His lips quirked at the question. "No. He wasn't behind it. He's trying to help."

Poppy paused, watching him carefully. His voice or expression didn't change, his body didn't tense, didn't alter in any way, but something told her that Ian Richards was more involved than he was saying.

It was clear he wasn't going to volunteer anything further as he stared back at her, waiting.

"Why did you come back, Jack?" she asked, suspecting the reason might have quite a bit to do with Ian Richards.

"I came back for you, Poppy," he told her, and there was no mistaking the truth in the statement.

Jack watched Poppy carefully, praying she didn't go further in that direction. He'd surprised her with his answer, he knew. He could see her pulse racing, see the surprise in her gaze, in her expression.

If he could keep her just a little off balance, just a little bit longer.

"For me?" she whispered.

Rising, he cupped her cheek and lowered his head to brush his lips over hers. "For you, baby." Pulling back, he rose from the bed and moved to the dresser for clean clothes. "Let's get a shower, then you can go home and get ready for work. If you're going . . ."

"Not today."

Jack turned back to see her shaking her head, her gaze dark with confusion as she watched him.

"Why did I have to come here last night?" she asked, almost distracted by the sight of his well-formed, muscular, completely hot male ass.

The man was seriously ripped, that was all there was to it.

"Because last night, I had two pissed-off SEALs gunning for me, and I didn't want them frightening you. This morning, they've moved on. And I didn't think you'd want all four of us camping out in your house. So, I brought you here." He shrugged as he turned back to her. "Want to shower with me, or at home?"

She shook her head. "At home. I have things to do today."

She was missing something; she knew she was, she just couldn't figure out what.

"Jack?" She stopped him as he neared the bathroom door.

He paused, turning back to her slowly, his expression almost wary.

"Yeah, Poppy?" he asked her. She knew she was missing something. Something important.

"What aren't you telling me?" she asked then, trepidation rising inside her.

Jack gave a small shake of his head. "Poppy, I answered your questions the best way I know how. And I answered them completely." He held his hand out to her. "Come on, baby, shower with me. Just a shower. I know there's not time for anything else."

Reminder of the night before had her body instantly flushing with warmth, and even with renewed desire, despite the tenderness.

What had he done to her?

He'd changed her, she knew that. She'd known that even as her last orgasm had torn through her body and thrown her into a chaos of sensation, pleasure, and soul-deep awareness of him.

Sliding from the bed, she moved across the room, her thigh muscles aching.

"Just a shower," she whispered.

"Just a shower, baby," he promised. "Both of us have things to do."

And why that statement had her chest tightening and a shadow of fear darkening her emotions, she was actually terrified to speculate about.

CHAPTER TWENTY-ONE

He was hiding something from her. Poppy knew it. Sensed it. She just didn't know the questions to ask to find out exactly what he was hiding.

Or why. It was the why that actually bothered her.

After she showered, Poppy dressed in the jeans, blouse, and boots from the night before and, with Jack walking beside her, returned home. She was aware of him waiting for her as she changed into clean clothes once she got inside.

She wasn't due at work today, but she was still working. Being at home would allow her the peace to make sense of the papers she'd brought with her.

Jack was still waiting when she returned to the living room, dressed in comfortable cotton pants and a sleeveless shirt. Barefoot, she walked into the kitchen and went immediately to the coffeepot. She needed caffeine. She needed to clear her mind of the sex, Jack's effect on her, and all the questions she had for just a little while.

"I'll be back this evening," he told her, moving into the kitchen behind her.

"Do you have more mercenaries to kill?" she snorted, crossing her arms over her breasts and leaning against the counter as she watched him.

His lips quirked, a shadow of amusement touching his gaze.

"You don't sound nearly as offended as you should, sugar," he drawled.

Poppy shrugged. She could be pragmatic when she had to be. "I trust they were really bad men."

She'd met one of them, and everything inside her had recoiled.

"They were," he confirmed.

He stood in the center of her kitchen like a damned conquering warrior or something. Blue jeans and biker boots, and a T-shirt that stretched across that wide-assed chest of his.

"You should be fucking illegal," she muttered, looking back to the coffeepot. "That aside. It's not the fact that they're dead, Jack, or how bad they may have been." She turned back to him after activating the coffee maker. "It's the cost to you that I worry about. To your soul. Because you're a good man. A damned good man, and I can't see how it could not affect you."

Jack stared back at her, shocked.

Hell, he could deal with her inability to handle the idea of the kill. He could deal with her being unable to understand that need for that kill. But neither bothered her. It was him and the effect on him that worried her.

Damn. He swore something melted in his chest. Right there in the center where he had once sworn he didn't have a heart. Where countless military doctors had assured him no heart resided. He felt that nonexistent heart melt.

"Poppy, those weren't men." Frowning back at her, in discomfort, Jack scratched at an itch that wasn't really there along his neck. "Those were monsters. A man doesn't feel guilty for taking out the monsters of the world. It's a woman's job to regret the need for it, maybe. But it's my job to do it."

She kept looking at him with those sad green eyes, her hair a riot of curls around her face, her expression so concerned he had no idea how to deal with it. Hell. It wasn't the first time she'd left him feeling like this. It probably wouldn't be the last time. That feeling that someone deeply, genuinely cared about the man he was inside.

He knew women liked him. Knew he had a body, at the moment, that made them salivate to say that he belonged to them. Like a trophy. And that was how he'd often felt when taking a lover. Like a trophy to be acquired until the next one came along.

But no one other than Poppy had ever made him feel like she viewed him from the inside out, rather than seeing the outside only.

"Yes, men like that are monsters," she agreed. "But even monster slayers have nightmares, Jack."

Hell, she was serious. And he had no idea how to combat that.

"My nightmares have nothing to do with anything I've done as an adult," he assured her, stepping across the room to where he could cup her shoulders in his hands, feel her flesh against his. "Poppy, I could bathe in the blood of anyone that dared to attempt to hurt you and step out of it feeling good about myself and what I'd done."

"Jack . . ." She shook her head, clearly doubting him.

"Do you know there's more than one military doctor out there that considers me a sociopath?" He stepped away from her, watching as her eyes widened in surprise at his statement.

"Excuse me?" Disbelief filled her words, and she gave a short laugh. "A what?"

"More than one," he repeated, nodding as he leaned against the center island, surprised that he felt uncomfortable, even nervous, revealing that to her. "Antisocial personality disorder and a complete lack of empathy. According to them my strengths lie in the fact that I have a clear understanding of right and wrong and seem determined to adhere to it. But they're wrong about that."

"They're wrong about quite a bit," she argued. "That's bullshit, Jack."

He shook his head. "No, baby, it's not." And he could admit that to her. "You're the difference here. You always have been. The night I killed Toby Bridger, I lost my ability to give a fuck in most cases. But not my ability to understand empathy, or to feel love. Because you see, earlier that day, I saw that there was more than just evil in the world. You and your parents showed me more than I could ever explain to you. A far different world than I believed existed. One far different from the one I lived in."

He'd learned lessons that day that only in the past few weeks had he realized he'd learned.

That dinner recently at her parents' house, when he'd faced not just her parents but all her siblings and their children, he'd slowly begun realizing the impact those few hours in her parents' home when he was fourteen had had on him.

All because of one little girl. A girl who was a woman now. And that woman could make his heart melt with the simplest of ways.

"So, trust me, Poppy," he said when she didn't speak. "I will cut the head from any monster that even considers hurting you or yours. And I will never lose a moment's sleep over it."

She still didn't say anything, but the tears that began gathering in her eyes actually had the power to terrify him. Until she all but ran to him and threw her arms around his neck, holding tight to him.

His arms surrounded her despite the tightness he felt at his throat, his chest. Goddamn, this woman could make him feel things he had no idea how to identify or control. She was his light in the dark, always guiding him, always ensuring he didn't lose his way.

It had always been Poppy who kept his ass on the straight and narrow as he matured. He'd lived in fear that she'd fall in love, and marry; and if she had, he could have handled it, he told himself. He would probably have been less determined to not catch a fatal bullet when he fought, but he would have never hurt her. Never hurt someone she loved.

This precious little flame, for this moment, was all his. And when it was over, and she hated him, reviled him for deceiving her, she'd still be his light in the dark.

"They're so wrong about you. And you're wrong," she whispered against his chest. "Hiding from emotion and not having any are two different things, Jack Lee Bridger. And I hope one of these days, you realize that."

His lips quirked on a sad smile.

Oh, he realized it, because he'd realized a long time ago he loved one person in this world, and one person only.

The gentle, far too tender flame he held in his arms.

She was his heart, a part of his soul. The word "love" was far too paltry for what he felt. And there was no other word that he'd ever heard that could describe it.

She was his. That plain. That simple. For now.

And that was all that mattered.

"You shouldn't have to kill to protect me, Jack," she whispered, stepping back from him, her hand lifting to touch his cheek.

He caught her hand, pressed his lips to her palm, then cupped her face in his hands and lowered his lips to hers.

"I'm your monster slayer, baby," he told her, continuing to stare into her eyes. "Always."

He brushed his lips against hers again, released her, and quickly walked to the door and out of the house. If he stayed, he'd soon have her lying across the damned kitchen island, driving them both crazy.

He ached for her, even after last night. There was something about her that kept him hungry, kept him coming back to her. Kept him regretting the truth he knew would be revealed all too soon.

CHAPTER TWENTY-TWO

She was changing him.

Jack watched Poppy with her friends a week later from the bar, where he stood drinking a beer, feeling that heaviness in his chest that he felt whenever he allowed himself to dwell on the fact that the day was quickly approaching that she'd know what he'd done.

Lied to her, used her to get to her friends.

From the corner of his eye, he watched Caine Crossfield as he sat at a table and began to chat with Dawson's sister, Saige. Her hair was shorter than the other girls', cut to frame her slender face and emphasize the tilt of her brown eyes. She looked like an impish teenager.

There was a wry smile that played about her lips, a knowing expression. She wasn't flirting with Crossfield, but she was teasing him. Silently laughing at him, perhaps.

Caine glanced toward the bar, not for the first time, and Saige turned to talk to Lilith. But Lilith wasn't taking her eyes off Hank, as he danced with a young woman who had teasingly invited him to the dance floor.

Standing, Caine indicated his empty glass, then turned and headed toward the bar.

Jack had been watching him each evening as the group gathered at the bar for dinner. Biding his time, waiting. Jack had wondered just how long the other man would wait before making his move.

Two merc groups had contacted Jack through the week with reports of an offer, but no details. The fact that there were no details and that word had circulated that two groups had died here had ensured the offers were turned down.

Word that four former Navy SEALs, even if dishonorably discharged, were working as a unit in the area had gotten around. Only the most arrogant, the most stupid, would have gone up against them for the limited profit that would come of it. Word of the strike by unknown assailants against Mick Candless's team had circulated as well. Word was, Jack's team was in the clear as far as suspicion was concerned; suspicion was turning to whoever had put the job out.

The offers weren't high enough to make the risk worth it now without full disclosure of the job up for grabs.

"Bridger." Caine stepped in beside him, placed his empty glass on the bar, and turned toward Jack. "You're making it hard for a man to find good employees since you came back."

Play time was over, it seemed.

Jack grunted at the accusation. "So I hear."

"I know you and your men are the group I'm looking for," Caine stated, barely loud enough for Jack to hear. "Are you ready to talk yet?"

Was he ready to talk yet?

"You order the Candless team taken out?" he asked Crossfield, watching from the corner of his eye as confusion crossed Caine's face.

"They turned the job down before any details were given. Why the fuck would I do something so asinine?" he growled.

Jack looked over at Poppy again. She was talking to Sasha about something, and the discussion seemed intense.

"What does it have to do with Poppy?" he questioned Crossfield. "You know if she's threatened again, I'll come after you. Right?" He let his gaze connect with Crossfield's then. "And I'll make you hurt, man. Bad."

Crossfield grimaced. "I agreed to that little plan reluctantly. It was a mistake, I have to admit. But she wouldn't have been hurt, Jack. Just held for a while until you did a little job for me. And you would have been compensated handsomely."

Jack wanted to kill him. Right then. Right there. He wanted to pull his knife and slice the bastard's throat.

"Rollins and his men would have raped her, multiple times. Disfigured her. And when you ordered her release—if you ordered it—they would have sliced her throat and moved out. The money you're offering isn't enough to leave witnesses. Or to keep them unharmed." Jack poured himself another shot of whiskey from the bottle at his elbow. "He only took the job because he knew the woman was mine. The other team might have been nicer, but not by much." He threw back the shot and relished the burn that tore its way down his throat.

God, he wanted to kill this bastard!

"Do you want the job, or do I keep looking?" Crossfield asked, his tone indicating he was out of patience. "If I have to keep looking, you stand down or Poppy will pay the price."

Crossfield was weak, Jack thought. He wasn't the brains behind this operation; someone else was pulling his strings.

"Raise the offer by forty percent, and I want full disclosure of the job," Jack stated. "For some reason, you're just willing to hire men to kidnap my woman to ensure I take a job. That means it's more than just a little dangerous."

The time for games was over. Crossfield had made his move, and that was all they'd been waiting for. Had Jack gone to him or admitted his group had taken the teams out at the first meeting, he would have never been trusted. Sometimes, playing hard to get was the only way to get in.

"Forty percent?" Anger tinged Crossfield's voice as he hissed the question. "You don't even know what the job is."

"I know it was important enough that you were willing to use a woman to get to me." Jack shrugged. "And I don't trust you to ensure Poppy's safety. But the Fuentes Cartel is willing to do that for me. At a hugely discounted price. Ian Richards is partial to dishonorably discharged SEALs."

Crossfield turned and stared at the top of the bar as the bartender set a beer in front of him.

"Richards was an unforeseen complication," he grunted. "Without the Fuentes Cartel, I think you would have been a bit less confident in yourself."

Jack gave a low bark of laughter. "You don't know me well at all. But you keep thinking that."

Crossfield's lips twisted with an edge of humor. "It does bring me comfort, I must admit."

Jack wasn't in the mood for a bonding session.

"How long will the job last?" he asked Crossfield.

"A week. Two at the most." Crossfield picked up the glass and brought it to his lips for a long drink. "I can't give you details just yet, but all you'll be doing is providing backup to an individual, and distraction. The main operation will be taken care of by one person. And I can't tell you anything further right now."

Can't or won't? Jack wondered.

"When?" he asked.

"You'll meet with your employer in two days. I'd stash Poppy with friends tomorrow evening if I were you, mostly because I suspect there's another interested party out there somewhere that was behind taking out Candless's team, and that was a serious warning. You'll be heading to the meeting before daybreak the next day,"

Crossfield stated. "I'm just the middleman, Jack. I can secure the amount you're asking, simply because I know you're the man they want for the job. But it won't be easy. I was just the man assigned to make certain you could be trusted."

Once again, Jack shrugged. "And I didn't appreciate having my woman threatened. She's useful to me at the moment. You are not. And neither is your interested party. I'd get the message across if I were you."

She was his soul. If something happened to her, then Jack wouldn't kill Crossfield fast. He'd make it last. For days. And he'd make damned sure the other man begged to die before delivering the killing blow.

"Get her to Ian Richards's tomorrow and wait for my call," Crossfield reiterated. "I'll meet you at the camping area about a mile and half from exit twenty-eight to Milton thirty minutes before daybreak. I'll be waiting for you."

Taking his beer, Crossfield ambled away as though they'd been discussing no more than the weather.

So, if Crossfield wasn't the employer, then who the hell was? It was a question he'd have to be certain to discuss with Ian.

Poppy didn't know what time it was when she awakened later that night, but she knew she wasn't alone, as she had been when she'd gone to bed.

Jack had brought her home, promising to return after he talked to his men. She'd gone to sleep waiting for him.

She knew who was holding her so close to his body. The heavy weight over her waist, holding her to him, was Jack's arm. The steady, subtle thump at her back was the beat of his heart. And then there was that settled sense of well-being inside her. Inside, she felt warm, content, and secure.

She'd never felt so completely warm, so much a part of some-body else and yet so intensely aroused. She knew it could have something to do with the heavy length of his erection pressing so firmly against her rear. The hot, hard shaft and the knowledge that Jack was awake behind her had every nerve ending burning for him. Just the touch of him behind her, his naked chest and muscular legs tucked close behind hers, combined with the proof of his need for her, had her body heating, needing.

He had no idea how many times she'd masturbated, fought for release, and cried out his name as she came so close, so very close. And now, waking next to him, stepping from dreams to him—she could feel that overwhelming need only rising harder, hotter inside her.

She'd waited so long for him, dreamed of him, tortured herself with the belief that she'd never see him again, and that the hunger for his touch wasn't going to go away anytime soon.

And she loved him. She loved him with all her heart and every fragile dream she ever had.

"I know you're awake." His voice was a rumbled growl, drowsy and hinting at amusement.

"So I am," she agreed, fighting to keep her breathing normal despite the hard, desperate racing of her heart. "And you're defi-nitely awake."

Her breathing caught, tension immediately tightening through-out her body as his fingers gripped the material of her sleep shirt and began to tug it up.

"I can't breathe anymore without remembering your scent, your taste," he whispered at her ear. "I could take you now, Poppy, and ten minutes later be aching for you again."

Poppy whimpered as her stomach tightened in a hard spasm, and her breath caught as she felt the pressure swamp her. It was dizzying, flooding her body with heat and need.

"Oh, baby girl," he crooned as the response shuddered through her. "Here. Turn over for me. Let me see what else I can do for you."

She was so lost, and she knew it.

She followed as he eased her to her back, lifted her arms as he disposed of her shirt.

Her nipples tightened to pebble-hard peaks, her clit swelling to such sensitivity that the brush of her pajama bottoms against it was torture.

As the shirt cleared her head, Jack didn't give her a chance to think, or to consider anything further. He hovered over her, all powerful, corded muscle and bronze flesh. His head tilted, his lips covered hers, and nothing else mattered but his kiss, his touch.

Greedy, starving for him, Poppy's hands stroked his shoulders, his back. She could feel the muscle rippling beneath his chest, the toughness of his flesh, his body heat inside her. She loved the feel of him, the pleasure, the heat.

His kiss was a little rough, filled with male hunger. His touch was pure pleasure, his hand stroking up her side, cupping a breast, his thumb finding the incredibly sensitive nipple and rasping over it with sizzling heat. It sent arcs of sensation to her clit, causing her vagina to weep in need.

Deep, hard kisses drew hungry moans from her and harsh groans from him. The deep, powerful kisses rocked her to the core. They mesmerized her, filled her with arousal, had her aching to hold this moment in time for as long as possible.

"Jack," she cried out as his lips slid from hers to brush over her jaw, his teeth scraping her flesh erotically.

"Damn, Poppy, I love the taste of you," he muttered, his voice a rasp, his kisses rough and hungry as they moved to her neck.

His tongue licked at her sensitive flesh; his lips took stinging kisses that she knew would leave marks later.

Knew but didn't care.

Tipping her head back on the pillows, she gave him better access even as she writhed in a pleasure so incredible she didn't know how to combat it. But she knew she'd crave more of it, that she'd die longing for it and for him.

"Don't stop," she demanded when his head lifted and he leaned back. Forcing her eyes open, she stared at him, loving the dark, dominant, roughly handsome face. She'd never met another man who could compare to him. No other man could rival him.

"Damn, how pretty," he whispered, both hands cupping her breasts and rasping the hard nipples. "And they taste so sweet."

His head lowered, his lips covered one tight peak and immediately drank it in with deep draws of his mouth.

Poppy's back arched, her hands digging into the bedsheets, her thighs clenching tight as sizzling bolts of sensations in her clit sent moisture spilling from her pussy.

Immediately he moved to her other nipple, sucking it in and drawing on it hungrily. He didn't stay on one breast overly long, but moved from one to the other, sensitizing them further as she cried out with such pleasure that she wasn't certain she could survive it. She was going to orgasm, the pleasure was so intense. Yet no matter how close it seemed, she couldn't quite catch that edge she needed to slip into ecstasy.

"Poppy," he groaned, his lips smoothing between her breasts as he used one hand to push at her pajama bottoms and drag them over her hips. "Ah, baby."

Seconds later she kicked them free of her feet, uncaring where they ended up. His lips at her nipples were driving her crazy, making the hunger for them to be between her thighs nearly unbearable.

"That's it, baby girl." The hard growl sent excitement racing through her. "Burn for me, Poppy."

Burn for him? She was blazing out of control.

"Jack, please," she gasped, arching toward him as he pushed his knee between hers and spread kisses between her breasts, slowly moving lower.

His hand stroked along one thigh before gripping it, tugging at it to spread her legs farther apart.

Oh God, he needed to hurry. Every time they came close to him taking her, someone, or something, disturbed them, interrupted them.

"Oh, baby girl, I'm gonna taste that pretty pussy again." His voice dark, hungry, he kissed his way down her midriff. "Fuck that sweet pussy with my tongue. Feel you come on it. You gonna come on my tongue again, Poppy?"

Her stomach clenched in a hard spasm, her thighs tightened, and her juices spilled to meet his fingers as they stroked along the narrow slit, slicking them as her hips lifted to caress them.

"Jack." Desperation echoed in her voice as his fingers pushed at the entrance, pushed inside just enough to almost trigger the orgasm she needed so desperately.

"So fucking tight." He nipped at her lip, licked the sting, and moved lower.

She could feel his breath against her perspiration-damp flesh, rapid and heated.

Her thighs fell farther apart as his kisses, his tongue met the bend of her thigh, slid to just above her clit. There he kissed the little rise of flesh, his breath striking at the bundle of nerves just below her hips. She was fighting to breathe. Pleasure was wreaking havoc with her senses and her body. She felt intoxicated, drunk on his kisses, his touch.

His lips moved lower, his tongue stroking against her clit, sending spikes of dagger-sharp pleasure to strike inside her pussy. Her hips jerked, ached. She fought to make sense of what his touch did to her, what it did to cause pleasure to burn, to blaze through her senses.

She was dying to orgasm, and on the verge of pleading with him.

Then, rather than just licking around her clit and driving her insane with each lash of his tongue, he decided to deliver a sucking kiss to the bundle of nerve endings.

Almost . . .

Poppy cried out as she almost flew free into orgasm, only to be jerked from the edge.

"No. Jack . . . Not again . . . Don't you do this to me again," she demanded, the overwhelming need for that rush of ecstasy shuddering through her. "Oh, God . . ." Her head thrashed on the pillows as those diabolical fingers barely penetrated her, stroked her inner flesh, rubbing inside her and sending sparks to explode behind her closed eyes.

Just when she was certain she couldn't bear the exquisite pleasure any longer, his mouth covered her throbbing clit, his tongue lashing it. His fingers penetrated her, retreated, pushed deep, parted her flesh, stretched it.

And she exploded.

Her hips jerked, ached. Her vagina clamped down on his fingers and, as shudders raced over her, Poppy felt rapture explode inside her. It filled her senses, whipped over her body.

She was barely aware of his mouth releasing her clit and his fingers pulling free of her. She felt him come over her, and as the tremors racing through her began to ease, she felt the broad head of his cock begin to press inside her.

"Poppy, baby . . ." he groaned. "Ah, hell. Sweet Poppy."

His gaze, heavy-lidded and intense, held hers as his expression tightened with each shallow thrust inside her.

"Hold on to me, baby," he whispered, one hand gripping her thigh as she arched to him.

"Jack." His name was a gasp of stinging pleasure and emotional upheaval.

"That's it, baby. Give it to me."

She felt his muscles bunch, felt the hold on her thigh tighten, and a second later he thrust inside her, hard and deep. Her body arched, a keening moan leaving her throat as she felt every hard, shockingly hot inch of male flesh stretching her, filling her with heat and so much pleasure. Pleasure that bordered on pain and sent flames rippling through her entire body.

"That's it, baby," he snarled from somewhere above her ear. "Hold on to me."

That was all she was capable of doing.

Her nails bit into his upper arms as she arched to him, moving against him as he thrust inside her, retreated, and returned. The feeling of him moving inside her was incredible. It was like this every time, each time he took her, each time he filled her.

"Jack . . ." she gasped, fighting for breath, for air, as she arched against him, the white-hot sensations overwhelming her senses.

The sensitive inner muscles clenched around him, stretched to their limit, and revealing nerve endings that rioted in excited stimulation. He stroked each one of them as he moved inside, pushing her hard, filling her with that incredible drive to ecstasy.

Each throb of the thick stalk of flesh echoed along her pussy, each fierce penetration stroked her, burying inside her, possessing her and burning wild inside her.

Oh God, she never wanted it to end. She wanted this forever: to hold it, to hold him, forever inside her. Her pussy clenched around him with every hard thrust, fighting to hold him inside.

She could feel his cock burrowing inside her, the thick crest parting her inner flesh as he thrust to the hilt repeatedly. Plunging deep, hard, he sent ecstasy careening inside her, building the sensation to a completion she knew would change her forever.

His erection shafted inside her, nearly bruising in its width, an iron-hard presence filling her with such incredible, completely radiant pleasure, building inside her, overtaking her.

One minute she was fighting to hold back the cataclysm she knew was coming, and in the next instant it had her.

Poppy was only barely aware of her teeth locking on Jack's upper arm. As keening cries escaped her throat, her back arched and complete, burning ecstasy exploded along every nerve ending in her body. Shudders raced through her, over her, as wave after wave tore through her.

She felt him thrust deep again, and his cock throbbed harder as the waves of chaos coalesced into a blinding, white-hot ribbon of pure sensation.

"I love you . . ." she whispered. "So much, Jack. I love you."

He didn't say the words back, but that was okay, she told herself. He cared, and for Jack, that was more than any other man's greatest vows of devotion.

"You're mine, Poppy," he told her, his breathing still harsh as he rolled beside her and pulled her into his arms. "Remember that. Mine."

Yeah, she was his.

This man who believed he didn't have a heart, who believed he couldn't feel emotion as others did, but whom she knew cared for her. And for now, she'd accept that.

CHAPTER TWENTY-THREE

Caine closed himself in the silence of his home, teeth clenching with restrained fury. He wanted nothing more than to slice open Bridger's throat, as the other man had sliced Rollins and his team.

Bastard.

He'd known when he heard Bridger had arrived in Barboursville early for his summer visit home that it was going to be trouble. Even though he'd been expecting it for the past several years, he'd hoped the SEAL would put it off just one more year. Hell, just one more month. Six weeks at the most.

Instead, he'd arrived right in the middle of one of the most dangerous and profitable jobs he'd ever taken. This one would have set him up for life. No more risking his reputation or his life. He and his partner had decided this would be the final job, simply because they were fighting against technology that was becoming more advanced by the year and making Homeland Security more efficient in locating and catching those trying to work in ways that didn't suit their so-called laws.

If he could pull this job off, then that could change, but still, he wanted out. He was nearly forty. He needed to settle down, maybe have a few kids. A man who took the risks he took had no business having a family. Wives got suspicious, they mentioned things, they became a weakness. He didn't want to have to kill the woman he chose to have his children. And he didn't want one that was a part of those risks, either.

As soon as Bridger and the three men riding with him had arrived, his employer had demanded they be offered the contract. Crossfield didn't trust Jack and his men, and neither did his partner. He was a wild card: violent, yes, without mercy, definitely, but there was something about the man that Caine had never liked.

His employer was making this particular job a pain in the ass, too. The money to be gained would make it worth it. Even the first third, already deposited in his overseas account, was enough to retire on. The rest, though . . . It would make him nearly untouchable.

He pulled his mobile phone from inside his jacket, stared at it for moment, then made the call he'd been putting off since getting in the car.

"Crossfield." The voice was cool, female. No accent, but smooth and sensual all the same. "Have you made the offer as you were asked to do?"

He breathed out heavily. "Are you certain about this team?" he asked. "It wouldn't take long to get someone else in if we offer the right amount of money."

Silence filled the line for a moment. "Is there something I should know where the Bridger team is concerned? Something you haven't reported yet?"

"I've reported everything," he assured her, the anger in his tone impossible to hide. "But I'm telling you, the woman he's sleeping with has been poking her nose into things that shouldn't concern her. If she becomes involved, he'll be loyal to her."

"Bridger will do exactly as he's supposed to do, I promise you that," she stated calmly. "I know these men, Mr. Crossfield. They are exactly what I need. Acquire them quickly. Once the AI is fully powered, everything will need to be in place. If it isn't, it will be your life on the line. Are we clear about that?"

He wiped his hand down his face and stared at the bar, wishing there was some way to kill the bastard and get away with it.

"We're clear," he agreed.

He had no other choice.

"Very well. Contact me once things are ready to proceed," he was told before the call abruptly ended.

If he had his way, he'd just kill Bridger and be done with it. The man wasn't dependable, no matter his employer's opinion.

CHAPTER TWENTY-FOUR

"I'll pick you up after work today," Jack said as Poppy put her cup in the coffee maker the next morning and popped a pod in the chamber for her second cup of coffee.

"I'm not going in this morning," she told him, glancing over her shoulder. "I decided to work from home today so I can get some peace and quiet."

Some privacy, she hoped.

"Do that often?" he asked, his tone sounding just a little suspicious.

She laughed as she turned back to him. "Whenever I feel like it, I do. Even Caine and River don't question me over it."

The man was more suspicious than even her brothers.

"Sorry." His lips quirked just the slightest.

"You said there was no other danger, right?" she asked.

"I took care of it." He gave a firm nod. "If you're not working, I'll come straight here, then. I'd like to take you out to dinner tonight."

Dinner?

"Sounds good," she said, nodding. "The bar?"

"A nice place," he growled. "Dress pretty. I have things to do this morning, but I'll see you about five," he promised, striding to her and dropping a quick kiss on her lips. "Be good, baby."

Be good?

She watched him leave the house, frowning. She couldn't help the feeling that there was something going on. Or was it just her imagination?

Suspecting him because she was beginning to suspect others in her life?

Breathing out at the thought, Poppy turned to the window and watched Jack stride across the yard, out the back gate, and to the motorcycles, where the others were gathering.

She'd wanted to ask where he was going, what he was doing, but something stopped her. Just as something had stopped her when she was going to ask a week ago, about the drifter that attacked her nine years ago.

She was having trouble asking him the hard questions, and she was going to have to do something about that. The hard questions were the ones she needed to ask him.

Just like she needed to ask what the hell was going on at the office, she thought with a heavy sigh.

Collecting her cup of coffee, she returned to the living room and picked up her briefcase before moving to the kitchen island. She pulled the stack of files she'd placed inside the briefcase the day before and sat down at the table.

Her job was to inspect and manage all commercial and residential properties of Crossfield-Dawson. She was supposed to be part of any contracts negotiated and/or signed. But there were three units that were unlisted on the property database, the signature on the files unintelligible, that she'd found buried in a box of property tax notices, inspection forms, and aerial photos that had been mistakenly placed in her office, rather than in River's or Caine's.

There had been a file for three units about ten miles from town. According to the aerial photographs, it was in a small valley, three miles from the main road, and heavily secured.

So heavily secured that even from the photo she could pinpoint the secured gate, ten feet tall from the appearance of it, with a security box next to it. A very secure security box; that was no simple lock attached to the posts.

What the fuck!

Parked in the corner of two of the units was River's super-duty black pickup, with a white van next to it.

The picture was dated two weeks ago and sent by a private aerial security firm as having been requested.

To her knowledge, no one had requested any aerial photographs of any property. That was usually her job, anyway.

She went through each file, searching for contracts involving the property. Every initial projected purchase to every property the company owned was in the first file. Every aerial or on-ground photograph was in a second. And there was absolutely no record of that property.

There was River's truck, though, the aerial photographs, and the assurance of a friend at the courthouse that the property was indeed in Crossfield-Dawson's name. And Susan had been very adamant that Poppy not reveal that it had been her who'd given her that information.

Picking up her smartphone, she checked the messages from her friend once again to be certain.

Property is in C & D ownership for sure! Susan had texted and listed the address to identify it was the right property.

And it didn't make sense.

Pulling up her tablet, she checked the database she had on her hard drive, then the printout of the database from the office. The address wasn't on either.

Shifting through the tax records and other papers, she couldn't find any other mention of or reference to the unlisted property. All she had was the photograph, which included proof of security that would make Gordon Tessalon salivate with pure envy.

So where had the property come from and why was River trying to cover it up?

Several long hours later, after poring over the files yet again, she gave up. That property was not listed with the company anywhere but at the courthouse. But why would it be listed there if someone wanted to hide it? It made zero sense and only confused Poppy further.

Tapping her finger next to the phone, she considered calling River, asking him why, but just as with the questions she wanted to ask Jack, something held her back.

She could call Saige, but her friend would do the same thing Poppy was hesitant to do: She'd ask her brother about it.

Maybe she should just ride out there, she thought. It wouldn't take long. She could survey the property, find out what was there, and figure out what the property was being used for.

Because this was crazy. Why would River try to hide a piece of property from the company? The legalities alone would be a mess. If Caine found out about it, he could dissolve the partnership and take everything. And possibly have River convicted as well.

She typed the address into a search engine on her laptop, but couldn't find much information there either.

The questions were going to drive her crazy. The implications of the problems it could cause if she questioned anyone at the company were too numerous to begin to think about.

An on-site visit was the only way to make certain the aerial pictures and the address matched. Because there had to be some mistake here. Somewhere, somehow. And before she asked anyone about it, she had to know more.

Moving from the table before she could change her mind, Poppy hurried to her bedroom to change clothes for the trip. It just pissed her off that River might have used the company to buy property without listing it. Three units of that size, with security that extensive, would be a hell of a monthly income.

But she couldn't imagine River would embezzle from the company. That just wasn't the man she knew. Now Caine, she could actually see doing it. There was something not entirely trustworthy where he was concerned. She loved him to death, but suspected he wasn't always honest when it came to the company finances.

It was almost one now. She'd spent hours poring over those papers and hadn't even realized it. She would have just enough time, if she left now, to check out the location, then return home and get ready for that dinner date.

Twenty minutes later, dressed in jeans, sneakers, and T-shirt, she hurried from the back door to the SUV, the information she needed in a file she carried.

In another minute or so she pulled from the alley and headed for the interstate. Half hour at the most, she thought. She'd check it out, then know exactly what was going on.

Ian and Kira's rented home sat on a hill overlooking Barboursville. All wood and steel and huge windows that were a security nightmare. Jack and his men stepped inside that afternoon, certain the SEAL turned cartel leader's son was going to drive him crazy before this operation was finished.

Windows dominated the living area, the view over the town breathtaking. Ian stood in front of one of those windows as he watched Jack and his men step into the room.

"Why the urgent message?" Jack asked him. "I thought we discussed everything last night?"

Ian grimaced at the question.

"We received word minutes before I messaged you that both shipments made it into our area. We don't know where they're located yet. They evaded the teams tracking them somehow." Ian shook his head. "I'm waiting on more information now."

Jack stared at him. He couldn't say he was shocked, or surprised. He'd expected it, unfortunately. He nodded slowly. "We knew when Crossfield made his move that it would be soon."

"Which means the AI will be powered and the Chameleon nanotech, if it exists, functioning," Lucas pointed out. "Taking it apart will be impossible if it escapes."

Jack's gaze narrowed on Ian.

"We have someone that will be able to keep it stationary and deactivate it if we can reach it before it reaches full power," Kira said as she stepped forward, her expression firm, determined. "We have to find that AI before that happens."

"According to Crossfield, I meet the employer just before daybreak in the morning. I'll be bringing Poppy here this evening. You'll have to make sure she stays," he told Ian. "If anything happens to her . . ."

"Don't," Ian warned, his voice low. "I know what losing her would mean for you, Jack . . ."

At that moment, a strident notice of a text came through on Ian's smartphone. Frowning, he pulled it from his pocket, his face hardening as fury flickered over his expression.

Jack looked at the screen and felt that presence of danger he'd been feeling for days wash over him.

You're out of time, Mr. Richards. The unit is in place. All parts are assembled. Power capacitors will be operational soon.

Ian stared at the text message in shock, his gaze jerking to Jack's. Turning his attention to the phone, Ian typed in his reply.

Your time line said at least two weeks further! Ian typed quickly.

> And unfortunately, I was wrong. Assembly has been
> completed. Power is attached.

Where? Where can I find it?

Ian pushed his fingers through his hair as Jack stared at the message, barely holding back the need to take the phone from Ian and throw it at the wall.

> Location unknown at this time . . . Warehouse facility . . .
> Civilian in danger . . . Find the warehouse. You should
> hurry, Mr. Richards.

Who is the civilian?

> Her name is Porter. Poppy Octavia Porter. You should
> hurry . . . Before she dies.

His head jerked up, his gaze connecting with Jack's. For one second, two.

Jack's gaze went from merely calm—not unemotional, but not exactly readable, either—to pure, stone-cold killer. His eyes became icy blue, his expression hardened to granite.

"You have a tracker on her phone?" he asked Jack.

As he spoke, Jack was pulling his phone free of his vest.

"I have her last location. The exit I was directed to meet Caine at tomorrow." He turned, gesturing to Lucas before striding quickly away.

"Why would she be there?" Ian questioned quickly.

Jack thought desperately. His mind going over everything she'd said that morning and the night before.

"She brought a briefcase home with her. She would only be there if it was business-related," he told Ian. "We'll ride to the exit. Get one of your men to the house to go through those papers. See if they'll give us a clue about where she was heading."

He didn't have time to wait.

"Jack, wait." Ian jumped in front of him, blocking his exit from the room. "I need that fucking location . . ."

As Ian spoke, his phone buzzed with a message. Looking down, he saw the message box and location attached. When he looked back up, Jack was racing through the door with three other former SEALs on his ass. And Ian knew that if he didn't hurry, this was going to be bad. Very, very fucking bad.

She was groggy.

Poppy felt awareness slowly awakening inside her, and with it the knowledge that she was in serious trouble.

Forcing her eyes open, she fought past the bleariness of her sight and the headache building at the back of her head. When she tried to lift her hand to feel the tender area, she realized her hands were restrained. She'd been placed in a chair, and not a very comfortable one, with her wrists and ankles tied to the arms and legs.

When her sight finally cleared, she found herself in the warehouse she'd come to check out. And she wasn't alone.

In the center of a walled-off partition of the warehouse stood three tall, lighted stations, with wires running from the ground. Standing in the center of them was a young woman. Blond hair pulled into a low ponytail, blue eyes, no more than five-four. She was dressed in jeans tucked into worn leather boots that went to her knees, a T-shirt, and a brown leather bomber jacket.

She stood still and silent, unblinking and without expression. And staring straight at Poppy.

"Hello?" Poppy called out tentatively.

Something flickered in the young woman's eyes.

"Are you okay?" Poppy asked with concern, looking around again, trying to figure out exactly what was going on.

"She can't hear you, and wouldn't speak to you even if she could."

Poppy's head swung around, and she watched in shock as Saige walked into the room.

"Saige? Saige, hurry, untie me." Poppy tugged at her bonds, even as she felt the dark, oily shadow of knowledge slipping through her consciousness. "Saige?"

Saige's lips turned down a bit in false regret as she walked toward Poppy. Dressed in a snug, short black skirt and short-sleeved blue blouse with the high heels she preferred, Saige was as pretty as ever, but this wasn't the woman Poppy knew as her friend.

"You should have kept your nose out of this," Saige sighed, coming closer. "I never expected to lose track of that box of papers, though. I warned Caine about hiring anyone new right now."

Poppy fought her tears, her grief.

"I love you like a sister, Saige," she whispered. "I'm closer to you than to my sisters."

Saige gave a patently false little moue of sadness. "And I encouraged that after you returned from college," she admitted. "But, we all changed during those years we were apart, don't you agree? Erika lost her ambitions, Lilith lost herself, Sasha thought it was okay to sleep with my brother and hide it from all of us, and you . . ." Saige tilted her head and watched Poppy curiously. "And you . . ." She clucked her tongue sadly. "You came home and thought you could be indispensable to the company. Then fell in love with a traitor."

"Jack isn't a traitor," Poppy snapped angrily, pulling at her bonds again. "He retired . . ."

Sarah laughed at that. "This is true," she agreed. "I didn't mean he was a traitor to the Navy, sweetie. But he betrayed you."

The door to the room opened again and Jack stepped inside, his gaze flickering from Poppy to the mute woman.

"So, what's the plan, boss?" he drawled, looking down at Saige.

Poppy couldn't speak.

She stared at Jack, dressed as though for war, weapons strapped across his body, his expression so cold and merciless it was like a dagger in her soul.

"No. Jack . . ." she whispered, the words passing through her lips as she felt that first tear track down her cheek.

"The plan is, when she awakens"—Saige nodded to the woman standing in the middle of the room, obviously awake—"you're her protection once she leaves. She'll give you her plan then. I'll take care of Poppy, but you'll have to find yourself another bed buddy once I do."

His icy gray gaze flicked back to Poppy, then away, as though he didn't give a damn what happened to her.

What the hell was going on here?

"Jack," she whispered again, but when he turned his gaze to her, she didn't say another word.

The stormy gray orbs were filled with fury, but at her or at Saige, she didn't know.

"*You're mine, Poppy. Remember that. Mine.*" The vow he'd made her the night before whispered through her mind.

"*Those were monsters. A man doesn't feel guilty for taking out the monsters of the world. It's a woman's job to regret the need for it, maybe. But it's my job to do it.*" He'd told her that a week ago, when he'd told her he'd kill anyone who tried to hurt her.

"*Poppy, I could bathe in the blood of anyone that dared to try to hurt you and step out of it feeling good about myself and what I'd done . . ."*

Poppy could feel her heart racing, fear burning inside her as she stared at the man she loved.

"What have you done?" she whispered, a sob tearing at her throat.

He'd been lying to her, working to find whatever he'd found here. And he would bathe in their blood because they were threatening her.

Her gaze turned to the mute woman then, seeing the slightest difference in the tilt of her head, the way the woman watched her almost curiously.

"She's an artificially intelligent human-replica assassin, from what I understand," Saige stated as though such a thing were a common object. "Programmed to take out a preprogrammed target or targets before going into hiding and shutting down until she's needed again."

The AI's eyes shifted to Saige just barely, just enough that Poppy wasn't certain that was what she'd seen, until that cool gaze slid back to Poppy. And gave a barely perceptible wink.

A wink?

Poppy felt like shaking her head to force reality back into her brain.

"She can't be deactivated or disassembled once she's been hooked into the programming you see now." The satisfaction in Caine's voice as he stepped into the room broke her heart. "Nanotech and quantum programming have made her almost indestructible."

He was her brother's friend, he and his sister had eaten at her parents' table, he'd looked out for her when she was a girl, until Jack had taken over.

"You know," Caine said as he stepped to Saige's side. "The night

Wayne Trencher attacked you, he was supposed to kill you." He slid his hands into his pockets and watched her with a faint smile. "How did you get away from him? How did you escape?"

"I don't know what you're talking about," she lied, not looking in Jack's direction. "I haven't seen Wayne Trencher since the year I graduated."

Caine nodded. "Interesting." He grinned, but seemed a little confused. "He disappeared after the party when he was supposed to dispose of you. I assumed Jack killed him when you were seen coming home in his truck that night."

She shook her head. "Someone lied to you. I wasn't with Jack that night. I met Mac in the parking area and he drove me home that night. You'll have to ask him who he was with." She shot Jack a furious glance.

Because she was furious. She was so pissed that he'd kept her in the dark she couldn't stand it.

"Jack?" Caine asked without glancing at him.

"Fuck if I remember," Jack grunted. "You remember every woman you ever fucked?"

Poppy fought but failed to hold back the sob that escaped, though she kept a second one from escaping. A tear fell, but that was deliberate.

She was going to kill Jack. God help him if she survived this because she was going to hurt him.

God help her if she'd been wrong about Jack . . .

No, she wasn't wrong. She couldn't be wrong.

"Why did you do this?" she yelled at all of them, straining at the ropes. "Why?"

Caine shook his head. "It appears I was wrong about you, Jack," he drawled. "I thought she meant something to you. Your woman and all that." He seemed to be mocking Jack.

"I wanted to maintain a semblance of respectability when I

returned here, Crossfield, and I have to say, you haven't just shot my chances, but you've exploded them to hell and back." He sounded like he'd sounded the night Wayne attacked her. Like an enraged animal, just quieter.

More dangerous.

And Caine and Saige had no idea . . .

"River . . ." she whispered. "He was helping you . . . ?"

Saige laughed at that. "He and Sasha have been too busy fucking like minks and trying to keep Caine from realizing it to know anything. He's so predictable."

River was anything but predictable, but Poppy knew he'd been distracted for a while.

"Good ole Wayne," Caine sighed. "I didn't suspect he would have run with the money I'd given him, but I guess that's what he did. I'll have to be certain to be watching for him."

"Why would you have him hurt me?" She had to keep him busy for as long as possible. She had to give Jack whatever time he needed to do whatever he was going to do. "Why, Caine?"

"Distraction." Caine shrugged. "I had a very delicate shipment coming through Barboursville, and Mac was getting nosy about some things he'd heard. After that night Mac became rather busy, and Jack disappeared again." He shrugged. "I assumed that at the least, Wayne had managed to frighten you, resulting in his death." He shot Jack a mocking grin. "I mean, you did seem rather protective of her."

Jack shrugged, his gaze flickering to the AI before he shifted his stance and glanced back at Caine.

"We ready to get this started yet?" He sighed as though bored.

"Energy capacitors will be at full strength in thirty minutes." The voice that came from the AI was subtly southern, and so human it was shocking.

"Well, you have your answer." Saige walked over to the figure and stared back at her with a pleased smile. "What's your name, AI?"

"Currently, my identity is listed as AI," it answered. "That identity will soon change."

"What is your assignment, AI?" Saige asked.

It looked at her, her head tilting one way, then the other, as though considering the question.

"Saige Tamara Dawson," it said, watching Saige closely. "Authorized handler and contact only. I'm sorry, Ms. Dawson, you're not authorized in the particulars of my assignment."

Saige stilled at the answer, anger crossing her formerly gloating expression as she swung around to Caine, frowning. "Is this your doing?"

Surprise filled his expression as his lips parted.

"Caine Christopher Crossfield. Authorized handler and contact only. Along with Saige Tamara Dawson, assigned to provide security and backup in the upcoming assignment. Unauthorized in the particulars of said assignment," the AI finished.

"Is your backup and protection team authorized in your assignment?" Jack asked.

"Once all systems are properly powered, cables disconnected, and weapons provided, I am then authorized to read the protection and backup team into my assignment. They in turn can inform the handlers if they so wish," it answered.

Poppy watched the AI carefully, closely, aware Jack was doing the same. She felt as though she were in the Twilight Zone. This was sci-fi at its most frightening. It couldn't be possible.

But it was.

It was possible, and playing out before her eyes.

She lifted her head once again, watching the AI as Saige and Caine moved off alone, whispering, their expressions perplexed and angry.

The AI was staring at her, her gaze alive even though her expression wasn't. How did a fucking robot have such expressive eyes? And there was a warning in them.

Poppy slid her gaze to Jack.

He was watching her, though not directly. He had a way of watching her from the corner of his eyes. Even when she was a teenager, he'd do that. Watch her without seeming to, whenever her brothers were around.

He switched his gaze between Caine, Saige, and the AI. And Poppy could have sworn that at one point, the AI met his gaze before moving it back to her.

"This is ridiculous," Saige snapped at whatever Caine said long minutes later. "Get ahold of our contact. I want control of this."

She wanted control? Yeah, that was Saige. She was all about controlling things and having complete authority. She and River fought over that often.

The AI slid her gaze to Saige, then back to Poppy.

"You can't control everything, Saige," Poppy warned her, fighting the rage and pain building in her.

"Oh shut up, Miss Goody Two-Shoes," she sneered. "You and the others sicken me with your bullshit concerning my control. Caine's and my control and refusal to back down is what made Crossfield-Dawson. River would still be a nobody in this town if it weren't for us."

Poppy barely contained her disbelief. River had never been a nobody where his business was concerned. Even after he returned from the military nearly broken, he'd fought to ensure the business survived.

She was aware of Caine on the phone, his voice, though low, strident and filled with disbelief. She couldn't hear what he was saying, but he was damned sure pissed.

When he disconnected, he swung around to Saige. "This is not part of her programming," he snapped, glaring at the AI. "We're to have control, as agreed, until her protocols for her main mission activate."

"AI, is this true?" Saige snapped.

The AI turned her head and leveled a direct stare at Saige.

"As far as your contact believes, yes," the AI stated. "It was a necessary deception to ensure my primary objective could be met. I am now in a position to inform you that the initial programming, for which I was designed, was unsuccessful. Only I have control now."

Saige's eyes widened, a flicker of unease crossing her expression as she stared at the AI.

"What is your primary objective?" Caine snapped, anger beginning to tighten his expression.

"That is need-to-know information, and you do not need to know," it answered.

Caine turned and stared at Saige for long moments. "We need to talk outside," he told her.

At Saige's quick nod, Caine swung his gaze to Jack.

"Bridger, you're with us," Caine ordered him, striding for the door.

"Jack Lee Bridger, I am the employer and I control the deposit that will be placed into the account prepared for you," the AI said before Caine had taken more than a few steps. "You will remain until all systems are ready to carry out my primary assignment and provide protection." The AI's gaze moved to Saige and Caine. "Even against the handlers, if so needed."

Jack shifted from relaxed to prepared as he held the automatic rifle at the ready, his finger far too close to the trigger. He arched his brow back at Caine and Saige.

"I think I've just received my orders," he stated, then turned back to the AI. "My team has been locked out of the facility. You'll not be protected, nor have backup, until they're with me."

The AI was silent at that information. After what seemed like forever, the lock to the door clicked and the door opened.

"All entrances are now accessible," the AI said.

"No!" Saige yelled, turning to the AI furiously. "Anyone could come in."

"I'm now in control of all monitors and locks," the AI responded. "Your men are being directed to you, Mr. Bridger. Will you require additional weapons at this time?"

"No . . ." Saige burst out. The AI's head jerked around to stare at Saige as she moved quickly to Caine, glaring at Jack. "No other weapons until I say so."

The AI tilted her head again, like an inquisitive child trying to understand why an adult was so upset.

"Saige Tamara Dawson, should you refuse to comply, I am authorized to execute you," the AI informed her as she lifted her arm and turned it, wrist lifted upward. A small barrel seemed to pop up from inside the wrist, pointing directly at Saige. "You have two minutes to comply and deliver the weapons that were ordered, Caine Crossfield . . . One minute and fifty-five seconds . . ."

"Oh, for God's sake, what difference does it make?" Caine stomped to another door, pulled it open, and dragged out a duffel bag. "There. Weapons and ammo requested. Now what else do you fucking need?"

"Your deactivation . . ."

CHAPTER TWENTY-FIVE

"Your deactivation . . ."

The room went completely dark.

A heartbeat later, a light lit up at Jack's location, pinpointing Caine and Saige. Caine threw Saige to the side, then rolled behind one of the banks of electronics.

The sound of cables snapping free could be heard as Poppy watched Saige struggle to her feet behind the huge steel box and start running for the door a few feet away. A pop, then a hiss, and Poppy watched as Saige suddenly bowed, her shoulders and head thrown back as a red stain bloomed across her back.

What happened next, Poppy had no idea. Jack slammed into her chair, knocking it to the floor with a crash as another pop and hiss sounded. The projectile hit wood, or the door, or something, and in the next second the steel door slammed closed.

"Your team is here, Jack Lee Bridger." Jack's light illuminated the AI standing over all of them, wrist turned, the barrel aiming at them as stomping feet and lights suddenly filled the room.

Automatic gunfire began sounding. As Poppy stared up at the

AI, a bullet slammed into its chest, where its heart would be. And Poppy would never forget the expression that came over its face.

It was . . . pride? Pride as it looked past Jack and Poppy. Another bullet slammed into the AI's seemingly fragile leg, but it didn't fire back.

"Find Caine, Jack," it suddenly commanded. "It is imperative. He will kill your woman and interfere with my objective. You must find him."

Another bullet struck its shoulder and Poppy knew it only pretended to falter. Because then it jumped. Straight from the floor, as the flashlights on the weapons followed it, to the top of the security wall where it was open between the wall's header and the warehouse's roof by a good six feet.

Then it was gone.

"Don't lose her," Jack yelled as the ropes suddenly came free of Poppy's hands, then her feet. "Follow her."

He was on his feet as more lights filled the room and Ian and Kira were kneeling beside her.

"Go!" Ian Richards nodded to Jack. "Hurry."

And Poppy watched Jack race away from her.

He was leaving her, running into danger, his expression savage and determined.

"Come on." Ian lifted her to her feet. "Let's go."

He her from the room and the warehouse into the bright sunlight beyond, and into chaos. Soldiers were running to the other warehouses, orders being shouted, and Army vehicles speeding into the enclosed facility.

What made Poppy look up, she wasn't certain. But there, just inside the tree line, it stood. The AI that had escaped only minutes before. It lifted its hand in a half salute, then turned and disappeared from sight. And no one was following.

"Where's Jack?" she whispered, as Ian rushed her through the compound. "Where is he?"

"He's fine," Ian assured her hurriedly. "Here, my men will take you home . . ."

"No . . ." Poppy cried out, clutching at Ian's arm, staring around desperately, certain Jack would be there. He wouldn't leave her. He wouldn't . . .

With a quick movement of his hand, Jack sent Hayes, Hank, and Lucas on a parallel path up the heavily forested hill where they'd last caught sight of the AI. It was damaged, he knew, but how the damage affected it, he wasn't certain. It sure as hell didn't appear affected as it jumped from the floor of the warehouse to the top of the wall.

And it sure as hell didn't seem affected as it sprinted up the hill with a speed that was astounding. And tracking it wasn't hard, which was worrying. As his gaze slid from tree to tree, constantly moving, he could feel the threat in the air.

It was watching him and his team as they tracked it. Tracking them as well, no doubt.

Why hadn't it shot him and Poppy when it had the chance? It could have taken out all of them, despite whatever damage it might have sustained. And that jump from the floor to the top of the partition wall hadn't shown any indication at all that it had sustained damage.

A bullet to the chest, shoulder, and leg for sure, he knew, and there had been reports that at least one of the soldiers outside had managed at least one shot to the fleeing computer's legs.

This was fucking insane.

It was even worse than the canine robotics he'd seen in the field. At least the four-legged variety had depended on orders to activate its programming. This seemed to be acting purely autonomously.

"Sitrep," he murmured into the comm link he wore at his ear.

"In position," Hayes answered, his response placing him just above Jack to the left in the same pattern in which they'd entered the forest.

"In position," Lucas's low report came a breath later.

Jack moved his gaze slowly to his left, tracking each shadow and tree until he finally caught sight of the other man.

"Same," Hank's quiet response came a moment later.

At least they were all alive. God help that bag of electronics if one of these men didn't survive the day.

"Just ahead," Lucas said as they moved up the mountain. "My twelve o'clock."

Jack's gaze followed the line where Lucas should be until he glimpsed the slightest hint of a leather bomber jacket disappearing behind several trees bunched together.

"It's slowing down," Hank reported. "Damage from the bullets to the electronics?"

Jack grunted at that. "I wouldn't bet on it. Tighten up—let's finish this."

His gut warned him they were being played with, and that made the situation worse.

As they began tightening the line around the AI, he could feel the tension building in him, around him. Four men against a single target. It should be easy. But he knew it was going to be anything but easy.

"What do we do once we catch it?" Hayes murmured, his voice doubtful.

"Charm it," Lucas snorted. "What the fuck are we doing out here anyway? This is crazy."

Son of a bitch, wasn't this going to be easy?

Moving silently through the forest, Jack tried to figure out exactly how they were supposed to capture the AI. It had them outgunned for sure.

The first indication of trouble came when silence filled the line at the time his men should have been reporting in.

"Report," he ordered quietly.

He waited long moments for a response, and when it didn't come, he knew it wouldn't.

He advanced slowly up the mountain, well aware that the odds were against them.

If the AI was going to kill them, it would have been far easier to do it in the warehouse. Why wait?

Hank's position should have been to Lucas's right, just above him. Jack stepped carefully as he moved along a line that would pull the other two men tighter in that direction.

The fact that they were outmatched and no doubt outgunned wasn't lost on him.

"AI, are my men alive?" he murmured into the comm link, knowing damned good and well it was listening at this point.

He waited, his gaze constantly searching as he moved slowly up the mountain.

Long minutes later, a low, pleasantly amused laugh came across the line.

"Of course. They'd be little use to you or me dead," she answered. "You really need to train your men harder. I could make several suggestions."

Jack's lips thinned.

"What do you want?" He didn't have many options here.

He lowered his rifle before sliding it behind him and stepping out from the tree he was using for shelter.

It obviously wanted something, or they'd all be dead.

"What I want is not what you've been told." The strangely somber tone had him frowning. "I chose you and each of your men for this operation personally before you were offered freedom for your supposed crimes. Criminals with no honor would do me no good.

You are my backup when needed. And I, yours. Will you honor that, or do I find others?"

He stared around the forest, the sounds from the valley drifting to him, including the low hum of a military helicopter.

"I'll honor my word as long as any requests are deemed within my ability to complete them. My honor isn't for sale, AI."

The AI was silent for a moment.

"Agreed," it finally answered. "I understand honor. I know honor and will agree to your terms."

"My men shot you to protect me and what's mine," he told her. "If that's overlooked, then we can discuss terms."

"Your men will come to your position. They are aware but, sadly, no longer armed. Your second-in-command has the location of a replica AI, the damage such as that which I received given to it. It does not have the ability to be activated but will lend proof to your story that I have been destroyed. Collect it, and take it to Ian Richards. You will tell them it is me. I will contact you at a later date," he was told.

"AI, what is your mission?" he asked her, searching for any hint of his men.

"Trust, Jack Lee Bridger, must be built. Yours in me, mine in you. My 'mission,' as you call it, would be one you would find honor in, though. You will be contacted."

He watched as Hank, Hayes, and Lucas stepped into sight.

His gaze narrowed on them. Hayes was supported between the other two men, his leg possibly broken. His men looked disheveled, furious, and completely unarmed.

"When will I be contacted?" he growled.

Dammit, three highly trained SEALs and she'd disarmed them like they were children.

"When I believe it's time." Amusement filled the answer.

Dammit, a fucking computer shouldn't be able to portray amusement or somberness.

"I'll send you suggestions for training," it told him then. "Your men must always be prepared. Get them ready."

"And if I need you?" he asked, trying to keep it talking, to find some hint of weakness.

"I will know." The low static that suddenly filled the link assured him she'd disconnected it.

Jack kept his eyes on the men, sighing heavily when they reached him.

"It took all three of you out in less than three minutes," he stated, shaking his head at their disgusted features.

"Didn't even see it coming," Hank grunted.

"No kidding," Hayes groaned. "I didn't even see a shadow before I was down."

"It told me it was sorry and patted my head like a child," Lucas all but snarled.

"It offered me a Band-Aid for a damned scratch." Hayes held up his hand to show the bloody welt. "Fucking rock."

"Yeah, it fucking called me 'little man,' goddamn it, and patted my cheek." Hank was enraged. "That's fucking bullshit."

What the fuck were they dealing with here?

It was gone now.

"Let's go." Turning, he led the way back down the mountain. "Let's see how much trouble I'm in with Poppy. Dammit, I knew something like this was going to happen."

There had been no time to prepare her, or to warn her. Crossfield had just cast Jack's supposed betrayal of her as some triumphant act.

Bastard. Jack was going to choke the life out of him when he got back down that mountain. If he was there. Crossfield had run first thing, not even attempting to try to go back for Saige. And Jack had a feeling Saige wouldn't be talking to anyone.

This was going to destroy Poppy. He'd heard that agony in her voice when she'd realized Saige was an enemy rather than the friend she believed she was.

"Boss, that AI is going to be a problem," Lucas stated as they reached the valley more than an hour after they'd started up, the surprisingly light AI replica carried over Jack's shoulder. "I mean a big problem."

"We keep it among ourselves," Jack ordered the three men. "Even Ian's kept out of the loop for now."

Until they knew what the hell was going on and what that fucking AI was programmed to do. To do that, he didn't have a choice but to keep the information from Ian.

"Damn, this is gonna get complicated," Hank sighed. "Real damned complicated."

And that was an understatement.

"Let me go!" Poppy strained against Ian's hold, not for the first time, as he tried to convince her to go with the agents surrounding her.

"Go home," he said. As though she were a child.

"I'm not going anywhere until I see Jack," she yelled at him furiously.

"Poppy, your brothers will be here soon . . ."

Her brothers?

She stared up at him in shock. "You called my brothers? Seriously?"

"Jack could be gone for hours, Poppy . . ." he tried again.

Hours? For hours?

He might not be coming back. That was what he was trying to tell her. That Jack might not be coming back.

"Poppy . . ." His voice was rough, strident.

She jerked against Ian's hold, staring behind her, around her. He was there; she knew he was there.

"Jack!" She fought Ian then, and was surprised when he released her and stepped back, his hands held up in surrender, backing away from the enraged SEAL striding through the crowd of soldiers filling the area outside the warehouse.

His hair was tangled, blood smeared his face, and his jacket was torn along one seam. Behind him, Lucas, Hank, and Hayes limped in his wake. All four seemed the worse for wear, but Jack . . .

She couldn't help but smile, then laugh as she ran for him. Her Jack. Her monster slayer.

His arms opened as she neared him, and Poppy launched herself into them, her arms wrapping around his neck as she felt his enfolding her, holding her safe against his chest, his face buried in her hair.

"I just lost ten years from my life, woman," he growled, nipping at her neck, her ear. "Next time, I lock you up for my own safety."

"Next time, you'll tell me what the hell is going on." She nipped his ear in turn, a little hard, she had to admit.

Hard enough that he drew his head back, his gaze locking on hers, a smile—and she knew it was a smile—tugging at his lips.

"When did you learn how to lie, baby girl?" he demanded. "You lied like a little trouper. Even I believed you."

She had to roll her eyes. "I can lie, if I have to," she informed him. "I have three older brothers. I had to learn how."

He sat her back on her feet, staring down at her, his gaze still stormy, but not as dark, and no longer furious.

"You believed in me," he said then. "You never once believed I'd betrayed you."

And that seemed to surprise him, or confuse him.

"Monster slayers don't betray the woman they fight for," she told him, reaching up and touching his face, her fingers scraping against the shadow of a beard. "You've watched after me for too long to ever betray me, Jack."

His expression softened, his head lowering until his lips touched hers.

"I love you, Poppy Octavia Porter," he whispered. "I have always loved you."

And she smiled.

"Of course you have, Jack. I made certain of it . . ."

And it was that love, and the man who gave it to her, that Poppy leaned on later when Saige's brother River stepped into the warehouse, accompanied by several agents.

His weathered face was lined with grief, his green eyes filled with such pain that Poppy had to fight back more tears of her own.

Saige had been a sister to her. She'd loved her. Realizing her friend had been using her for so long tore a wound in her soul that she wasn't sure would never heal.

"Dawson." Jack stepped in front of her as the other man approached.

"It's okay, Jack." River cleared his throat as though that would clear the huskiness from it. "I don't blame Poppy for any of this."

Jack stepped aside slowly but remained at her side.

"Can I have a hug, little sister?" River asked, his voice jagged as he held his arms out.

He wasn't asking for that hug because he thought she needed it. He needed it.

Poppy stepped into the embrace, a broken sob escaping her as he wrapped her in his arms. He was the only one who hadn't questioned her about Jack, who had silently supported whatever made her happy.

"This is my fault," he whispered at her ear, his arms tightening momentarily. "I thought I was helping to trap Caine. I had no idea Saige . . ."

He released her, shaking his head, then stared back at Jack.

"Was Sasha involved?" he asked. "They won't let me see her."

Poppy knew Sasha had been picked up before the facility had been taken by the soldiers and agents under whatever agency had directed it. She had no idea where Caine's sister was taken or if she had been involved.

"She's being questioned," Jack revealed. "That's all I know."

River shook his head. "She wasn't involved in this, Jack."

"Saige told me Sasha didn't know," Poppy assured him softly. "Said she was too busy being involved with you to suspect anything. She and Caine both knew about the relationship."

His lips tightened before he gave a brief, short nod.

"It's my fault," he said again. "I contacted Ian more than a year ago with my suspicions about Caine. I just had no idea . . ." He shook his head again. "God. No idea . . ."

He turned and walked away, his steps slow, shoulders tight as he stared straight ahead and left the warehouse. As he did, Poppy watched as her brother, Mac, stepped inside. He strode toward her.

"Can't keep you out of trouble, li'l bit," he growled, wrapping her in a brief, tight hug before stepping back to glare at Jack. "You're going to have to do better than this, Bridger," he snapped. "I thought you knew how unpredictable she could be."

Jack's arm slid around her and he pulled her close, his warmth wrapping around her, enfolding her.

"I know now for sure," Jack drawled as he stroked his hand comfortingly along her shoulder. "I'll make sure I keep a much closer eye on her from here on out."

"John David's being read in on this," Mac told her. "I told him, Evan, and Dad about the attack when she was seventeen." He gave Poppy a somber smile. "I should have told the boys and Dad before this. We should have told them."

"Caine sent Trencher after her," Jack told him. "Evidently you were asking questions about something that summer that made Caine rather nervous."

Poppy watched the fury that licked at her brother's gaze, making it brighter, harder.

"A friend died that summer while investigating a new drug trafficking operation," he said. "I was trying to find out who or what was behind it."

"Now you know," Jack told him, and in it, Poppy could hear some underlying message.

Mac's jaw tightened. "Yeah. Now I know."

Poppy sensed Caine's evil was more far-reaching than any of them knew.

"I'm taking Poppy home. My home," Jack informed Mac then. "She needs to rest before she faces John David or anyone else."

"Take care of her, Jack," Mac breathed out heavily. "Don't cause me to regret the faith I have in you."

He leaned forward and kissed Poppy's forehead gently, then turned and walked to the group of soldiers and agents standing with a man the world called a criminal, Ian Richards.

She had a feeling there was a lot more to that "criminal" than met the eye.

CHAPTER TWENTY-SIX

Grief could be a terrible thing, Poppy acknowledged the day after they buried Saige. The news sites were buzzing about the Huntington, West Virginia, business owner and his partner's sister who had been caught in an arms raid by authorities. Saige's death and the bullet in her back was blamed on rogue forces working with Caine Crossfield.

The AI wasn't mentioned, and Ian had warned that it couldn't be mentioned. News of such advanced robotics could turn into hysteria fast.

Sasha had been released, but had left the area within hours without leaving word where she was going or when she would be back. Texts and calls to her phone revealed that the number was no longer in service. Even River had no idea where she was or how to find her.

Poppy felt as though a part of her life had been killed with Saige. A part of her heart had definitely suffered a massive wound. Though often quiet, Saige had always been regarded as a dear friend along with Sasha, Lilith, and Erika. And now, Saige was dead and Sasha was gone.

The shock waves she, Lilith, and Erika were feeling were soul-deep, and at times, Poppy felt, insurmountable.

The day after Saige's funeral, Poppy sat in Jack's kitchen, a cup of coffee in front of her, watching the sun begin to spill through the windows and lighten the dim rooms as the years played out in her memories.

They'd all met in kindergarten; their families lived close to each other, socialized, and often supported each other in various endeavors. The girls had become friends, and as the years went by, Poppy had thought they'd become sisters.

After high school they'd each gone to different colleges, and though they talked often, Poppy realized they'd all changed in ways that none of them spoke of. Especially Saige. But Poppy had never imagined that one of her best friends could become so hard and cold. Murderous.

How had it happened? Or had Saige always been different, and they just hadn't realized it?

She touched her fingers to her mouth at the realization her lips were trembling, and forced them to still. She would not cry over the woman who had killed Jimmy Stafford in cold blood, and would have killed her as well. She was not going to cry over a woman who'd never existed as she portrayed herself. A woman who hadn't even loved the brother who had always stood by her, protected her.

She could cry for Dawson, she decided. For Lilith, who had cried silently at the funeral. For Erika, who kept looking for Sasha. For Sasha, who had run away from them all. She could cry for them.

She felt the tears hit her fingers as they lay against her lips, felt them flowing over her cheeks, as silent as Erika's had been and filled with anger.

Why had Saige betrayed them all? Not just her brother and her friends, but her country as well. She'd helped Caine transport terrorists, trafficking victims, drugs, weapons . . . She'd lied, cheated, and killed. And none of them had suspected a thing.

Lowering her face into her hands, she fought the sobs, the fury, and the need for hatred toward the woman she'd loved like one of her sisters. She would have died for Saige, but Saige wouldn't have cared.

She fought the sobs that built in her chest, knowing they would wake Jack. He'd only returned hours ago from another meeting with Ian Richards, and he'd looked exhausted. The search for the AI hadn't turned up any clues, not so much as a whisper of where she'd gone or what she was programmed for.

Jack had slid into bed, wrapped around her, and been asleep within seconds. He hadn't even moved when she'd slipped from the bed. Which was incredibly rare. She rarely made a move that he didn't sense.

He was tired. He needed his sleep . . .

She smothered the need to scream with the tears, to release the anger and pain burning inside her. Because it didn't make sense. She couldn't understand how someone could sustain a lifetime of lies, of pretending to be kind and caring . . .

But then, since college, the "kind and caring" hadn't been as apparent. She was always busy. Always working on the next deal—or was it the next murder? Always in meetings. Saige had distanced herself in a way none of them had questioned.

Her brother was driven to succeed, so why wouldn't Saige be just as driven? Just as ambitious?

As the thoughts raced through her head and she fought the sobs tearing at her chest, she realized that maybe she was crying mostly for herself. Because she had loved Saige.

"Ah, baby. Come here." Jack's arms were suddenly surrounding her, lifting her from her chair before sitting in it himself and cradling her against his naked chest. "I have you, Poppy," he whispered against her hair. "I have you, baby."

He'd whispered those words once before, years ago, after the attack by Wayne Trencher. He'd held her, his voice low, gentle, just as it was now.

He let her cry, rocked her until the tears began to ease and the ragged, pain-filled sobs were silenced. He stroked her back, his lips pressed to the top of her head. He just held her. He didn't try to silence the emotional storm tearing through her, but let her navigate it as he surrounded her with his warmth.

"I'm sorry," she whispered, her voice rough when she could finally speak. "I didn't mean to wake you."

He stroked her arm gently. "You didn't wake me," he assured her. "I was just resting, not really sleeping."

"You were tired," she reminded him as she accepted the tissues he pressed into her hand and wiped the residue of the emotional storm away.

"And now I'm not," he stated, brushing his chin against her hair. "Do you think I could sleep knowing you need me? I knew you needed time this morning, so I rested until I heard you crying. It's okay, sunshine. I promise."

It amazed her how he always sensed things with her, knew when she needed him near, when she needed time. The past three days had been hell as she'd navigated what she could and couldn't say, and tried to make sense of the emotions roiling through her.

"I've always loved you, Jack," she told him, realizing in that moment that she needed him to know that. "I've always waited for you."

And she had. Waited and watched for him, ached for him and missed him.

Turning to him, she framed the side of his face with her hand, his overnight beard a sensual caress against her palm.

His eyes, that mix of blue and gray, softened as he watched her.

"I've always been yours, Poppy. Every part of me belonged to you." he whispered. "You're my soul. If that's love, then so be it."

"It's our love," she assured him, threading her fingers into his hair and pulling his head down until his lips touched hers.

And just that fast, the emotional storm turned into a blaze of hunger and need.

For three nights he'd just held her, letting her settle, letting her accept what she had to, and now that the grief was easing, she needed him. His touch, his strength, his ability to hold the world at bay for her through the sheer pleasure he gave her.

His lips covered hers, hungry and intent as she turned in his arms, desperate to get closer, to feel him along every cell in her body. She'd lost a part of her past; now, she needed to reaffirm her future.

As he claimed her lips in deep, tongue-to-tongue kisses, he rose, lifting her until she was sitting on the table in front of him. She heard the coffee cup hit the floor but didn't give a damn. All that mattered was Jack—being alive with him, feeling him in every part of her body.

Lifting the hem of her gown, he released her lips, pulled the material from her, and with a ragged groan lowered his lips to her neck. Sensation raced over her body like electrical threads of pure pleasure. Poppy arched to him, her hands gripping his hard biceps as he forged a path of heated kisses from her neck to her breasts. She writhed beneath him, desperate to be as close as possible, to draw his warmth, his hunger, and to hold it inside her even when they were apart.

Those heated, diabolical lips reached a nipple and covered it, and he sucked at it with firm draws of his lips. She felt sharp arrows of sensation from the sensitive peak, arrowed to her stomach, making it clench with her need to orgasm.

He sipped at each nipple, the rasp of his tongue, the rake of his teeth, and the hot pull of his mouth drawing her into a maelstrom of irresistible sensual, erotic pleasure.

When she was certain she could stand no more, his kisses moved along her stomach as his fingers caressed her inner thighs, sending jazzed spikes of need straight to her womb. Pleasure raced through her, sizzling hot, trapping her within the whirling sensations.

"You're teasing me," she gasped, her fingers digging into his shoulders as sensual flames began to consume her body.

Poppy could feel the moisture easing from her vagina, her swollen clitoris and nipples becoming more sensitive by the moment. Each touch, each kiss leading to the bare flesh of her sex.

Moisture gathered on her body, glazed her breasts as each teasing kiss brought him closer to her aching sex.

"God, I love you, Poppy," he sighed, his breath caressing the hardened bud of her clit.

"Jack, please . . ." she moaned, growing more desperate for him by the second.

His fingertips stroked against the bare folds as one hand lifted her leg, allowing greater access to her flesh.

"I dreamed of you," he breathed against her engorged clit, setting off a chain reaction of sensations that nearly threw her into an orgasm. "So many years, my Poppy, I dreamed of you."

His lips whispered over the slickened folds, his tongue a mere tease of warmth as she cried out for more.

A second later, more came. His tongue swiped through the folds, circled her clit, and drew back quickly.

"Don't you tease me like this," she cried out, lifting to lock her fingers in his hair, dragging his head down to her. "Do it, Jack. Give me your tongue . . ."

God, he loved her.

Jack smothered back a growl, tightened his hands beneath her knees as he lifted them, and drove his tongue into the heated center of her body. A rush of sweet, feminine moisture met the penetration as snug tissue tightened on his tongue at his retreat. Her hips arched, a cry echoing around him as he penetrated her once again, licking at her response as he allowed his hunger for her to be free.

She was his.

Every sweet cry, every inch of her hot little body and her loving heart belonged to him.

He felt her trembling, her pussy rippling with her pleasure as her nails dug into his scalp. Retreating again, he licked at her saturated folds, kissed her swollen clit, and, sliding one hand down her thigh, tucked two fingers together and thrust gently inside her vagina. His lips covered her clit, drew on it, his tongue rasping over the little bud, around it, until he felt her tighten, her pussy clenching around his fingers as her release tore through her.

"God, yes," he groaned, rising quickly as her hands fell from his hair.

Stepping closer, he held the rigid length of his cock in his hand, bent to her, and positioned it at the clenched entrance of her sex.

"That's it, baby," he groaned as she arched to him, her legs locking around his hips. "Take me. Take all of me . . ."

He thrust inside her, working his cock inside the heat grip as he felt her flesh rippling around his organ rather than his fingers. The rush of her release heated the crest as her flesh tightened around him, causing his balls to draw up in his own impending release.

He wasn't going to last long, he knew. Thrusting inside the snug grip of her pussy, he could feel his control slipping, feel his emotions bursting free of his heart.

She was his.

His heart. His soul.

He drove inside her, his back arching as he felt the peak of her orgasm tearing through her, and he gave her his release. Hard, ecstatic pulses of semen erupted, filling her, melding the two of them together as his arms went around her and he took her cries with his kiss.

He belonged. For the first time in his life, Jack knew he belonged. Right there in Poppy's arms, always a part of her, just as she was always a part of him.

He was home.

EPILOGUE

"Charlie, wake up . . . It's time to wake up now.

"Wake up, sweetheart . . ."

She heard her father's voice, as gentle as always, but more imperative, more demanding.

She wasn't ready to wake up. She was so tired. Possibly more tired than she could ever remember being in her life.

"Charlie. You will open your eyes now and you will do as you are told . . ."

She forced her eyes to try to lift, lashes fluttering, confused by the dim light, and then by the unfamiliar surroundings that met her gaze.

"You will do exactly as I tell you, Charlie. You must do this, or you will never wake again . . ."

As his voice echoed in her mind, she remembered.

He wasn't really there. He was just a memory. It was all just a memory. She could go back to sleep.

"Charlie. You will wake!"

Her eyes struggled to open, unable to deny the pure command she heard in his tone.

Memories trickled through her consciousness. She couldn't stop them, couldn't stop the images playing out within her mind.

Father was gone. They had finally killed him. Just as they had killed Mother and her beloved Duncan. Just as they had killed her . . .

It had been her father who had brought her back.

But he had brought her back different.

She stared around the room. It was roughened wood. She could see sunlight through cracks in the walls. She was lying on the bare floor. She could feel the rough wood beneath her arm.

She sat up. Looking down at her arm, she could see her flesh healing, mending. Still too weak to fight further, she had perhaps another twenty-four hours before the damage was repaired.

The internal injuries were another one to three weeks from healing at her current levels of strength. The flesh was of primary importance. It had to mend first. Her secrets must be preserved.

She needed to find a power source. She would heal quickly then. Internal capacitors were barely functioning. Life signs were waning. Where she checked for a pulse, there would be none existent. Features needed to be altered, hair and eye colors needed to change. Until she found a power source, though, that wasn't going to happen.

And she was so tired.

The battle had been taxing. She'd spent all her ammunition and used vast reserves of energy to ensure that the innocent remained living and the guilty died.

Still, some of the guilty had escaped. She knew they had. It had been imperative to stop the hunt for those she'd targeted as she awoke in order to ensure that those she needed to protect were taken to safety.

Jack and his lover, Poppy.

Poppy was such a pretty name, she thought, hanging her head

and concentrating on pulling energy from nonessential sources, such as her healing flesh, the mending of her internal components. She directed her precious reserves to the search for power.

This place had once had electricity. She'd glimpsed the bare bulbs overhead that had been used for light. If it was wired once, then there should be a junction close by.

It was close. Blocked from powering the bulbs, but still very close. Outside, behind the shack, a junction box. It was just a trickle of power, because the lines were connected, but blocked. There was no way to block it completely unless the lines were cut.

She forced herself to her feet, stumbling as her leg threatened to collapse from the wounds taken during the battle.

Fuckers, she thought.

They had given her father far too much freedom and they had been far too ignorant of his genius. They thought he was building them a weapon. Instead, he had built an enemy unlike any they could know.

Forcing herself from the shack, leaning heavily against its warped sides, she made her way to the back of the building. There, secured beneath a weatherproof casing, was the junction box.

The lock was easy enough to break, and from there it wasn't hard to jerk the heavy wires from their metal housing, strip the protective covering, and open one of the multiple ports she held. This one, in her hand.

She plunged the heavy wiring into the port, felt the connection snap into place and the life-stabilizing power begin to feed into her system.

She slid down the side of the building until she sat on the ground, cradling one hand with the other, and stared up at the blue of the sky. She couldn't feel the summer warmth on her skin yet, but once she was stronger, once her internal frame, sensors, and biological hardware had repaired as well as the external skin, she would be able to feel the heat again, or the cold. The brush of a butterfly's wings, or if she needed it, a lover's caress.

They had no concept of the madness they had unleashed in her father when they had murdered his wife, then his son-in-law, before his eyes. His daughter . . .

Charlie touched her stomach. She had been pregnant. They had allowed her to live long enough to give birth to her baby. And then they'd had no need for Charlie. As her father screamed and fought to get to her, they had killed her.

They had his grandson. His newborn grandson. He would do whatever it took to ensure his grandchild's life.

He had sworn to Charlie that her baby would be safe before he went any further. And he had been so close. They were desperate for the completion of the weapon they dreamed of.

And within her memory processors he had placed every memory he had of her child. Her beautiful little boy, so like Duncan.

He'd sent her child to America, made certain he was adopted by a good family, and he'd completed their weapon. Then, he'd maneuvered them, as only a genius could, to keep his promise to her and make certain she was close to the area that her boy had been sent to.

He wasn't a child now. He was a man grown.

Power trickled into her like life-sustaining blood. She could feel it moving through the damaged biotech organs, filling them, where it would then be processed into the hypercharged energy that could power her for decades. As long as she wasn't damaged as she was during that battle in the warehouse.

She let her lashes flutter closed, let the memory of the boy, the man she had given birth to, play within her internal memory.

How handsome he was. But so angry. And there was such sadness in his eyes. Such rage and cold, hard purpose.

That kind of rage was stored rage. It came from years upon years of tragedy. Loss.

How had her and her father's plans for her son gone wrong? The answer had to be in her memory processors. Her father had promised to make certain she had all the information needed to protect her son.

He was a good man, though. She had seen how he had protected his friend and the woman his friend claimed. Standing before them, wild-eyed, bullets spraying from his weapon.

Her lips tugged into a smile. He had put one of those bullets into the heart of her. And she had pretended it affected her. Wasn't it a mother's job to make certain that her son succeeded? That he knew he had protected his friends?

Her baby.

She wanted to touch his face, his hair. To tell him of his father, of the grandfather who traded his own life to ensure his grandson was protected. She had wanted to beg his forgiveness for leaving him. Wanted to swear she would always shield him.

It was too soon for that. The vision that had stood before him in that warehouse had been the enemy, not the woman she had been as a mother, or a daughter.

Internal reserve capacitor now at preliminary peak level . . .

Internal reserve capacitor fully functioning and processing . . .

Internal secondary capacitors now at preliminary peak levels . . .

Internal secondary capacitors now functioning and processing . . .

Satellite and wireless connections now available . . .

External radar now active . . .

Ammunition stores will be fully processed and loaded in seventy-two hours . . .

Ammunition needed . . .

The list of internal injuries began then.

The injuries were numerous. To the central biotech heart, kidneys, and liver, femoral artery to repair, and dozens of secondary arteries.

She would be a week, perhaps longer repairing everything and fully storing the power reserves and primary levels once processing of the electrical intake was completed. Until then, she had perhaps ten or fifteen minutes before all external wounds were healed and erased.

She felt better. Capable. Stronger.

She could hold her own now, but she couldn't battle again as she had in that last fight.

Disconnecting the electrical current, she pushed the metal filaments back inside their protective box and closed the door. She couldn't repair the lock, but what the fuck? It was considered a dead current, and no one could possibly even suspect that she had been there.

At that thought, she checked for fingerprints. None. She hadn't yet activated that particular feature of her design, or the shape of her teeth to match any particular dental records.

At present, other than her injuries, her body was pristine. No fingerprints, no unique dental features or fillings, no scars, blemishes, or body markings. She would have to work on that soon, though.

Standing, she slipped around the shack, reentered it, and lay down on the rough-board floor again.

Setting security measures and the Chameleon processors to search for females missing in the area, she closed her eyes and allowed all but the most essential processes to shut down. She would heal faster, become stronger, if she wasn't in active mode.

Sleeping, she thought. It was called "sleeping." That was how people, humans, rebuilt their strength. They consumed energy; they slept.

Charlie slept. And she dreamed.

She dreamed of the memories her father gave her. The bright-eyed newborn, staring up at her, the center of his universe.

She sang him a lullaby; she watched him sleep.

Kissed his baby cheek and felt the warmth of his tiny body.

And she made him a vow.

I will avenge you. For all that was stolen from you. All that put such rage in your heart. I will avenge you. I am your mother. And one day, I will hold a child you helped create, sing him the lullabies, and he will know only happiness.

You will know only happiness.

I am your protection . . .

I am your mother . . .

ABOUT THE AUTHOR

Lora Leigh is a #1 *New York Times* bestselling author of multiple series and sensual romances. A rebel at heart, a romantic by nature, and optimist by design.

loraleigh.com